Make You Love Me

ALEXANDRA GRACE

Book One in the You & Me Duology

Make You Love Me
Copyright © 2024 by Alexandra Grace

All rights reserved.

No part of this book may be reproduced or transmitted in any form or by any means, electronic or mechanical, including photocopying and recording, or by any information storage or retrieval system, without permission in writing from the author.

This is a work of fiction. Names, characters, businesses, events, and incidents described in this publication, except for those known in the public domain, are the products of the author's imagination. Any resemblance to actual persons, living or dead, or actual locales or events are entirely coincidental.

Content Warning: Some coarse language and casual drinking, mentions of past abuse and loss, steamy kisses, mentions of intimacy (off page), car accident.

Cover design by Haya In Designs
Edited by R.M. Proofreadereditor

Follow me on Instagram and Facebook: @authoralexandragrace

Website: https://authoralexandragrace.carrd.co

You & Me Duology

MAKE YOU LOVE ME

HOW YOU SEE ME

Other Titles by Alexandra Grace

(The Journey Series Prequel Novella)
A JOURNEY WORTH TAKING

(The Journey Series Trilogy)
A JOURNEY SPARED
A JOURNEY TO LOVE
A JOURNEY HOME

(The Journey Series Book 4)
A JOURNEY BEYOND

For those who never give up on true love.

Chapter One

Jordan

Everyone, at some point in their life, will be slapped in the face by the same unapologetic reality—we're not infallible, bad things happen to good people, and we aren't allowed a say when our time is up.

This is that moment for me.

A warm fluid streams into my eyes, but with my arms pinned under a web of metal, I can't wipe it away. Slashes on the side of my head burn and pulse with every labored heartbeat. It's all I can feel. Most of my body is numb, only a few random tingles in my thighs and back confirm my fate hasn't yet been sealed. I refuse to go out like this. Not before I've had a chance to live.

Panic grips my lungs before the smoke, and I'm suffocating in the thick plume laced with the smell of oil and gasoline, clouding the cabin. That could only mean one thing…the bomb inside my metal coffin has been activated. Maybe there's no hope for me after all.

The irony of this is not lost on me. Although I managed to escape the explosion that claimed the lives of most of my former unit years ago, it appears to have caught up with me. It's not an enemy ambush this time around, but this feels all too familiar—unpredictable, indefensible, criminal, tragic. Maybe one's fate can't be skirted by dumb luck more than once.

When I bought my teenage dream car—a 1965 two-door, poppy red Mustang with an automatic V-8 and white vinyl seats—I thought I had the rest of my life ahead of me. The seller, a gray-haired grandmother, purging her late husband's belongings to pay for the European cruise he refused to take her on over their forty-plus-year marriage, had different circumstances, but she and I faced the same pivotal life moment: the conclusion of years spent serving others and prioritizing everyone but ourselves. Now, freedom granted us the opportunity to shape our lives according to our own choices and wishes. And my list of things to accomplish is long.

Yesterday, Sergeant Montgomery handed over my discharge papers, and the first thing I did was purchase my dream car. The same one that a scrap yard would now reject. After being struck, rolled, and skidded to a stop against a light pole, it's as useless to anyone as a smoked cigarette.

Damn it. I loved this car. The asshole who hit me had to be going close to sixty. Like any responsible driver, I was following the law and running just two miles over the thirty-five mile per hour speed limit on the way to celebrate my first official day as a civilian. My destination—McDonough's Irish Pub in downtown Richmond, Virginia, only a few blocks away from where my beautiful car is now pinned to a pole.

I should be trying to figure a way out before the engine goes up in flames, but all I can think about is how pissed my sister will be when she finds out.

If I am hell-bent on buying a car, my sister said the day I signed the certified check, at least buy something *safer*. I understand her concern. We lost both our parents back in high school to a horrific crash not too different from this one, and since then, she refuses to drive, begging me on a regular basis not to either. Until yesterday, it's been easy to honor her wishes.

In the military, there was usually someone else with the keys—higher-ranked or trained personnel for Humvees, helicopters, and tactical vehicles. Rarely did I have a choice in the matter, and I didn't mind. But after eight years of following orders and doing anything my unit and country required, I wanted the freedom a running motor and four wheels provided. I wanted the damn keys.

Funny how one decision, one moment can bring all your plans to a screeching halt. And if I don't survive this, my sister will hate me for the rest of her life.

"Jordan!"

Remember that tube feature on playgrounds where you speak into one end and the person on the other end, yards away, can hear you? That's what my name sounds like. A distant, hollow version of the person's voice traveling through a metal pipe to my ears.

"Jordan, can you hear me?"

I can…barely, I want to say…but I…

"Jordan, it's me, Hayes."

I startle back to consciousness. Who? Sergeant? Why is he here? Where am I?

"I'm calling an ambulance."

Ambulance? What hap—Oh, God. The crash. I'm still alive, somehow. But for how long?

"Jordan, stay with me, buddy."

I want to, but it's not that easy. I can't see anything. Feel anything. I'm covered in something slick and sticky, and I'm afraid it's blood. *All* my blood by the sheer amount of it coating my skin and clothes.

"Tell my sister…I love her…and I'm sorry."

―――――

"Until when?" I hear a strained male voice ask.

"Until he's stable. He's had multiple significant surgeries and lost a lot of blood." The second male, firm in his delivery, doesn't sound quite as tired. He sounds more like the military doctors I've encountered while serving—half drill instructor, half lifesaver, matter of fact approach, unimpressed tone, no sugar-coating.

"Has anyone called his sister?"

Josie? The beeping sound coming from the machine to my right picks up speed with that little doozie of a question.

"Yes," the second man says. "She's on her way. Should be here tomorrow."

"Tomorrow? It doesn't take that long to get here from New York. She too busy to be bothered?"

No. She just hates cars.

"Apparently, she's taking the train."

Ha. Sounds like her. Dire emergency? No problem. One ticket for the slowest possible transportation, please.

"The train? You've got to be shittin' me."

Ahh. Sergeant Montgomery. Should have recognized that broody magnificence from the years I spent hearing it day and night. The man's resumé for Jordan Jones rescues is both extensive and impressive. But even after adding this instance to the column of relevant hero experience, the list pales in comparison to the fifteen years he's dedicated in service to his country.

"I could have picked her up and brought her back quicker than that," Sergeant Montgomery continues, his trademark crankiness at an all-time high.

"Still can," the second man deadpans. I can only assume he's the doctor on call with the unfortunate duty of dealing with my self-appointed security guard.

Sergeant lets out a long sigh and stalks across the room, his rubber-soled boots sounding more like steel on the soft linoleum floor with each sharp step.

I'd love to measure the deep line between his eyes to know just how serious my situation is. But I can't open my eyes or there's something covering them, keeping me in the dark. I'm glad my ears are working, though, even if there is an annoying ringing sound accompanying the world around me. Maybe I'll also be able to move or speak soon to let everyone know I'm still me inside this shell of a body. Since I can't, at least the incessant beeping on the heart monitor is enough to tell them and me that I'm alive.

"I don't want to leave him." Another sigh from Sergeant. "I'll stay until she arrives."

Oh, shit. If I could, I'd beg Sergeant not to leave me here alone with her. At least until she calms down, and I can defend myself. Josie is the only family I have left, and although she's only two years older, she sure acts like a fiery mother hen when someone or something threatens my wellbeing.

It took over a month to convince her that my joining the military would be a good thing…not a death sentence. That I'd have an entire unit of brothers to fill in for her while we were apart. She even came with me to talk to the recruiter to see for herself. God, she's the best. She loves like no one else, and I wouldn't be the man I am today without her.

But I'm not looking forward to the lecture she's surely crafting on the way here. I already know what she's going to say. Cars are dangerous. She doesn't trust me with a golf cart, much less a bullet on wheels with 1960s technology and safety standards. I'm too reckless, too trusting, too fearless.

So, yeah. I'll be hearing plenty about all the dangers of the world and how my shortcomings exacerbate them all. I just hope I've slipped back into unconsciousness before she gets here.

———

Something's wrong. It's as if I'm lying on a bed of smoldering embers, my skin blending into the fiery heat. My screams are silent, lost in the inferno. When I force my eyes open, there's only a void that swallows everything. Flames overwhelm my senses, reducing me to ashes carried away by the wind.

———

"I don't know what to do. After this last episode, I'm barely hanging on." Josie's voice is muffled by the ringing in my ears, but I can hear her. Is she here? Why isn't she in New York? Where am I?

I open my eyes to darkness, except there's a small light on my left. It moves as no light should and a glow trail shines after it like a shooting star. I blink hard to clear my vision and the glow disappears. The outline of her face appears. She's holding a cellphone in front of her, knees pulled up to her chest.

"I've started looking for an apartment. Mom and Dad's house isn't livable." She pauses, listening through earbuds to the other person. Is she moving to Virginia? Why is she renting an apartment here?

"No. Jordan wanted to fix it up and maybe he will one day." Her voice sounds unsure, hoarse, and weary, and I wonder why. She's always so cheerful—the quintessential, carefree artist who can see the good in everything. She's pure, unbridled sunshine in a tiny package. The same feeling you get from looking at her paintings. But she's none of those things at this moment.

"Yeah, right," she says, and her scoff keeps my eyelids from closing. She's pissed, and it's not my fault this time. Well, at least until she realizes I'm eavesdropping. She mentions the asshole she lives with, and it all comes together.

"Ryder wouldn't know a hammer from a screwdriver if his life depended on it. But it doesn't matter, we broke up."

Hallelujah.

"Or rather, he said my choices were bringing him down, and he wanted his freedom back."

Ass.

"Yeah. He enjoyed throwing his infidelity in my face. I hate what brought me home, but I'm grateful for the excuse to leave. I'm better off without him. We were too different for it to work."

More like she's too good for him.

"He never loved me. Just loved how I looked on his arm and felt in his bed."

Okay. I've heard enough. "Jo Jo?"

"Oh, my god." Her phone rattles on the floor as the vinyl couch cushions squeak. She's next to me in seconds and flips on a light above us. "Jordan, I'm here."

"Why?"

"What do you mean?" The whites of her eyes are bloodshot, her skin splotchy. Josie will cry at anything that moves her, upsets her, frustrates her, or scares her. I know her signs and see them all in her now.

"What's wrong?"

"Jordan, sweetie." She sniffs and sits next to me. "You're in the hospital. Don't you remember?"

My eyes cut to the right to see more stark white walls, a TV, a sink, and several life-monitoring machines. No. I don't fucking remember. My heart rate spikes as I try to think back, and the beeping monitor next to me picks up speed.

"What happened to me?"

"Let me get the doctor." She moves off the bed, and I grab her wrist to stop her.

"No. Tell me what happened."

"I will. I promise," she says to pacify me. It doesn't work. "Let me tell them you're awake first."

"Why?"

"Jordan, you've been in and out of a coma for two weeks. Your doctors need to know you're awake and communicating." She leans close to press a kiss to my damp forehead, and I hear a click.

Damn her.

She sits back on the mattress, the alert button in her hand. "I'm so happy to see those beautiful eyes of yours again. You had us so worried."

"Jo, I—"

Two nurses rush into the room and start checking my vitals. I want to scream for them to get out, but their kind, empathetic smiles shut me up. After all, I feel fine. Well, other than my bones aching like they were pushed through a shredder and my head pounding at a nauseating pace, I…feel…fine.

The heart monitor's pace switches from rhythmic to erratic as my vision blurs. I hear echoes of tools being dropped onto a metal tray, footsteps running in all directions, and frantic voices. Someone yells my name before it all goes silent.

"Good news," Josie says, but with the siren going off in my ears, I can't tell if she's talking to me. I open my eyes and roll my head until I find her on the couch again, talking to someone on the phone—her best friend Grant, most likely.

It's daytime, and she's wearing her usual patterned leggings that don't match her oversized sweater, which, of course, is hanging off her slender shoulder. Her feet are bare. I swear the woman hates shoes. And her wavy blonde hair is wild, tied into a loose bun on the top of her head. She reminds me of Mom when Josie and I were in elementary school, my most vivid memory of her.

"He's still hanging on," she continues. "Guess it really is impossible to kill a Marine." She chuckles at her joke, but it's not her authentic laugh. The real one could short circuit light bulbs.

Wait. Did she say *kill*? Did someone try to murder me? I dreamed recently of a car crash. Of metal crushing my body until I passed out. It felt too real, too vivid, for a dream. But that could be from all the medication flowing through my veins.

"Not until he can stay conscious for more than a few minutes. All day, preferably. He's got a long road of rehab ahead of him." She twirls a curl of hair around her finger as she listens. "Not sure. I bought a few paint supplies last week and have some commissions lined up. Everything I own is in New York." Another pause. "That would be great, but I can't ask you to do that…Are you sure? Looks like we'll be here a while, so anytime that works for you. I don't have a lot. Just clothes and art supplies. Ryder furnished the flat…I hate dumping this on you…But it will be nice to see you and show you around Richmond…You should reserve a hotel room, though. The apartment I rented is a one bedroom and not exactly the Fifth Avenue standards you're accustomed to…Thank you, Grant. Try not to go all RuPaul on Ryder. He can't help who he is…I know. I can't and won't stop you. Just watch your back…You're the best. You know that, right?"

I don't make eavesdropping on my sister's conversations a habit, but since I have no idea what's going on, I need every clue I can get. The main thing I want to know, besides the name of my would-be murderer, is where the hell is my girlfriend? Does Nora not know what happened to me? Wouldn't she be worried that I've gone missing for weeks? Getting back to normal would be easier if I could hear her voice, look into her beautiful brown eyes, and feel her body against mine.

"Where's my phone?" I mutter, probably not as loud as it sounds in my foggy head since Josie doesn't budge. Determined, I push up onto the elbow not restricted by a sling, ripping the oxygen tube off my face. Flashes of light blind me, as does the pain in my abdomen and shoulder. Acid in my empty stomach rises into my throat.

"Jordan! What are you doing?"

Reading my face, she grabs a trash can along the way to me and holds it under my chin. I hurl my insides into it, but there isn't much since I can't remember the last time I ate.

"Are you crazy?" she exclaims, her voice sharp, as she reaches for the call button attached to the headboard.

"Don't you dare," I hiss through gritted teeth. "I love you, but I swear. If you touch that button, I won't speak to you for a month."

"Well, that's nothing new. It'll just be like the last few weeks." She holds up the button, taunting me with it. "I'm liking the quiet. Helps me paint."

"Shut up." I swallow the razor blades in my throat and beg whoever is using my ribs as a punching bag to take a break.

"What possessed you to do that?" she asks, helping me lie back onto the pillows.

"I want to call Nora."

"What for?" Reaching over me, she returns the button to its perch.

"She's probably wondering what's going on." But then again, I don't know what I'd tell her since no one's told me.

"You need to focus on getting better right now. Stop blacking out all the time."

"Not my choice."

"I know."

I resign to bribing a nurse for my phone later when Josie leaves me be for a few minutes. She's not a fan of Nora, given our history, but things are different now. To change the subject, I nod toward the stack of canvases propped up against the couch. "What are you working on?"

"Just a few commissions and a little something for the staff taking such good care of us."

"Us? You still look perfect." Her smile emerges, as I knew it would, and I'm reminded of how amazing she is. I don't tell her that enough.

"After all this time, the staff and I have become friends. They keep me grounded every time you give us a scare. I want to leave them a gift when we finally break out of here." She strolls to the stack of paintings, pulls one from the pile, and spins it around to show me. "It's the view from your room at sunrise. I haven't added the final touches yet."

"It's stunning as always, finished or not. Can you really see the river from here?"

"Yep. Ignore all the smog and it's quite the view."

"Funny. Speaking of ignoring things," I venture as she returns the painting. "It's time you told me what happened. I can handle it."

"You haven't been very convincing of that lately."

"What are you talking about?" I suck in some air, and it only burns a little on the way down to my chest. "I'm strong as an ox."

"More like a baby giraffe."

"Maybe so, but at least I'm your favorite animal."

"And my favorite brother."

"Enough of the flattery," I get out before a coughing fit sends jabs and searing punches along my ribcage. No matter how devastating the pain may be, I still catch her trying to call in reinforcements. "I'm not coughing up blood and don't need another full body inspection." My voice is strained but firm.

"Fine. But there's one nurse who might be disappointed. She seems to give you extra close attention."

"Are you done?"

She shrugs, not looking the least bit remorseful, while I pretend the boxer hasn't returned to finish me off. Between each jab, I can only manage shallow inhales and jagged exhales.

Josie collects my hand, bringing my attention back to her. She's so petite, my hand covers both of hers. "You were in a car accident just over three weeks ago, hit behind the driver's side by a drunk driver. Hayes Montgomery…he's your sergeant, right?" she asks, and I nod. "He witnessed the crash and called 9-1-1. Since he couldn't get to you, he made sure the other guy didn't flee."

"How broken am I?" I ask, motioning to the cast surrounding my lower left leg. "Feels like all of me."

"You're probably feeling the two broken ribs and internal bruising. The sling is for the separated shoulder. Surprisingly, no broken bones anywhere else. But there are some pretty nasty marks on your left side and hip that will be around for a while. The doctors did a great job cleaning you up on the inside, but the brain injury has been the scariest."

I can't remember much from that day, just snippets that feel conjured from a dream. Maybe I did dream them, but at least there's no murderer on the loose.

"Was there a fire?"

"Not that I'm aware of. You don't have any burns."

"That's good. How long until I'm back to normal? Can I return to service after or am I beyond repair? My buddy Jackson's injuries were so severe they didn't give him an option."

"Return?"

New questions bombard my thoughts, and I can't get them out fast enough. "Wait a minute. Who was driving the car? Are they okay? Did they survive?"

"You were driving, Jordan. Don't you—"

"I was? Whose car?"

She stares at me, confusion creasing the skin around her eyes. "Give me a second."

"Where are you going?"

"Jordan, just…" She holds up a finger, telling me to wait patiently. But how can I when she's acting so strangely? Like she's scared. "I'll be right back." She jogs to the door and out, letting it rattle shut behind her.

While I wait, I shuffle through my memories, trying to remember the crash. I don't remember driving or getting hit. I vaguely remember Sergeant Montgomery's hollow voice calling to me in the darkness. Where was I going? Where did I get a car? Why wasn't I on base?

My head spins faster than my stomach can take. Hauling myself up by the short bed railing, I lean over and vomit into the can on the floor. And just my luck, Josie returns in time to see me hanging off the mattress, too weak to put myself back where I came from.

"Oh, Jordan. I'm sorry." She tugs on my uninjured shoulder with the help of someone behind me.

Embarrassment hits me like a cherry pie to the face—I hate cherries *and* pie. Uninterested in seeing the pity in their eyes, I close mine as my head lowers to the pillow.

"Sweetie, are you okay? Say something," Josie urges, and I despise how fear shreds her melodic voice way more than cherry pie.

"What did the ocean say to the beach?"

"What?"

"You heard me." She loves my dad jokes. Since we were kids, I've used them to make her laugh whenever she's sick or scared. Now's probably not the best time to pull one out of the hat, but I will argue that there's never a bad time for a joke.

"He thinks he's a comedian," she explains and sighs. "What did the ocean say to the beach?"

I can almost hear her eyes rolling. "Nothing. It just waved."

Silence follows, then a snicker from someone on my other side before they both laugh.

"Hardy har har," Josie placates, all fear in her voice successfully eliminated. "It's time to behave yourself. Doctor Elvis is here."

My eyes fly open. "Did you say Elvis?"

"She did," Dr. Elvis answers, and she's a woman. Totally unexpected, and I love it. "It's a nickname. Way more fun than Doctor Elvira Ellis."

"Ahh. Elvira and Ellis together…brilliant." I swallow the bitter taste in my mouth, and like the perceptive mother hen that she is, Josie hands me a cup of water. "Thank you. Tell me, Doc. When can I get out of here?"

"You've made impressive improvement this week. Your test results look good, and making jokes is a new concussion symptom I haven't experienced before. Does he always do that?" she asks Josie.

"Oh, yeah," we say in unison and so in tune it would be easy to mistake us for twins.

"I look forward to hearing more in the coming days. We don't expect you to need any more surgeries, but I'd like to get another x-ray or CT scan to make sure. Since you're still vomiting, we need to monitor you a little while longer. Let's get you some lunch and see if you can hold it down."

Dr. Elvis turns and nods to a nurse, who I didn't notice standing beside the door. She scurries off to take care of the silent order.

"Now, give me your best jokes while I finish looking over your chart."

Chapter Two

Jordan

"Are you ready to get out of here, little brother?" Josie asks as she closes the last of our belongings and the shiny new wheelchair in the trunk of our Uber ride. Sergeant Montgomery offered to give us a ride, but I refused without mentioning it to Josie. She may be the best sister ever, but she's never been good at accepting help.

She's been that way all her life, even before our parents died while we were in high school. In elementary and middle school, our parents would leave her in charge of me and the house while they worked double shifts. After she graduated, Josie did the same, working multiple jobs and selling paintings to keep me out of foster care, put food on the table, and pay the bills.

It's why our parents' house is in such disrepair. Neither of us knew anything about plumbing or construction or yard work. Plus, it's sat empty and forgotten for the past eight years while I served, and Josie chased her dreams. A neglectful combination no structure can survive, no matter how good the bones are.

I plan to fix it up with the money I saved and maybe one day start a family there. Nora is not one to jump on the commitment train—or the kid train—but I can be very convincing when I want to be.

As we travel through Richmond and typical traffic for this time of day, I watch the world around me and wonder why she's not answering my texts or calling me back. Josie said she heard Nora left town to deal with some family drama in Northern Virginia. Her mother is a bit of a handful, and Nora's always putting her life on hold to pick up the pieces when her mother goes off the rails. But why keep me in the dark about that? She knows I will support her through anything.

Of course, Josie keeps telling me to stop worrying, but it's not like Nora to ghost me. Okay, even I can't think that with a straight face. Our relationship hasn't exactly been fairytale-like. Although I like to think of myself as her prince charming, she's slow to acknowledge the princess she is to me. She's too busy taking charge of her life like Mulan to wait around for a prince as Cinderella did. But that's okay. A strong woman is sexy.

Badass Marine training aside, maybe I'm the princess in this relationship. After all, she swept me off my feet the moment we met with her quick wit and caramel eyes. I love how she doesn't hold back, her foot always unapologetically on the gas pedal. I may not always like what she says and does, especially when she's being stubborn about her feelings for me, but I appreciate not needing a translator for her thoughts.

After we met at the Marine Marathon years ago, we got together occasionally when she was in the mood, and I had a night off. My favorites were the weekends we met up before I deployed. Her appetite for me was insatiable, like she wanted as much of me as she could get in case it might be our last.

A shiver runs down my spine and activates my lower half. Good to know *that* section of my body wasn't damaged in the crash.

Those days, separated from the outside world for forty-eight hours, we felt like a couple. Then, I'd ship off for eight weeks or more, and we'd start all over again when I returned. I didn't mind. Casual worked for us, and we didn't need labels, both content to use each other to satisfy our cravings, no strings attached.

But after my former unit—before I transferred to Sergeant Montgomery's—was attacked overseas, everything changed. The distance she put between us grew more than usual, and it took extra effort to close the gap. And when she finally let me back in, her emotions were unpredictable, and I couldn't gauge what she was thinking.

Eventually, after relentless pursuit, she agreed to be exclusively mine. It's not like we were sleeping around before that. She just refused to call me what I was—her boyfriend. On the other side of it, I labeled her my girlfriend every which way I could until she accepted it.

Things were good—*are* good—and as soon as I get her back in my arms, we can pick up where we left off.

Where we left off...

"I'm starving. Let's go get some dinner and a beer," I suggest, jumping out of Nora's bed as if my legs weren't weak from thirty-plus hours of extracurriculars.

It's late on Saturday, and we haven't left her bed since my leave kicked off on Friday morning. As much as I hate asking her to cover that gorgeous body, I need nourishment to continue what we started.

Plus, I have two other reasons for wanting to take my girl out tonight. First, I'm tired of keeping our relationship secret. We've been an official couple for two months, and there's no reason to continue hiding in her apartment. Second, she means more to me than our current arrangement, and I'm not sure she knows that. After four years of sneaking around and treating each other like a one-night stand on speed dial, I want more.

"We could go." She throws off the comforter, revealing every inch of her silky skin. "But that means covering up all this."

My fingers and other parts of me throb to touch her. But the mission has already been declared. The plan is clearly defined, and I've executed step one. Since a Marine never abandons a mission, she can't sex me out of following through on this one.

It would be tempting to let her try. I consider it until she flashes me a smile that isn't her usual come-ravage-me look. It's too smug, like she's exploiting my weakness and doesn't care if I know it.

Challenge accepted.

Tossing the shirt I collected from the floor, I leap on top of her. Greedy hands roam her body while I kiss her senseless—a little payback for the attempted diversion. I'm not the only one with weaknesses, and it doesn't take much effort to get her hips bucking against mine, begging me to finish what I started.

She thinks she's convincing me to stay right here to do what we're good at, but it's time for step two. "Put on your tightest dress." I trail kisses down her neck and breasts. "I want to see and feel every one of these delicious curves. Something that will take a long time to peel off you later."

"Are you seriously planning to leave me wanting?" she purrs, but the sensual tone isn't working—not enough to change my mind, anyway.

"Don't worry. I'll make it worth the wait." I smack her on the ass and crawl back to grab my shirt at the foot of the bed.

"Maybe I'm not hungry."

"Then you can decorate the table with your beauty while I eat."

"Not interested." She sits up, leans back against the headboard, and crosses her arms in a show of defiance, not bothering to cover up.

Her comfort in her skin is one of the many qualities I adore about her. She doesn't give two shits about me drinking her in every chance I get. Although, the opportunities she allows makes me think she likes it when I do. Our favorite pastime, other than the obvious, is to play cards, mainly various poker games. I've beat her a time or two. But I make little effort to win at sex poker—her invention—since her ideas for payment are infinitely more creative than mine. We play strip poker, too. The view may be spectacular, but it's not as much fun as the alternative. Nothing beats watching the most beautiful woman come undone under my touch.

Speaking of Nora's nude body. "And don't you dare wear anything underneath in case I change my mind."

A deep hum rumbles in her throat in response. My demands turn her on something fierce, but she holds back a reaction this time. Not what I hoped for, but exactly what I expected.

"If you insist on doing this," she begins with her usual rebelliousness. "I'll wear whatever the hell I want."

"Go ahead. Your expensive panties mean nothing to me, and I'll have no problem ripping them off you when the mood strikes. If you're willing to sacrifice them…"

I know my girl and love pulling her strings. After all, what happens when those strings snap is quite satisfying for me, too.

"Damn you," she growls and jumps off the bed to shower.

———

"We're here," Josie announces, interrupting my glorious daydream.

I crane my sore neck to see the red brick apartment towering outside my window.

"It's the only one I could find within walking distance to the veteran therapy center. Since we'll both be spending a lot of time there—"

"Other than dropping me off, why will you need to be there?"

She stares at me like she's trying to read me before answering. "I'm painting a mural behind their reception desk."

"Oh. That's great. We can go together."

"My thoughts exactly."

She climbs out, but not before instructing me to wait for her. Since I'm twice her size, it takes plenty of maneuvering, pauses, and readjustments before I'm sitting in the wheelchair. Every inch of me screams from the jerky movements and her compact frame trying to support me. I'm afraid she may have a few new bruises just from this one exercise.

"My bad, sis." I breathe deep, which hurts like hell, too.

The next several weeks of recovery and physical therapy may test our sibling relationship. We share everything. We've been best friends all our lives, but there are some things my sister doesn't need to see.

I chuckle to myself, thinking about my 115-pound sister trying to get my slippery naked self out of the tub, and all the jokes I could make afterward. Even more hilarious would be her comebacks, falling just off their intended mark. She's too sweet to make crude jokes, but she doesn't know that.

Maybe sponge baths are a better idea.

"277 Smithfield Avenue," I repeat out loud a few times to commit it to memory.

"What are you doing, silly?"

"Memorizing our new address so I can send it to Nora. Dr. Elvis said it might be hard to remember things for a while."

With a curt nod, Josie lifts our bags from the trunk and drapes the straps over the wheelchair handles. She doesn't want me dating Nora, and that's fine…for now. She just needs to see Nora and I together to understand that we have more than a random hookup relationship. And now that Josie's moved to Richmond, she'll get to know Nora better and, hopefully, let go of the resentment she's harboring for no good reason.

She pays the driver and pushes me up the ramp to the main entrance with everything we own either hanging off my chair or sitting in my lap.

"Thankfully, we're on the first floor," she says, stopping outside apartment 103. "The living room has sliding glass doors facing the courtyard."

"Sounds wonderful."

"You haven't seen it yet."

"I'm sure it's fine, Jo Jo, and temporary, right? You'll be moving back to New York after I'm self-sufficient, and I'll go back to Quantico." I pause, confused why her eyes are glistening. Is she worried about me getting hurt again? Does she not want us to be apart? Is she embarrassed about the apartment? I focus on the last since we'll have plenty of time to talk about the rest. "Plus, this will feel like a luxury apartment compared to what I'm used to."

"We'll see." With a sniff, she inserts the key into the lock and pushes open the door. "Well, at least it smells better than the last time I was here."

She rolls me over the creaky hardwood floors to the center of the small living room. I can see the entire apartment from my vantage point. A small galley kitchen with off-white flat cabinet doors trimmed in medium-stained wood. The new white stacked washer and dryer at the end of the counter standing out like a spotlight. The curtainless glass doors Josie mentioned and the courtyard beyond to the left. Two doors leading to a bedroom and a bathroom on the right. And not a single piece of furniture.

"At least I came with my own chair," I joke.

"Don't."

"Big city luxury in my mind."

She rids me and the chair of our belongings and sets them on the floor. "You have more imagination than I thought you did if that's what you see here."

"I'm used to wobbly folding tables and sleeping on the floor or on cots that feel more like a bed of rocks." I hold out the hand that's not trapped in a sling, and she slides hers into it. "Because you're here, this will feel like home."

Her body reacts to the *home* comment before she hides behind a smile. But knowing her as I do, I notice the eye twitch, her muscles tightening ever so slightly, and the pad of her thumb rolling over her fingertips in slow circles. Her stress signals. Regret punches me in the gut for using the word in jest.

We lost everything that represented a traditional home the day our parents died. As if high school wasn't hard enough, we were dumped into the foster care system before our young minds could process what happened. We were expected to be model students, refrain from causing any disruptions, and go about our lives as if our hearts weren't ripped from our bodies. From that moment on, *home* became each other.

"You're not sleeping on the floor in your condition," she informs me, fully recovered.

But I'm still mentally punching myself for the careless slip. We've always protected each other, and in this situation, she's the vulnerable one. It's like we're teenagers again—the last time she changed her life to support me. I need to do better and stop making it harder on her.

"I'll grab two air mattresses until we can buy some beds," she continues. "You'll take the bedroom."

"Absolutely not."

"Jordan, I'm not backing down on this." Her free hand finds her hip as she glares down at me. It's the stance she takes when she's in sacrifice-myself-for-others mode. It's the most stubborn one. So, I try another route.

"But what about the safety of my eyes whenever I want a late-night snack?"

"What are you talking about?"

"All the hot guys you'll be bringing home and getting to know in the living room." I wiggle my brow and wait for the joke to settle into place. Punchlines usually register for her well after delivery.

"You're ridiculous," she says finally with a huff. "If you didn't have a concussion, I'd smack you on the back of the head like Dad used to do."

"Since you can't retaliate, I'm not shutting up until you take the bedroom."

"And since I'm in control of your transportation, you'll go where I take you each night…which will be the bedroom. I win." With a toss of her hair, she saunters toward the kitchen.

"What are you doing?"

"Grabbing my phone. The mattresses can't order themselves." She shuffles through her bag, pulls out the phone, and starts her search. While she shops, she rambles about what she finds or whatever pops into her head to fill the silence. "When do you want to visit VETS? They'll take care of all your appointments after we sign up and provide physical therapy, mental health counseling, and anything else you need."

"Doesn't matter. When did you want to paint the mural?"

"Crabcakes," she says with the punctuation of a curse word, warming my sore body like a heating pad. "All my supplies are still in New York…at *Ryder's*." Her eyes circle to the ceiling, then back to her phone.

"Why did you say his name like that?"

"Like what?" she asks, her disdain glaringly evident.

"Like you're mad at him." If they're over, it will be the best news I've heard in forever. The rich bastard is such an arrogant tool and not even close to good enough for her. "I thought you two were all in."

"I was mostly in. He was all the way out and just hadn't told me yet."

"What'd he do?" There goes my easily excitable blood pressure.

"Calm your stallions. He just cheated and sent a text to break it off." She went back to scrolling as if none of what she confessed bothered her, but I know better. The bastard did more than wound her pride. "It's not worth causing yourself a headache over."

"I have a headache 24/7. So, too late. He really ended it over text? Such a heartless coward," I bark out. "When was this?"

"It doesn't matter."

"When Josie? Before or after you came here?"

She looks up from her phone to meet my heated gaze, and thankfully, her eyes are dry. At least she's not wasting any tears over him. "After. But that—"

"Damn that asshole. How long had he been cheating? Did you know?"

"I did." She holds up a hand to stop the next outburst forming on my tongue. "I was working on getting out. New York is expensive, and I had nowhere else to go. From the penthouse, it was a two-block walk to a job I loved. I had space to paint with wall-to-wall windows overlooking the city. I had no bills and the best wine to drown my sorrows. He was kind enough not to kick me out, even though we had grown apart. You can think less of me if you want for not jumping from that into homelessness."

She's not telling me the complete story, protecting me as usual, but I don't push her. "Josie, I could never think less of you. What about Grant? Couldn't you have stayed with him?"

"He may be my best friend, but he's also my agent. I'm sure living together would be frowned upon."

"Well, how are we going to get your stuff…if it's not in a dumpster?"

"It's not," she says flatly.

"How do you know?"

She looks up again. "Grant collected it and is bringing it here soon."

"Good. Did he give that asshole what he deserves while he was there?"

"He did."

"Guess I'll let him back on my good side then."

Chapter Three

Nora

"I need to talk to you," my boss says as I rush by. Emily Vane is the co-owner of the Veterans and Exercise Therapy Services Center I manage. The concern in her eyes has me curious, but it also activates my fight or flight reflex. Flight it is. Plus, I have a good excuse.

"Would you mind if I find you after class? Since I've been out, it took longer to get caught up at the front desk, and now I'm running late to teach the Chair Yoga class."

Emily checks her watch and sighs. "Okay. It's urgent but can wait a bit. I'll be in my office."

"Thanks." I rush through the fitness equipment in the main workout area and into the Will Mason Multi-Purpose Room to find I have six class participants. Some are younger with leg or hip injuries. Others are older, nursing chronic pain or healing from recent surgeries. All were ordered to be there by their VETS physical therapist as part of their treatment. All are veterans, male, and based on their sulky postures and exaggerated scowls, think yoga is stupid. But I love a challenge, and this lot of broody heroes have no idea what's in store for them.

I saunter to the speaker system in the opposite corner with a broad smile, making eye contact with each member. I have a mission to accomplish, and I'm going to deploy every tactical weapon I have at my disposal to do so. Mood lighting. Soft instrumental versions of popular rock and pop songs. And gorgeous female anatomy that deserves to be admired.

By the end of class, these defenders of freedom will have gained languid muscles, improved movement and strength, and a new appreciation for the benefits of yoga. They won't be coming to class next week with those frowns. I'll have eager students, excited about this part of their ongoing recovery.

Time to initiate contact and get working on the mission.

"Alrighty boys," I say to the twelve skeptical eyes directed at me. "Let's warm up those muscles."

For the next twenty minutes, we breathe and stretch together—each one following instructions to the letter as though I'm their commanding officer. It's one of the many things I love about working at VETS. Every member getting help here is either active military or a veteran. Every staff person and volunteer come here because they want to help and serve others. Respect and courtesy, duty and honor make up the core of the people, the organization, and the nonprofit's mission. I've never seen a place overflow with selflessness and benevolence like VETS does. It's breathtaking, and I'm instantly inspired the second I walk through the door.

Movement outside the classroom steals my attention, and as my eyes land on a familiar face, my brain jumbles. I can't remember which exercise I am leading or what I'm supposed to say next. Emily's giving a facility tour to a couple: my ex and a gorgeous, petite blonde woman pushing him in a wheelchair.

I can't breathe. Why is Jordan here? What happened to him? Why didn't I know he is a member here now? Is that his girlfriend? Shit. I want to look away, but I'm drawn to them, curiosity overtaking confusion. This visit must have been what Emily wanted to tell me this morning.

As he and his companion head toward the therapy wing, following Emily's directions, she glances my way with an apologetic grin. She doesn't know our full story, but she has enough details to know this surprise warranted a warning. After all, we hooked up at her and Jackson's wedding and activated quite the gossip chain since many attendees knew we'd been broken up for months.

Regret consumes me for not knowing about his injury. In my defense, we haven't kept in touch since the wedding ten months ago. But it's not like he means nothing to me.

God. Why does my chest feel like it has an arrow in it? It's pierced through skin, bone, and heart. I could have better prepared myself for the strike had I known he was coming in today. If it hadn't been for my mother's ridiculous drama, I would have.

Today is my first day back to work after taking a long weekend to talk my mother off yet another imaginary ledge. She was served her fourth set of divorce papers, which means her world is ending…again. That's why I missed Jordan's registration. Why I hadn't had time this morning to review the new member list and get up to speed.

Now that I think about it, my best friend could have warned me well before now. Sydney should have known, not only because she's VET's accountant but because she's close to Emily, Jackson, the front desk staff, and literally everyone in this damn place. Everyone knew this new member came with a warning label, and only Emily was brave enough to bring it up…albeit a little too late.

Did everyone's phone break simultaneously where no one could send a simple text?

> **Literally Anyone:** Warning! Ex-boyfriend and you will collide unexpectedly tomorrow. Your world will be rocked, and you won't know which way is up. Have a nice day.

Yet, with or without the warnings I wish I'd received, I still should have known. It's Jordan, for goodness' sake. Something significant and potentially horrible occurred in his life, he's in my city, and he seeks services from my employer. At that, my hand presses against my stomach as it twists with guilt.

To make matters worse, my sick brain is running through all the possible causes for his obvious injuries, military-related or otherwise, and his upcoming recovery. I wonder if he'll be able to return to the career he loves. If the woman he's with will take care of him, and if they're close like we once were. And with that thought, I'm forced to remember the shambles I made of our relationship and how it's reduced us to strangers. An ache I don't recognize pushes through the chaos, bringing me back to—

Someone nearby coughs, and I glance toward the only noise in the room. The music stopped and only a few of my new yogis remain, quietly removing themselves from the awkward end of class.

Shit.

"You okay, Miss Nora?" asks one of the older gentlemen, a Navy veteran, as his dark blue and gold embroidered hat tells me.

"Yes, thank you. I just need a moment."

"Not a problem since time is up. Great class today." He winks and rolls himself out.

"Sydney." I jump up to go search for my best friend slash keeper of heart-wrenching secrets, but stop in the doorway to check for equally gut-wrenching ex-boyfriends. With none in sight, I head for the administrative hallway and burst into Sydney's office without knocking. "Sydney Norman, I can't believe—"

The stunning blonde who had accompanied Jordan on the tour now sits in front of Sydney's desk as if waiting for me. I take longer than necessary to shut the door, sensing this is a closed-door type of meeting. Plus, I still need the moment I didn't take earlier to gather myself.

Shit. Shit.

"Hi, Nora," the woman says flatly. "I thought it was time we talked." She doesn't stand to greet me, only eyes me with suspicion and a forced smile. Her face looks familiar, but I can't place her. Thick, perfect curls framing her slender face; a deep dimple on her left; big blue eyes—Oh, god, it's Josie. Not Jordan's new girlfriend, but his protective, despises-me-with-every-fiber-of-her-perfect-little-body older sister.

Shit. Shit. Shit.

"It's nice to finally meet you, Josie," I lie. At any other time in my and Jordan's history, I believe I could have won her over as I do with my stubborn yoga students. She seems like a decent person from the things Jordan says, but no amount of shmoozing could make her like me after what I did to her brother.

"Have a seat, Nora," Sydney urges. I narrow disapproving eyes at her sympathetic tone yet follow her directions, grateful she's here to keep me from saying something I'll regret. I can always count on her for a good kick in the shin whenever I'm being a jerk or have said something I shouldn't. Unfortunately, her big, fancy-ass desk separates us and leaves me on an island. I'll have to fend for myself or take my chances swimming for some distant, unknown shore when this conversation turns rocky.

"I'll cut to the chase," Josie begins. "Since Emily is busy with Jordan, I gave the details to Sydney to pass along to both of you. If I'm gone much longer, he'll start asking questions."

"What's going on? Is he okay?"

She scoffs, surely not believing my concern is sincere. "He will be. Until then, I need you to do something."

I glance at Sydney, and she gives me a tight-lipped grin, indicating my choices between right and wrong are limited. "What is it?"

Josie lets out a long breath. Asking me for help causes her a great deal of discomfort, and I don't know how to interpret that. Her face scrunches like the words are bitter on her tongue. "I need you to pretend you and Jordan are still a couple."

"What?" I shoot out of my chair. The arrow is back and has set my entire body aflame. "What the hell for?"

"Sydney can tell you why. I don't have time to explain it again."

She stands to face me squarely. She's only an inch or two shorter than me, but she's got a fierceness I wish I had in this moment. Mine seems to have melted into a useless confused pile of—

"Will you do it? For him?" she asks.

"Not until you tell me what's going on."

"She'll do it," Sydney says, and my eyes shoot daggers at her. She hadn't moved from her seat, but with this betrayal, she might as well be standing beside Josie.

"Good. I'll leave her in your hands." Josie turns to me and points a slender, unpainted fingernail at me. "You better not do anything to make this worse."

"Worse? How can it possibly get any worse?" I say as she storms across the room and lets the door shut in her wake. "What the hell, Sydney?"

"Sit down."

"That's the third time you've told me what to do since I walked through that door. I don't want to sit. I want you to tell me what's going on before I lose my shit right here."

"Jordan was in an accident," she begins, staring me down. She's adored Jordan since we all met at the Marine Marathon and tells me all too often how I feel when I can't admit it to myself. Sometimes I wish she didn't know me so well. "It nearly killed him. Josie said his heart stopped several times."

My weakened body lowers to the seat despite my stubborn pride. The thought of losing him, whether I want a relationship or not, is more than I can bear. He's an amazing man. I've never thought or said otherwise, but having a future with him isn't possible for many reasons. Not to mention my steadfast refusal to give my heart to a man of the military.

I saw first-hand what that did to Sydney. Her future bliss was all planned out with her Marine. After watching his absence rip her to pieces repeatedly and supporting her each time, I can't subject myself to the same torture. I won't.

"The last thing I want is for anything to happen to him," I say, still shaking from hearing the news. "But what does this have to do with me? And why did Josie say I have to pretend nothing over the last year ever happened?"

"In addition to his physical injuries, he has post-concussion syndrome and lost part of his memory."

"Which part?"

"The last year. He thinks you two are in the middle of the six months you were actually dating in your five-year on again off again relationship."

"Well, that explains a lot." I stalk to the large window and stare out at the mid-September morning, seeing none of its beauty. Fall is usually my favorite time of year, but under the weight of what Sydney and Josie expect me to do…

"Why can't she tell him we're not?"

"Doctors recommended letting him remember things on his own time frame to keep his stress low." She crosses the room to sit on the window seat in front of me and takes my hand. Josie shouldn't have left Sydney to bear the brunt of delivering this news alone. None of this involves her—other than being my punching bag or support system during this farce I want no part in.

"The trauma of knowing something happened and not remembering it," she continues, "and all the resulting questions could impede his progress or cause more strain than his healing body can handle. Until he can remember…"

"We all have to pretend I didn't break his heart?"

"Appears so."

My gaze drops to her. "This is fucked up, Sydney."

"It is. And it's going to be hardest on you. Would you rather put him through the alternative?"

"Of course not." My legs waver under me, and I sit beside her. With my head on her shoulder, she gathers me closer. "How long do they think it will take?"

"There's no way of knowing. The brain is a curious beast."

"Curious beast?" I glance at her with full-blown skepticism. "Have you switched your romance novels with nonfiction textbooks? That doesn't sound like the romantic I know and love."

"Since when do you acknowledge my romantic side?"

"You just didn't sound like you."

"What would have sounded like me?" Sydney asks, laughing.

"I don't know. Something over-the-top hopeless, like in a Hallmark movie or like Emily."

Sydney scoffs. "Nothing comes close to Emily's romantic side. Even I look at her like she's crazy sometimes."

"Can't blame her, though. Jackson is stupidly hot."

Ignoring me because she's happily engaged to her own beautiful veteran, and Jackson is her son's godfather, Sydney circles back to Jordan. "So, you'll do it?"

I sigh. "Doesn't sound like I have a choice."

"Not really." She tugs me into a hug. One I didn't realize I needed until I'm snug in her arms. "And you know why?"

"I'm afraid to ask."

"Because you still care for him."

I start to pull away in protest, but she squeezes tighter.

"And I bet this little exercise makes you finally admit your feelings for him."

"Alright, that's enough." Breaking free, I make my way to the door. Little does she know I'd long ago fallen for Jordan and look where that got me. "I said I would pretend to be his girlfriend. No one said anything about love."

"You're right. No one did…except you."

———

Alone in my office, avoiding reality, I'm unable to focus on anything except Jordan and our predicament. When he texted over the last few weeks, I assumed he'd been drunk at the time or sleepwalking or doing something that impeded his good judgment. Especially since the messages were sometimes incomprehensible or written in an odd shorthand.

It never crossed my mind that the texts might be sincere. That he truly thought his heart was still intact, and I hadn't shattered it for a second time almost ten months ago. Which is exactly why I didn't answer any of them.

In his current mindset, I can only imagine the hurt and fear that's crept in while I've remained silent. Snatching up my cellphone, I reluctantly open the text app to reread his messages.

Jordan: wher r u
Jordan: ned to talk to u im n rchmd dnt no y
Jordan: herd u went home hope ur ok
Jordan: plz call me hard to txt
Jordan: gttn out soon
Jordan: hm n richmond 277 smithfld ave 103

Each awkward word he sent stabbed at my conscience. I wish I knew what happened to him. I was too stunned by Josie's request to ask questions after she left. I'll corner Sydney before she leaves, but right now, I know what I must do. My thumbs hover over my own tiny keyboard, not knowing how to begin.

Me: Hi. I'm sorry I missed your texts. Are you OK?

This is cowardly. I should call or go see him…or better yet, wait until I've wrapped my head around how to act like a girlfriend around him. My thumb reaches over the keyboard to hit the delete button and accidentally scrapes the *Send* button.

Shit. Shit. Shit. Shit.

Three little dancing dots pop up, showing he's typing, and my heart jumps into my throat.

Sh—

Jordan: its bout time where hav u ben i miss u im ok only puked thre tims toda

Me: Is that good?

Why is this so hard? Oh, right. Because it's an absurd plan and only a matter of time before he remembers. A secret hidden in the shadows of his mind and poised to make itself known with the power of a grenade. The devastation could be the same, or worse, the third time around.

Jordan: trying to typ bettr

Me: You're doing great.

Tears pool and blur my vision. What the hell? I can't remember the last time I cried. Maybe in elementary school when my parents told me they were divorcing? Whenever it was, it's not something I do. I've never been prone to showing that kind of emotion, but what we're doing to Jordan is wrong. My heart cracks just thinking about it, and that truth grenade hasn't even exploded yet.

Jordan: when can I see u?

Something in my stomach flutters as I stare at the question. I don't know if I can keep up this charade in person. It's one thing to text lies, it's another to say them to his face. To see his reaction to me and the promises my presence makes when I have no intention of following through.

I don't want to do this. I don't want to hurt him again and myself in the process. I don't want to touch him and feel his love, knowing how it will end.

But still I answer…

Me: Soon.

He doesn't respond. I stare at the phone, envisioning him hunched over and unconscious in his wheelchair, and all I can think is I hope he's not alone. I hope he's safe.

Chapter Four

Nora

"I've been trying to avoid the subject of your reincarnated relationship with Jordan, but it's obvious your attention is there…as it should be," Sydney says, but I'm barely listening. This lunch is turning into another situation I don't want to endure now that Jordan and my fake girlfriend status has entered the conversation. Yet, it's not as if it hasn't been constantly weighing on my mind.

Like the best friend she is, Sydney took me to lunch to give me an opportunity to talk about it.

"When are you going to see him?" she asks carefully.

"When I'm forced to."

"Delaying it is not solving anything."

"Sure, it is. The longer I wait, the more likely he'll remember, and this whole damn ordeal will end." I take a sip of water because my throat feels like I ate fresh-off-the-skillet fajitas instead of a cool salad. "He can go back to hating me, and I can go about my life as if none of this ever happened."

"Are you sure that's what you want out of this second chance?"

My answer is a solid, you-know-me-and-don't-be-ridiculous glare. Plus, responding would only dignify a question that never should have been asked.

"Fine. I'll tuck that away for another time."

"Or never."

"There will come a time when this conversation ends differently. I'll just keep my comments to myself until—Hey, is that Josie?"

My eyes follow where she's pointing through the wide front windows of the restaurant, and I see Josie carrying four too many grocery bags. More like she's dropping four grocery bags. Cans and apples roll across the sidewalk. Boxes tumble out of flimsy, overstuffed plastic bags. As her head drops back in exasperation, I get what feels like a steeled-toed boot to the shin.

"Go help her," Sydney says when I don't jump up with eager excitement. "It will do you both good to get to know each other."

"Syd—"

"Go!" She *nudges* me with her hard-ass boot again and stupid me doesn't dodge it despite knowing it was coming.

With a long exhale, I slide to the edge of the booth, rubbing my sore leg under my jeans before standing. "I hate you."

"Love you, too," she sing-songs as I storm out of the deli. This is our regular go-to lunch spot for escaping the hustle at VETS. What I wouldn't give to escape the uncomfortable confrontation I'm about to thrust my stupid self into against my better judgment.

"Need a hand?" I hear myself ask, but it sounds hollow, like an unbalanced voiceover. Like someone else is hastily covering up what I really want to say with what I should say.

"That would be—" When she sees it's me asking, her tone and demeanor switch from friendly appreciation to stubborn refusal. "I've got it."

"Come on, Josie. Let me help by giving you a ride. How were you going to carry this back to your apartment?"

"It's not that far, and if the bags hadn't ripped..."

"Jordan's not alone, is he?"

She lets out an audible exhale and collects the can of green beans that rolled against the light pole base. "No. Jackson's with him."

"I didn't mean to offend you, it's just..." Feeling awkward, I stack the boxes of cereal and pasta into a tower and lift them into my arms.

"It's what, Nora? You were worried about him?"

"Yes, actually."

"That's new."

I take a moment to calm my rising temper before my tongue says what my brain is thinking. Rarely do I bother with that, but the shitshow casserole has already been assembled, and I don't need to mess it up further by adding my salty seasoning. "Josie, just because our relationship didn't work out doesn't mean I didn't care for him."

"Well, your actions said otherwise."

I swallow the pile of salt my attitude poured into my mouth in response to the comment and try again. "My car is right there." Her head swivels to take in her saving grace a few steps away. All she has to do is accept that the devil isn't the one offering it and get in.

"Okay," she surrenders, shifting the heavy bags in her arms. I take a few to relieve the load. "I'd appreciate a ride. Thank you."

"You're welcome."

We drop the groceries into the trunk and take off without further incident and in haunted house silence. But now that I have a captured audience, I attempt to file down her hatred of me. "How's the apartment?"

"It works."

First pass at it, complete failure. As I search for another safe topic, she sits up suddenly, her eyes zeroed in on something in the distance.

"Oh! A yard sale. And they have a table." Lost in her excitement, she seemingly forgets who she's with, and sweetly asks, "Mind if we stop?" She leans on the dash to get a better view of the items as I pull up behind another car and park. "Thanks."

The door flies open, and she rushes across the small grassy area before I turn off the engine, leaving me behind. Guess we're doing more shopping on our four-block drive.

When I catch up, she's already clutching a stack of yellow, orange, and brown dishes straight out of the seventies.

"I love anything vintage," she says to the older woman with a button-down plaid shirt, jeans, and fanny pack behind the table, tracing the edge of the table she saw from the road. It's antique mahogany in exquisite condition, with carved legs and six matching chairs. "How much is it?"

"Four hundred," the woman says, but Josie's shoulders slumping in response has her adding, "or best offer."

"On second thought, it might be a little big for our apartment. It's beautiful, though. I'll just take these." Her smile fades to disappointment as she tosses a bundled set of silverware onto the bowls, juggling the heavy stack like a clumsy waitress. They shift and lean as she reaches for her purse.

"Why don't I hold those?" Her head swivels in surprise at my presence, and without giving her a chance to be stubborn, I secure the dishes in my arms.

"There's another sale down around the corner if you're interested," the woman snaps the tension between us, and Josie passes her a ten-dollar bill.

"Thanks," she says and turns to me. "I'm going to jog over there to see if I can find anything else for the apartment."

"Sure, but why do you need all this? Aren't you moving back to New York when Jordan returns to the base?"

"Sydney didn't tell you?"

"Tell me what?"

"Let's put those in the car and take a walk."

I follow her back to the car, too stunned by her tender delivery and warning about more secrets to think for myself.

The next yard sale is within view when she finally breaks the silence. "I'm staying in Richmond for the foreseeable future, and Jordan's not going back."

"What?"

"The accident happened on the day after he left the base for the last time, honorably discharged by choice, of course. Not because of his injuries, as you probably think."

"I didn't know he...I thought he wanted to make the military his lifelong career. And that he'd go back to serving after he healed."

"That's what he thinks, too, thanks to his symptoms." She sighs. "Part of me thinks he retired for you."

We reach the sale, and as I follow her past each table, disbelief has me seeing none of it. There's no way he left the military for me. We hadn't spoken for over nine months. If anything, he did it to forget me.

"Jiminy crickets! Look at this quilt." Her excitement grabs my attention. She traces the intricate pattern with a finger, checks the price tag, then tucks it under her arm before moving on. "Since I didn't hear otherwise," she says without looking away from the items, "I assume you decided to do what I asked."

"I have," I manage while trying to ignore the nerves that feel more like blood-thirsty vipers in my belly. "But not without a mountain of reservations. This could end far worse than if we just told him the truth."

"Possibly, but it's up to you to ease him into it and make sure he doesn't come out of this more damaged."

"How in the world am I supposed to do that? He's going to be—"

"Ooo. Stainless steel pots."

"Josie." I gently grab her arm and turn her to face me. I need advice, even if it's from the queen viper herself.

"Just make him fall out of love with you." She shoots venom at me with her blistering glare. "You've done it before. You can do it again."

"That's not fair."

"What's not fair? The truth?"

"You don't know—"

"Oh, yes, I do."

I glance around, and thankfully, the only other shoppers are an older couple, paying us no mind. The home's residents are another story. But Josie barrels on as if she wants the entire block to know what she thinks of me.

"I was there for him when you weren't." She steps closer to challenge me, and I hold my ground, respecting her strength.

She's scrappy, smart, and fierce despite her small stature. And if she didn't use her disdain for me as a weapon, I might actually like her. But we're nowhere near that now.

On the surface, we're not so different. While I haven't fought for everything in my life as she has, no one's handed me anything either. My own battles have hardened me, and my work ethic has rewarded me. I protect my friends and family, too, just as she is protecting Jordan.

"You want to talk about fair?" The folded quilt she's hugging to her chest fills the inches between us. "What about Jordan? He served eight years for his country in the most dangerous situations and returned with not one blemish. Less than forty-eight hours after he leaves, he's almost killed by a frickin' drunk driver. He doesn't remember any of it, or that he's moved on from the one person who broke him more times than any drill instructor or weapon ever could. So, tell me, Nora. How fair is that?"

"It sucks, Josie, but this situation is not my fault. It was your idea to bring me into it, and I'd appreciate it if you'd stop treating me like the enemy."

She stares me down as she backs away to resume shopping. "Alright," she says easily, picking up a small wooden cutting board to examine the dents and grooves on both sides. "Answer this question first…truthfully."

"I have nothing to hide."

A smirk lightens her eyes when she glances my way. "Did you ever love him?"

Damn. Anything but that. As promised, I answer honestly, giving her insight into something no one else knows. "Yes."

"Then why did you do it?"

"Do what?" I stall. I know what she's asking, and I can't avoid her question, thanks to my *I-have-nothing-to-hide* arrogance. My eyes blur over the eclectic arrangement of trinkets on the table.

"Don't give me that shiitake."

"Shiitake?" Snapping out of my sulk, I pinch back a laugh. Is she really so perfect that she can't taint her flawless lips with a curse word?

"You know what I mean."

"It's shit. Mushrooms don't have the same effect as a steaming pile of—"

I gasp when my eyes land on a rainbow squishy toy in the shape of a pile of poop. It has a goofy smiley face on it that matches my gratification over the impeccably timed irony. I snatch it up and display it proudly on my palm. "I'm getting this for you."

She giggles before remembering she despises me. "You're avoiding the question."

"No. I'm hopefully making you hate me less."

"I don't hate you."

My throat tosses out a *yeah-right* scoff as if I have no control over my body.

"Truly," she insists. "I just don't trust you with my brother's heart."

Can't blame her.

"He seems to have a softness for you." She adds a light blue shower curtain and matching bath rugs to her arms. "Or a high tolerance, depending on how you look at it."

It comes out like she's talking through something she doesn't understand, so I choose to believe she didn't mean it as an insult. After all, she'd protect Jordan with her life and only sees good in him. If I allow myself to see her point of view, she's right to guard him. He *is* one of the purest, kindest, sweetest souls, and I'm none of those things.

Chapter Five

Jordan

"We're here," Josie says as she enters the front door. "We? Who'd you pick up at the—Nora." At the sight of her entering the living room, my system snatches the air from my lungs and slaps me in the face with it. I'm not ready. I mean, I've been begging to see her, but I haven't prepared my heart for the jolt her presence always gives me.

While I search for a thread of control, my eyes take in every inch of her. Her soft white sweater, cropped at the waist of her black high-rise jeans. The light freckles on her nose and the lone mark above her top lip. Her long dark hair tied up into a ponytail, exposing the soft skin of her neck and my favorite place to kiss. She's holding bags and something else, but I can't focus on it because her glistening eyes have met mine and put me in a chokehold.

"How did you two—"

"It's a long story," Josie dismisses, but Nora pipes up to fill in the blanks.

"She tried to carry the grocery store home in a few bags, but some of them ripped. I witnessed the disaster and saved the day with my car."

Josie grins, but it looks painful. "And she was patient enough to let me pick through a couple of yard sales on the way."

Seeing the two of them together for the first time mesmerizes me, but my attention keeps gravitating back to Nora. She's a beacon of light in the shadows the accident cast over my days, and I'm captivated, drawn to her like a wayward ship in the night.

"I heard voices. Everything okay?" Sergeant Montgomery asks as he exits the bathroom, whipping me out of my stupor.

"Yes. It's—"

"Hi, there." Josie steps around the kitchen counter and tosses me a confused glance. "I didn't know we had a visitor. I was about to ask where Jackson disappeared to," she says.

"Something came up at VETS," Sergeant Montgomery answers, saving me from having to muscle up the words. "I arrived to see how Jordan was getting along before he left."

"That's great."

"I should get going. Jordan, I'm glad to see you're upright and all in one piece. You had us worried."

I shake his hand, grateful to call him my friend and sergeant. But with Nora moving around the kitchen in my periphery, I'm not fully present in the conversation.

"Tell the guys we'll celebrate big when I get back," I say at last.

"What? You're—"

"Thank you so much for stopping by…Hayes, is it?" Josie waves for Sergeant to follow her. "Let me walk you out."

I don't like the look on her face or the warning her eyes are giving him, but they step outside together (also odd), leaving me and Nora alone. She looks over the bags at me, then around the room. It feels less empty now that her sweet vanilla scent has filled the space.

"How have you been?" I ask for lack of anything else coming to mind. Her beauty has a way of knocking me senseless with or without brain injuries.

"Good." She removes a can of green beans from the bag and sets it on the counter. "I'm loving my new job."

Why is she still so far away?

"You have a new job? Where?"

"At VETS."

"Really? That's great. I guess I'll be seeing you there a lot. Are you commuting? That's a long way to—"

"I moved here."

"Oh. When?" My dumb concussed brain isn't putting the pieces together. I have so many questions and each one makes my head pound. When did she move, and why didn't I know? My hospital stay lasted only a few weeks. How did she get a new job and move cities in that time frame, and why didn't she tell me? Has this been in the works for a while? Was she planning to break it off before the accident? Is that why she's so distant now?

"Jordan," she says, a little too weary for my comfort, as she continues to unload the groceries. "We can talk about me anytime. Now I want to know how you're feeling."

"I'd feel a lot better if you were beside me instead of over there."

After what seems like months of separation instead of mere weeks, I'm itching to touch her again. My heart rallies in anticipation as she takes a step closer. And another. She reaches the edge of the kitchen on her way to me when the slamming front door sends her back.

Josie appears and takes us in with caution before resetting her face with a wide smile. "Is that sergeant of yours always so grumpy?"

"Yes. Nothing makes him smile except a lot of booze."

"Sounds like a real bore…except at parties." She shrugs and joins Nora in the kitchen. "Wait until you see what we found at the yard sales. Next find will be furniture, I know it."

Nora's eyes drift to the only so-called furniture in the open living room and kitchen area—an air mattress in the corner where I convinced Josie to let me sleep for easy wheelchair maneuvering. I wonder what she's thinking. She knows my family history, but my present situation might be bleaker than she's prepared to deal with. Good thing it's temporary.

"I have some furniture I'm not using," Nora says, concentrating on Josie. "You're welcome to it."

"Thanks, but I'm sure I'll find—"

"Don't be silly. It's all just sitting in storage and in great shape. I rather someone use it."

Josie sighs. "Okay. If you're sure."

"I bought a new set right before my mother rid herself of all the furniture she and her soon-to-be ex-husband bought last year. But guess who gets to do all the actual ridding?" Nora points a thumb at herself and adds a sarcastic grin. "You'll be doing me a favor."

They share a smile, and watching my two favorite girls become friends soothes the ache in my chest.

"And you'll be happy to hear that my mother's last husband owned an antique dealership. The house was furnished with pieces she picked out from the store."

"Get out!" Josie pushes on Nora's shoulder, soliciting a laugh from them both. "Where is this storage unit? I'm dying to see what you have."

"It's in Northern Virginia. Just two hours from here."

"Oh." Josie's shoulders slump, and I know why. It's the burden bearing her brother's name.

"Why don't you go next time I have a long schedule at VETS?" I suggest. "I can eat lunch and keep myself busy there until you get back."

"We'll see," Josie says, balling up the empty plastic bags and tossing them under the sink. "Thank you, Nora. It was kind of you to offer."

"Or I can take some muscle with me and let you shop by video chat," Nora suggests.

"Not loving the sound of that," I chime in jokingly—sort of—but they're lost in making plans and didn't hear me.

"We can bring back whatever you want in a moving van or truck."

"*I do love* the sound of that," Josie says, mocking me with a wink.

"Great. I'll let you know when I have time to run over there."

"Hello," I call to get their attention. "Remember me?"

Their eyes land on me in unison.

"Got anything to eat over there? I'm starving."

Nora

"Can we talk?" Jordan asks me after Josie takes our empty dinner dishes to the kitchen. "Maybe outside?"

"Sure," I say with more enthusiasm than I feel, rising from the floor and taking hold of the wheelchair handles. Josie flashes me a half warning, half pity glance as we pass the kitchen, and I'll take it. After our escapades today, she no longer hates me (as much), and I need her. Neither one of us wants to hurt Jordan. It's why she sucked up her distaste and asked for my help.

While I try not to jostle him, that's what happens when I push the chair over the floor groves of the sliding glass doors and into the courtyard. "Sorry. Guess I need to work out more."

"You're perfect," he says with such conviction that the gloom I feel about the upcoming conversation twists and burns inside me. Tentacles wrap around my heart and squeeze, reminding me of why I shouldn't be there. Why leading him on and pretending everything between us isn't broken is cruel and so terribly wrong.

After setting the brake and closing the door behind me, I sit on the short brick wall, separating their small patio from the next, to gather myself. But flashbacks from our last conversation take over my thoughts and steal the air from my lungs—his glistening eyes when I refused his second proposal. The resolve that hardened his body, telling me he'd never ask again. The heartbreak I felt watching him walk away for the last time. Both of us will relive that pain over again when his memories return. He'll feel deceived and manipulated—and he'll be right.

I can't do this. I can't lie to him again. He needs to know what happened between us. He needs to hear the truth. But no matter how much this hurts, I can't say any of that today. He's unstable, and Josie would have my head if I broke our agreement without speaking to her first. I'll talk to her to—

"I've missed you," he says, stealing my hand and my focus. His eyes are soft, loving, and processing my every movement.

Straightening, I hide behind a smile. "And I'm glad you're safe."

"In the hospital, all I could think about was getting back to you. I think you saved me."

He raises my hand to his lips, sending fire and ice down my back. I don't know what to make of it. Goosebumps prickle my skin as his gaze heats my core. I'm used to seeing desire and complete surrender in his twilight blue eyes, but it's the absolute adoration I see now that has tears burning my own.

What the hell? Not again. I'm the one who mops up everyone else's tears and talks them through whatever issue caused the emotional breakdown. Sydney affectionately named me her therapist in college. Usually, after my *clients* talk it out, they realize the issue, person, or hurt wasn't worth crying over. But Jordan has always been worth it to me. I just couldn't give him what he wanted and deserved. The other problem, he's never been able to see me for who I am. He doesn't know *I'm* not worth the love he offers…but he will.

"How's your mom?" he asks in that selfless way of his.

"Now that she's signed the divorce papers, she's hit the I-hate-men stage. It won't last more than a week."

"I can't remember his name." His brow pinches as he weeds through the lingering fog and memories. "Was it Terry? No, Todd."

"Brent," I correct, instantly regretting it. Since he doesn't remember the last year, he won't know my mother's latest marital victim. It could raise a few flags.

"Oh. Right," he says, but his face doesn't match. He's confused and questioning himself.

"I'm glad I'll be seeing you at VETS," I say to change the topic. "With us both in the same city again, we can spend more time together." After the words spill out, I realize I meant them.

"Me, too. I wish I could do more than just sit here." He winks, but I see the anguish behind it. He's used to being active, a necessary piece of a system—part of something great—and feels empty without it.

"You'll heal and get back on your feet before you know it."

He nods. "Having this special time with you and Josie is the only thing making the pain, nausea, blackouts, and incessant itching all worth it." A sideways grin lifts his cheek before he shifts into the chair.

"You're blacking out?" I ask, the news settling like a load of bricks.

"Yeah. It's why Josie won't let me be alone."

"Don't blame her."

"I love her and appreciate her taking care of me, but I hate not being able to do anything for myself. Do you know how weird it is to be bathed by your sister?"

Despite my growing concern over his slow recovery, I laugh. "I imagine it's not pleasant for either of you."

"Thankfully, it's just a sponge bath, but I much rather you do it."

His eyebrows wiggle, and the thought of touching his naked body does something to my insides I can't decipher. Is it desire, dread, excitement, fear? All the above?

"We'll see," is all I can muster out of my muddled brain. "Is there anything else I can do to help?"

"You're doing it now."

His gaze locks on mine, sweet and sensual. It's how he used to look at me before an engagement ring complicated our arrangement and sent us into another round of arguments and breakups. Before I freaked out and turned into a runaway bride without a wedding ceremony. My heart revs at the possibility of him asking that impossible question again during this charade.

"What's wrong?" he asks, holding my clammy palm against his chest.

The pace of his sprinting heartbeat matches my own. How will I live with myself if I hurt him or cause more health issues because I can't get a grip?

"Nothing," I say with a conviction that even I believe. "I just haven't adjusted to all this yet." It's the truth, just not the truth he understands.

"Me either, but I like to look at it as an extended leave. We get more than a weekend together—a month, possibly more—and I'm looking forward to it."

"You're the sweetest, you know that?"

He pauses, pinning me with an incomprehensible stare. "You've never told me that before."

"What?"

Was I really that horrible to him? How could I never have told him how amazing he is? With frustration, I think back. Since we met, I refused to be seen with him in public, disregarded his feelings, and never appreciated the joy he brought into my life. I rarely, if ever, mentioned anything that involved my heart, thinking only of myself. His kind nature and tenderness were overlooked or discouraged on a regular basis.

So, yeah. I really was *that* horrible.

Fear and stubborn pride controlled my life, yet somehow, he loved me still. Shame shudders through my body, but it doesn't change the past or why that stubbornness was there in the first place. I never deserved him, and he is better off finding someone who does.

"Well, I should have," I finally say, knowing it doesn't make up for five years of keeping those words to myself. "You are one of the sweetest, most selfless people I know, and you deserve the world. I regret never telling you that."

"Okay." He drops my hand like it burst into flames. "Who are you, and what did you do with my snarky girl?"

My back straightens as I take him in. His playfulness is back, and I'm grateful. "I can bring her back if you prefer."

"No, not yet. I'm liking this new softie side, too."

"Don't get used to her. She only comes out of hiding in dire situations."

"I didn't know my situation was that grim."

"It's pretty bleak, but I have faith that you can turn it around."

"Wow. Softness *and* faith in me. I should have gotten injured long before now."

I pop a hand on his good leg. "Shut your mouth, or Josie will come out here and do it for you."

"Right. I don't—" The base of his hand flies up to his temple, and with a grimace, he rubs hard.

"Jordan, what is it?"

His body twitches, then convulses as if in answer. I shoot to my feet, my mind reeling with a thousand competing thoughts. Instinct kicks in, and I check my watch: 4:16 p.m. I try to keep him from slipping out of the chair but can't do it alone. I call out for Josie. When she arrives, she's in a state of panic and fear, but we work together to get him back in place.

"What's happening?" she asks, fear shredding her voice.

"It's a seizure."

"Is that normal?"

"I think it can happen after a brain injury. I've got him now. Call his doctor."

She rushes back inside to grab her phone. By the time she's connected to the on-call doctor at the hospital, Jordan's trembling body calms. Gently, I turn his head to the left and run my hand over his hair.

"You're okay," I whisper. "Relax. We've got you."

Josie lets out a long exhale and steps inside to talk privately with the doctor.

He lets out a moan before his eyes flutter open. Staying connected to him, I adjust my position so he can see me. "Hi, there. Everything's okay. Josie's here too, but she's talking to your doctor. Don't worry. You're going to be fine."

A tear escapes his eye, shattering any chance of me getting out of this arrangement unscathed. At a loss for words, I kiss his forehead, then his cheek, before pressing my lips softly to his. He's too weak to react, and with his eyes glassy and distant, I'm not sure if he comprehends my words or presence. Then, he reaches for me, and I take his hand, holding it to my chest.

"You're doing great, sweetheart."

Chapter Six

Nora

After getting Jordan to the air mattress in the living room so we can watch over him, Josie and I huddle in the kitchen with a bottle of wine and a box of chocolate chip cookies.

"He looks peaceful," Josie whispers, her hands wrapped loosely around one of the cups she bought earlier in the day.

I turn to take in the sight of him sleeping in the soft light of the sunset. "Did the doctor say he could have more seizures?"

"Yeah, but there's nothing we can do except help him through it...like you did. How did you know what to do?"

"My last job was at a rec center, and we were required to keep up various training: CPR, first aid, diabetes. Seizure care wasn't one of them, but I completed every certification I could find. It's probably what helped me get the job at VETS."

"Well, I'm eternally grateful. I don't know what I would have done without you."

With a grin, I pat her arm. "Glad to help. But you would have figured it out."

"Maybe. I'm an artist. I don't deal—" Her ringing phone cuts her off, and she checks the ID. "I need to take this."

"Sure. I should go home, anyway."

"No. Please stay," she says quickly. "I'll be just a minute." She pushes the button to answer the call but waits for my answer before speaking.

With my nod, she rushes to the bedroom to take the call. Looking around, I survey their living conditions, grateful Josie accepted my offer. The apartment is a cold, empty shell. With nothing to make it a home, or even comfortable, for that matter. No photos, decorations, furniture, curtains. My mother's stash should remedy that soon enough, or at least give them a head start.

Before I can grab my phone to open a game or social media app to keep me company, Josie tiptoe runs back into the room. She trips on the threshold separating the hardwood area from the kitchen linoleum, catching herself on the edge of the counter. She barrels on as if it never happened, her eyes staying on me as she grabs my arm and drags me outside.

"Oh, my goddess. Oh, my goddess."

"Goddess?" The strange saying stopped me in my tracks, and she waves it off.

"I don't know what to do. Help."

"Help with what? Who called?" I ask, trying to understand the root of her panic.

"Grant."

"Who's Grant?"

Her face scrunches as she realizes she's talking in riddles. "Sorry. He's my best friend and agent. I got in." She squeals, then slaps a hand over her mouth. Her eyes dart back and forth over the concrete as she processes what she learned from this Grant guy.

"That's great. Got in where?"

"The annual art show for alumni at my university in New York. It's a monumental event, and since I'm still a newbie in the art world, they stuck me on the alternate list in case someone drops out." Pacing now, her hands flap in the air as she tries to calm her restless nerves. "I never expected to get a spot. No one serious about their career turns this one down."

"That's great, but I'm confused. Why did you say you don't know what to do? You go, right?"

"The setup and opening event is next week. I'd have to leave in a few days."

"Oh."

"The good news is all my pieces are in storage in New York. The bad news…"

"Jordan."

She spins around to face me, tears pooling on her eyelids.

"Curators for a major museum in Las Vegas will be there. Grant's been shmoozing them for a feature exhibit for a year. They're slow to take a chance on me, but once they see my work featured at this show, Grant thinks it will be a done deal. That exhibit would catapult my career, possibly opening doors in Los Angeles, Chicago, Atlanta. All the big shows."

"Why are you wavering? Jordan will tell you to go."

"I know, but he needs constant care. Especially now that seizures have been added to the chaos."

I take a deep breath, already regretting what I'm about to say. "I'll stay with him."

"Nora." Her arms cross against the chill in the air, adrenaline no longer keeping her warm. "I can't ask you to do that."

"You didn't."

"Don't you think you two living together will only make matters more complicated?"

"Absolutely, but what choice do we have?"

"Plenty."

"Not from what I can see. You have a life-changing opportunity you can't refuse, and he'll never forgive himself if you do. He's going to expect me to be around more, anyway. It's the only answer that makes sense."

I barely get the last word out before she launches herself into my arms.

"Thank you. I'm so grateful." Peeling herself away, her hands linger on my arms. "I should only be gone for a week. Nothing can go wrong in a week, right?"

"Right. Piece of cake."

Oh, goddess, please help me.

———

We have four days to get ready. Together, we call Grant back and make arrangements. To get Josie to New York quicker, Grant will bring down her belongings, take her shopping, and help her pack. In addition to being her agent and friend, he's also her self-appointed stylist.

Once he's satisfied with her outfits for their expected appearances, she'll ride back with him instead of taking the train. She'll save money on a hotel by staying with him, an offer she couldn't refuse.

Before I leave, I reluctantly call Emily to ask for more time off work—the last piece of the puzzle. I promise to check in with staff, and work when I can. I hate asking. I had just returned from a long weekend to deal with my mother's latest drama, and now this.

Working at VETS is a dream, and I don't want to jeopardize my position. Yet, in true Emily fashion, she agreed without hesitation. Not only is Jordan a friend of Jackson's from their time in the Marines, both he and Emily are selfless souls, people who go above and beyond for everyone. She even offered to bring food or items for the apartment if needed.

On my way home, I ask Sydney to meet me out at a restaurant. It's late, and she has a son to think about, but I need a strong drink to soothe the nerves and my best friend to tell me I made the right decision.

"Where's your sweet boy?" I ask as Sydney slides into the booth at an Irish pub. I already ordered her favorite wine and began nursing a bourbon and Coke.

"Jackson took him fishing today, and he's sleeping over. With winter coming, he wanted to take one more outing on the boat."

"Damn. I'm sorry. Did I interrupt date night?"

"Maybe, but you would have dropped anything for me, as you have multiple times. I was happy to return the favor."

I smile, knowing we will always be available to one another. Our friendship is like a vine, deeply rooted, durable, and endless.

While we sip on our drinks, I fill her in on everything that happened since our lunch earlier that day.

"When I said to go make friends with Josie, I didn't mean take over as Jordan's caregiver," she says in disbelief. "It was incredibly thoughtful of you, but Nora…"

"I know, I know. What was I thinking?"

"Not about yourself, that's for sure."

I let out a sigh and gulp half my beverage. It burns on the way down, but losing control because I drank too much sounds better than losing it over decisions I made stone-cold sober.

"What made you do it?"

"I like her. She's strong and funny, and she needs me."

"And this has nothing to do with Jordan?" Sydney presses.

"I didn't say that."

"No. You didn't mention him at all. How'd he react to seeing you?"

"Shocked, grateful, sweet. He thinks he still loves me."

"He probably never stopped."

"There's no way."

Sydney shakes her head in disagreement. "I saw the way he looked at you at the wedding. Love like that doesn't vanish because of an argument."

I finish the drink and jingle the ice in my empty glass at our waiter standing nearby. The mention of what happened between us at Jackson and Emily's wedding ten months ago kicks my anxiety up a notch. "You don't know the entire story," my alcohol-loose brain makes me say, and Sydney slumps back in her seat.

"I'm your best friend. How can I not know?"

"I was too embarrassed to tell you."

Silence fills the space between us, despite the rowdy scene happening in the rest of the bar, and it's deafening. My secrets, hurt her, too, and if I could go back in time to handle it all differently, I would. Not only with Sydney, but also with Jordan.

"What happened?" she finally asks.

The waiter sets my second drink on the table, and I clutch it like it's a lifeline. "He proposed."

"Oh." She lets the news sink in, then leans her elbows on the table. "Obviously, you said no."

"Obviously."

"I wondered why the fire you two ignited that night fizzled out."

"There was no slow fizzling going on. It snuffed out the second that ring appeared. And it wasn't the first time."

She picks up her glass, then sets it back down without taking a sip. "He proposed before the wedding, and you didn't tell me then either?"

"It was before you moved back to Richmond, and we reconnected. I'm sorry, but I hated thinking about it then, even more than I do now."

"So, that's why you were so short and evasive when he showed up at our girls' night last fall."

"Yeah." I look down at the dark liquid in my glass and the taste no longer appeals to me. "That was the first time I saw him since his first proposal. He wanted to talk about it. I didn't."

"What if he asks again during all this? You will be spending a lot of time together, and he doesn't remember either refusal."

With a sigh, I push the drink aside. Getting drunk won't fix any of my problems. "It's my biggest fear. Strike that," I say, waving a hand. "*Second* biggest fear. I'm terrified of the day he finally remembers and realizes we've been lying to him. That I've been pretending."

"What if you develop feelings for him or accept the ones you already have before then? What will you do?"

"I don't have feelings for him," I say for the umpteenth time.

"You can keep telling yourself that, my friend. You're the only one who believes it."

"I hate you," I say jokingly. "And by the way, Josie believes me. Keep this up, and I might revoke your best friend title and give it to her."

She gasps and adds a dramatic slap of her hand to her chest. "You wouldn't dare."

"Watch me," I warn and stare her down until we both burst into laughter.

As we catch our breath, she reaches across the table for my hand. I take it, grateful to have a friend I can count on to always have my back, forgive me when I'm wrong, and laugh about it afterward.

"And I'm proud of you for what you're doing. It will be hardest on you, but despite knowing that, you're doing it anyway. No matter what's happened in your life, no matter your reasons for your decisions, you are a beautiful, noble, and compassionate person. And you deserve to be happy, too."

Annoying tears prickle my eyes, and I blink them away, shocked by their unwelcome appearance yet again.

"Thank you," I say, recovering. "And thank you for dropping everything to come here tonight."

"Isn't that what *best* friends are for?" She pats my hand and sits back, all smug in her title.

"Yeah, yeah."

Chapter Seven

Jordan

"I don't think this is a good idea," Josie says when Jackson catches us at VETS and announces that he and Sergeant Montgomery plan to save me from enduring a few hours in our blank and depressing apartment.

"Sounds perfect to me," I say a little too enthusiastically, and Josie shoots me a stern shut-up glare.

She fears what might happen while I'm out of reach, but she'll be busy preparing for her trip, her crazy friend will be here soon, and library books and watching movies on a phone are entertaining for only so long. I need a break.

"Josie, Sergeant has extensive combat medic training. He'll know what to do if something happens, and I doubt Jackson has forgotten all his training." I look up at my former unit commander, and he shakes his head. "I can't drink while taking medication, and it will just be dinner out. Nothing too wild…this time," I add, hoping to tickle a giggle out of her. It doesn't work. She's stressing about more than me these days and can't see that having one less thing to worry about for a few hours would be a good thing.

"Alright," she finally concedes. "Anyway, I know I can't stop you. You're a grown man. But promise me all three of you will act like it tonight." She wags a finger at me and Jackson like she isn't half of our size.

"Yes, ma'am," Jackson and I say together, stifling a grin.

"I'll be by to pick you up at six," he says to me before hugging Josie and heading back to his office.

"How was your therapy session today?" she asks as we push through the exit.

"Good. Doc gave me a few exercises that may help prevent seizures but says my head is screwed on tight. No worries in that department."

Josie's quiet as we make our way through the parking lot toward the sidewalk. It's odd for her not to ask follow-up questions, and I chalk it up to pre-show nerves.

"Are you excited about your trip?" I ask to get her talking.

"I am. I hate that you won't be there."

"I'll catch the next one. And the one after that. And the one after that." I glance back at her and she's smiling. Good. "You know it will happen. You're too good for it not to."

"Thank you, but you're biased."

"Maybe. I'm still right, though."

"Thank you."

"I'm excited for Nora to move in. When is she calling?"

Nora took a few friends to her mother's storage unit and promised a video chat so Josie could pick out what she wants for the apartment.

She stops to check the time on her phone. "In about an hour," she answers, pushing the chair into motion again.

"I'm glad you two are getting to know each other. Makes me happy."

No response.

"She's the one, you know?"

More silence. Odd. That statement would normally spark some kind of emotion from her.

Seeking an explanation for her lack of reaction, I shift in my seat to see her. Dark sunglasses cover much of her face, denying me the opportunity to read her. The sheer fact that she's stoic shocks me. After a few seconds of me staring, her head tilts toward me, and her frown softly curls into a placating grin.

"I know." She pats me on the shoulder.

Something about the way she says it makes me uneasy. Her voice inflections sound sad—not her usual irritation.

"I know you've never approved of our casual arrangement, but we're committed to each other and that's not changing."

Unnerving silence follows that declaration all the way to the apartment.

"Do you have a problem with Nora and me?" I ask when she parks me in the living room.

"No." It's the answer I want to hear, but I'd appreciate it not coming with an exasperated sigh. "It's just going to take me a while to fully trust her."

"I get that. If you were dating, I'd have a hard time trusting them, too. Never trusted that Ryder guy."

"Then I guess it's a good thing we broke up. He's enough to turn me off dating your species for a long, long time." She taps her chin with her finger in mock deliberation. "Maybe Grant has the right idea."

I snicker. "Any man or woman would be lucky to have you. But don't judge my gender by that one bad seed. If I had anything to say about it, he'd be kicked out of the club."

At that, an authentic smile brightens her eyes, only for them to dim again as she removes a few cans of vegetables from the cabinet. "Looks like you'll have to load up on calories at dinner tonight. Gonna be a corn and carrots kind of lunch."

"I have money saved, Josie. We can afford to buy groceries."

"Not an option. You have plans to fix up Mom and Dad's house and live happily ever after there with a family of your own someday. I'm not messing with your nest egg. You've worked too hard."

"So have you, Josie. I—"

"If I can sell a few paintings at this show and finish the mural at VETS, we'll be set for a while."

"Josie."

Ignoring me, she opens the two cans and dumps both into a pot. "I've got a few commissions in the works as well that will get us—"

"Josie!"

She drops the spoon she grabbed from the drawer into the pot and stares at me over the counter. "What?"

"You don't have to shoulder all this alone. I'm the reason you're here, remember? I'm the one who needs constant babysitting. I'm the reason your life is on hold. Let me help."

"No." She goes back to stirring the vegetables, but she's grinning. "You're my baby brother—"

"We're two years apart."

"Irrelevant," she quips with a shrug. "I've taken care of you since you were five years old."

"I know, and I love you for it, but you don't have to do everything anymore. Well, at least you don't have to *pay* for everything."

"Thank you, but I'll go grocery shopping before I leave."

I let out my frustration as sharp pains stab at my temples. "Josie."

"Mmm hmm?" The cooking vegetables and the remnant emotions of our debate have her attention, and she pays me no mind.

"Jo…" My head wobbles while the room converges into a kaleidoscope. Bile rises into my throat, and I fall forward, helpless to hold myself up. Footsteps on the hardwood floors echo in my ears. Overhead lights seem to dim and flicker until it all vanishes.

When my brain reactivates, I'm sitting in a red Mustang. The black leather steering wheel is warm in my hands from the mid-day sun shining through the windshield. The open driver's side window rustles my shirt, and I'm content—happy to be free.

I have several hundred dollars and the bucket list I scribbled on the back of a jewelry store flier burning a hole in my wallet. Both have me excited for the days and weeks ahead. The only problem is, I don't know which activity to check off the list first.

Cliff diving and wine tasting in Italy? Mountain climbing in Switzerland? Camel riding to the pyramids in Egypt? Skiing in Vale will have to wait until winter. Gambling away some of my savings in Las Vegas? Swimming with dolphins in the Caribbean? Feeling the mist on my face from Niagara Falls? White water rafting, cave exploring, skydiving? The world is waiting for me, and I can't wait to go…somewhere, anywhere.

Then again, restoring my parents' house is something I've been looking forward to for years. The sheer amount of manual labor needed to bring the old shack back to life isn't overwhelming. It's exciting. I've got the entire plan laid out in my mind. Marble countertops and a farmer's sink in the kitchen. Sanded and restained hardwood floors throughout. New electrical and plumbing. A coat of paint and a major cleaning will go a long way in transforming it into my new bachelor pad.

Wait…

Bachelor pad? Freedom to roam the world? What about Nora? What about my service? Forcing open my eyes, I see Josie pacing by the patio doors. It takes a bit to realize I'm no longer sitting in the sports car I've wanted since I was eight years old. Since Josie bought me a similar Matchbox car with the few dollars she earned selling her paintings to the neighbors.

She chews her fingernail with frantic abandon, lost in thought. The itching that never stops inside my cast registers with the realization that the car and my freedom were only a dream.

"Jo Jo," I manage, and she drops to kneel in front of me.

"Hi. How are you feeling?"

"Groggy. How long was I out?"

She twisted to check the clock on the microwave. "Long enough for the vegetables to get cold, but not long enough to miss Nora calling."

"That's good, I guess."

"I was about to contact Jackson and cancel guys' night."

"No. I want to go."

"Jordan." She rises and props her fists on her hips, disapproval scrunching her expression. "That's a terrible idea."

"I know you're protective, but I need to get out of here." I swallow the sour taste in my mouth. "I'll only be in the way and a distraction." I turn my hand over and prop it up with my elbow on the armrest. She reluctantly takes it. "You and Grant can join us after you finish packing, and we can celebrate your big break."

"I'd like that. But if you feel woozy even for one second…"

"I'll say something."

"Thank you."

"And thank you for all you're doing for me. I love you."

"Oh, Jordie. I love you, too."

———

Going out is exactly what I need tonight. There's great food for my empty stomach, a distraction everywhere I turn, entertaining conversation, and Sergeant Montgomery is a few beers away from smiling. It's almost perfect. The only thing missing is Nora.

I texted her and hinted that she should crash guys' night, but she was worn out from driving and packing and unpacking the furniture. It is a dick move for me to be out relaxing while she and Josie labor away at the apartment, but I'm less than useless these days. At least here, I'm not forced to face the burden I've become.

"Hi, fellas," I look up and see two women standing over the table with eager smiles. "Would you like to join our group?" The taller one points to two tables pushed together near the dance floor full of women in animated conversation. One looks over and wiggles her fingers at us.

"Taken," I say and shrug.

"Married," Jackson says, flashing the gold band. When did he get that? Why can't I remember his wedding? I had to be there, right?

I hear the woman say something like, "That leaves you," to Sergeant, but I'm too confused to process it. I want to ask Jackson about his wedding, but if I was there, he'd think I lost my mind. If I wasn't, what kind of friend does that make me?

My heart rate spikes with so many unanswered questions, and the sudden commotion of Sergeant's big body pushing back his chair and rising doesn't help. I watch him walk away in stunned silence. The shorter woman with long blonde hair and jean shorts wraps her arm around his and leads him toward their table. The taller woman on his other side says something to him, drawing his attention, and I'm speechless. For him to be social with strangers, he must have had more beers than I noticed. What else have I missed lately?

My thoughts continue to roam free with a bewildered abandon when another female interrupts with the same greeting.

"Hi, fellas." Turning toward the friendly voice, I'm glad to see I'm not stuck in a time loop. It's Josie with Grant trailing behind her.

"You doing okay?" she asks me, her hand falling to my shoulder. She gets my best smile, and it seems to convince her I'm not as messed up as I feel. Taking Sergeant's seat, she introduces Grant to Jackson. "Where's that grumpy sergeant of yours?" she asks.

"He found better company." Jackson points to him, sitting at the head of the table surrounded by adoring women.

"Can't say I expected that."

"Good for him," Grant chimes in with his usual flair. "At least we know one of us is gonna have a hot night."

"You better watch it. You're engaged," Josie teases him.

"Eric knows what he's getting." He motions to his body with both hands and settles back in his seat, all smug and comfortable. "And there ain't no taming this."

"Anyway." Josie rolls her eyes in jest and turns back to us. "What have you boys been up to?"

"We just finished eating when Sergeant's harem whisked him away," I answer.

"That's it?" Grant's displeasure with our easy-going flow is evident in his crooked frown. "No dancing or mingling or games?"

"Marines aren't good at those things," Josie teases.

"I have an idea to spice things up and get this party started." He retrieves the frozen margarita he brought from the bar and raises it. "We'll play truth or dare."

"Oh, Crayola. I'm out."

His head tilts to the side with annoyance at Josie's refusal. "Why?"

"Because you're ruthless and the only one who won't be embarrassed," Josie complains, knowing her friend well. "No one will get out of it without bruises."

"Bring it on," Jackson challenges, and Grant scoots to the edge of his seat, ready to make him regret that statement.

"Truth or dare?"

"Truth," Jackson decides quickly.

"Wildest place you've ever had sex."

Josie slaps a palm to her forehead, making Jackson chuckle. I feel the tightness in my chest give a little because I know Jackson, and his answer will not be as juicy as Grant wants.

"Dining room table," he answers pragmatically.

Grant takes him in with several slow blinks. "How can you look like that and not have any wild sex stories? Dining room table? That's all you've got?"

"It was quite the moment," Jackson jokes.

"Wow."

"Jackson was married to the Marines until he found Emily, so don't hold it against him," I urge.

Grant rolls his eyes. "Since you're a national hero, I'll let it slide this one time." He turns to Josie. "You're up, missy."

She groans out her displeasure and gulps down the rest of her pink, fruity cocktail. "Dare."

"I haven't even asked yet."

"And you know all my secrets."

"Oh, really?" I complain. "Are there some you haven't told me?"

She stares before turning back to her friend. "Let me have it." She winks over her shoulder at me, and I'm not sure how I feel about this. We tell each other everything…or so I thought.

"That disgustingly hot, muscley guy over there with all the chicks, ask him to dance."

"Hayes?"

"Sergeant?" I say at the same time.

"But he's so broody, and all those women will throw their ice-cold drinks at me." She shivers at the thought.

"Gorgeous broody men are so much sexier than cinnamon roll types…sorry, boys," he says to me and Jackson, and again, I don't know how to take it. I chuckle to myself.

"Does that mean we're cinnamon rolls?" Jackson asks him, amusement in his eyes.

"Oh, yeah. The sweet, gooey kind, fit for biting." He bares his teeth and laughter bursts from Jackson's chest.

"I've had my fair share of broodiness over the years, so I'll take it."

"Good. Now, get to it, sweetheart," Grant says to Josie.

"I don't know who's scarier—Mr. Grumpy or all those catty females sure to ruin my favorite top."

"Only one way to find out."

Josie rises from her seat, and my stomach churns. Her target is my sergeant. We're not even supposed to be hanging out together like this, but I assume we get a pass because of my injuries. Just a commanding officer checking in on his lieutenant. But he's six-three, two hundred and twenty pounds of muscle, and she's a buck fifteen soaking wet.

Sergeant would never do anything to hurt her physically. It's her heart I'm worried about. He doesn't hold back. The edges of his personality are jagged and sharper than she's used to. While she may act like she's sporting a tough outer shell, she's sensitive, and her tender side bruises easily. Without meaning to, he could leave behind a few blemishes and never know. One of Josie's most practiced skills—and the most dangerous in my brotherly opinion—is hiding how much she hurts behind a glorious ray of sunshine.

Watching her stroll over to him, the knot in my chest pulls tight again.

"And we have contact, boys," Grant commentates as Sergeant turns to find the tap on his shoulder came from my sister. "What is this? Another sexy woman wants me?" he says in a deep voice, pretending to be Sergeant. "He's contemplating. He's on the verge of denying the request. Choose one woman or ten? It's a no brain—Oh! What's this? That gorgeous ass is off the chair, his interest piqued." Grant's eyebrows dance at us before he returns to the play-by-play. "Lord have mercy, at full height, he is something to behold. What does he remind me of? Sexy Viking? Greek god? Oh, hot lumberjack. He could split a little something in two with just one thrust of his big—"

"Grant," I scold.

"What? I was talking about his wood splitting skills. But speaking of wood, she could use a little rough and tumble, if you know what I mean."

"I do, and I'd prefer you not talk about it."

"Sure. I'll keep my comments for another time when you're not so uptight."

"Or may I suggest never in my presence?"

Grant tosses me a *what-evs* look and returns his attention to Josie and Sergeant. "Well, look at that."

My eyes reluctantly follow his to find my sister's head resting on Sergeant Montgomery's chest and his hands intertwined on her back. A few measures of the ballad, playing over the loudspeaker, pass before she looks up at him and speaks. His brow pinches in the middle as he looks away in thought. She continues her speech and something she says has his gaze snapping back to her. He studies her before slowly responding with a nod. None of that exchange sits well in my gut. Doesn't help that instead of going their separate ways after the one-sided conversation, he follows her through the crowded dance floor and out of sight.

"Hmm. Looks like Jo Jo agrees with me," Grant says, spinning in his chair and sipping his drink. "Good for her."

If I had more than one good arm, I'd strangle that smugness right off his pretty face. Jackson clears his throat and hides a grin behind his glass of water.

"He has a reputation, doesn't he?" Grant asks Jackson, knowing I wouldn't dare answer that question. "Strong, silent type. Good with his hands…and other appendages."

Jackson chokes on his last sip and that's what he gets for not taking my side.

Several minutes string into twenty before Josie and Sergeant emerge from the crowd. She heads our way, while he stops by the women's table he abandoned to go with Josie.

"All hail Queen Josie," Grant teases, and her pink cheeks flush red with a satisfied giggle.

"Queen?"

"You, my queen, successfully plucked the town's most eligible prince from the ordinary townsfolk over there and showed them who's in charge. You were magnificent before, but now…" He pretends to bow to her, and my temper surges, especially when he asks, "Where did you two run off?"

"We didn't run anywhere. Why do you ask?"

"You had your hands all over each other and then you left together. In my book, that's running off."

Josie glances my way but doesn't meet my gaze. "We both needed a break from the noise, and I stopped by the restroom."

"Mmm hmm," he hums. "Well, now you've gotten it out of your system, it's Jordan's turn. Truth or dare?"

Despite my eyes are shooting darts at him, daring him to say another word about Sergeant and Josie, he holds his ground. "Truth," I answer.

"When was the last time you released that tension you've got bubbling inside your..." He waggles a finger at my lap, and my hand balls into a fist. There's something else bubbling inside me now, and it's about to boil over.

"Do you ever think about anything else?"

"Rarely."

"Grant, leave him alone. He needs to keep his stress level down."

"I'm not a child, Josie."

"Of course you're not," she placates, and for the first time, it makes me sick.

"It's my turn for a break. Jackson, would you mind taking me home?"

"Sure, buddy." He drops a few bills from his wallet onto the table and takes hold of the wheelchair handles.

Josie rises to come with us. "Stay. I need some time alone."

"Jordan," she says in protest, but we're already moving away from the table.

"What was that about?" Jackson asks after loading the chair into his truck bed and backing out of the parking space.

Giving myself time to cool down, I let out a long exhale, grateful to have someone other than Josie to talk to. "When Grant asked me that question, a vision of Nora and me flashed through my thoughts, and I don't know what to make of it."

"What was it? If you want to talk about it."

I nod. "We were in bed, and she was upset. She looked terrified and determined to push me away. In that moment, I was beyond angry. More like destroyed. Like a piece of my heart had been ripped out of my chest." What I saw in those few seconds brought on a pain so tangible, yet so unexpected, I'm still reeling with the aftermath.

"What do you think it means? Our brains can conjure up all kinds of things—I've been there countless times—but it doesn't make what you see real." He stops at a traffic light and looks my way. "What we've endured during our service, it messes with you. Not to mention your accident. How was Nora when you saw her?" He takes off after the light turns green.

"That's the thing. She was distant and cautious. I expected her to be more…"

"More what?"

I shrug, disappointment setting in. "Excited. Relieved. Affectionate."

"You know her better than me, but I've yet to see much emotion from her. She stays in control, no matter what."

"Yeah."

"Maybe she was overwhelmed from being the last to learn about the accident," he suggests.

"Yeah."

Each explanation, while adequate and believable, do nothing to ease the dread, tumbling like rocks down a mountain inside me.

We park outside the apartment building and make our way inside. After taking my meds, it's not long before they make me drowsy, and he helps me lie down.

"Thanks, Jackson," I mumble and drift off to sleep with a dozen more unanswered questions to add to the growing list.

But before focusing on answers, I need to make amends with Josie. I took my fears and frustrations out on her, and no matter what happened with Sergeant tonight, she didn't deserve my wrath.

Chapter Eight

Nora

Sitting in Jordan and Josie's apartment on their new-to-them loveseat, I sip my coffee and watch Jordan sleep. He's always been a peaceful dreamer. Soft breathing. Languid muscles. Limbs that never fidget or jolt.

Many mornings after spending the night together, his warm body and pine scent would register before the sound of his near inaudible inhales and exhales. But this morning, our first morning together without Josie, he's restless. Maybe it's from his medication wearing off and pain re-surging. Maybe it's a nightmare or vision from his past.

We've spent no time together since his first seizure several days ago, and he didn't contact me yesterday. Not one text or call. Under the circumstances, avoiding conversation makes things easier on me, but I grew concerned when Josie left this morning without waking him to say goodbye. She opted to leave him a note and her introspective mood put me in one, too. My thoughts are all over the place, and I'm not thrilled with being left here alone with no idea what to expect when he wakes up.

A quick glance at my phone tells me it's nearing the hour. His body may no longer be operating on a military schedule thanks to his three-week hospital stay, but Josie said he starts every day at six o'clock.

I watch the seconds tick by, and his eyes flutter open at 6:03. They land on me first, and there's bewilderment behind his stare that rattles my system.

"Hi," I say, needing to break the hold he has over me. "I brought muffins and bagels if you're hungry. Got strawberry cream cheese just for you."

He tries to push up onto his free elbow, but the loose bed sheet shifts, making him fall back on his pillow. Fingers pinch the space between his eyes as he takes deep breaths through the pain. This is only the third time I've seen his sunny temperament clouded with an emotion. He doesn't upset easily, but this morning, he is a lit match hovering under dynamite.

Unable to decipher what he's experiencing, I drop to the floor beside him. "What can I do?"

"Nothing."

"How about breakfast in bed?"

He doesn't grace me with a response.

"Okay. I'll pack it up, and we can go do something."

His hand drops, and his head rolls to face me, his brow still pinched. "Like what?"

"I don't know. What would you like to do?"

Rolling to the other side, he gazes out the window and ignores me.

"Do you still have that bucket list in your wallet?" I ask to get him talking.

"Yeah, but what good is it in my condition?"

"Plenty. Now, get up. I have an idea."

He turns back to me as I stand, prepared to make him listen.

"Why?"

"Come on. Let's get you out of your grouchy pants and into something a little more chipper."

His eyes narrow before the scowl is replaced by a playful smirk. "There's only one thing that could make me happy." He reaches for my leg, but I dance around it. "I'll lose my grouchy pants if you lose yours."

"But I'm not grumpy."

"You're always grumpy," he argues, and I take minor offense. So, I'm not the bubbly type like other happyish people I know, but that doesn't mean I'm grumpy.

"Fine. If I agree with you, will you attempt to get off this mattress?"

"Not until you tell me what we're doing."

"You're infuriating."

"No. It's called gathering intelligence. How else am I going to know how to dress for our date?"

"It's not a date," I contradict all too quickly, and he studies me with suspicion. It is how I would have reacted before we started officially dating, and it strikes an old wound. "I meant, it's nothing that requires special attire. Just bring a sweatshirt in case it cools down."

"Sorry, N.J., but you're going to have to grab it. Moving isn't my specialty these days."

"Right." I turn to head to his plastic bin of clothes, then turn back. "N.J.? That's new."

"Is it?"

"Yeah. You've never called me by my initials before."

"Oh. Well, maybe my brain is having a private seizure or something."

"Not funny."

"Sorry."

"Don't move. I'll grab you something to wear, then we'll get you dressed together."

"Nice. But you'll have to keep your hands off me. I'm in no condition to satisfy your cravings. Although, I'd love to try." He winks at me, and I storm off before he sees the battle I'm waging with my needy body.

It's been almost a year since we last gave into each other, and I haven't been with anyone since. He ruined me for all other men. After five years, he knows my every need before I do. He's discovered my weaknesses and learned how to best exploit them. He's given me years of incredible sex, and there's no coming back from that. I haven't even wanted to try.

Without giving it much consideration, I grab a pair of black shorts and a red T-shirt from the bin. I've always loved the way red looks on him. Reconnecting to the present, I return to the mattress and find him sitting up—his casted leg laid out in front of him, and his right arm perched on his other knee. How could I not hear him moving? Oh yeah, unfulfilled cravings can cloud the senses.

"Didn't I tell you not to move?"

"I'm stubborn," he says slightly breathless from the work but sounding more like himself.

"You don't have to tell me." Kneeling between his legs, I set down the clothes and dial up my resolve. "Walk me through this. How do we get you dressed without too much pain?"

"First and most importantly…" His serious tone grabs my full attention. "You kiss me right here." A finger taps against his lips. "To activate the endorphins and numb any pain that may come after."

"Right," I deadpan with an exaggerated eye roll, but find myself playing along without much consideration otherwise. Leaning forward, I give him a peck.

"That's not enough to numb a pinky finger."

"Well, it's all you—"

Before I can finish the sentence, his hand braces the back of my head and connects our lips. He's rough, greedy, and giving me exactly what I like. Desire heats my core, and God help me, I want what my body begs me to take.

But it would be wrong. This is wrong.

I drop back on my heels, adding some much-needed reason and space to the moment.

"Should we start with…um…your shirt?" I ask, trying to think of anything but the rock-hard body he gained over the last year.

Work emails. Insurance. Taxes. Puppies frolicking in wildflowers. Anything innocent, boring, and the exact opposite of this gorgeous man I'm about to strip down to his skin. Just the thought of seeing him shirtless is making me second-guess my self-imposed chastity belt. It's feeling more like a noose the longer his navy eyes sink into mine. Desire snaps into the air and sweat beads on my back. It's more intense than I anticipated, and for the first time in my adult life, I don't know what to do.

He smells amazing. And if he doesn't stop looking at me like he wants to rip off my clothes and make me scream in surrender, this week will either break me or my vibrator.

I'm frozen to my spot when his hand takes mine and wakes me from my stupor. His eyes never leave my face as he presses my fingers to the hem of the shirt he's wearing. More than anything, I want to look away, yet I don't. Can't.

I grip his shirt because I desperately need something to ground me. Something to help me feel like I'm not drowning in him. Careful not to touch his smooth skin, I pull up the fabric, slowly exposing two sharply defined abs at a time. I swallow—my mouth suddenly as dry as paper.

He pulls his right arm through the sleeve, and I push the shirt over his uninjured shoulder, admiring the solid frame. His chest rises and falls at the same rapid pace as my pulse. Freeing the shirt from around his neck finally breaks the hold his gaze has over me. Every smoldering nerve ending poking at me to act on impulse fizzles while I concentrate on unhooking the sling around his left arm. As I carefully slide his tender arm through the shirt, his body tenses from the movement, but he doesn't make a sound.

Instead, eyes dulled with desire continue watching my every move. Since I'm the only one who knows this is a temporary arrangement, I stay on task, determined to be the rational one.

Setting aside the discarded shirt, I rise to my knees to pull the new one over his head. Ten months of celibacy has me pausing and garnering a glance at the man before me. He's thick with muscle and broader than the last time I saw him like this. A thin layer of light hair glistens on his chest in the early sunlight. My fingers itch to touch it and feel the swell of his pecs underneath.

Squashing the thought because it has no business entering my brain, my eyes trail up to his strong jawline. The morning stubble gives him a different look than I'm used to—like he's thrown the military rule book out the window. Coupled with his new muscle and longer hair, this rugged rebellious style looks damn good on him.

His jaw clenches, a distracting motion while his hand wanders to my lower back. A subtle reminder to exercise control before we do something we can't take back. But that control wavers when I pull the shirt over his head, and his warm palm slips under my cropped sweatshirt. He cups my waist, his thumb gliding over my skin in long, languid strokes.

Blood momentarily stops in my veins and the rest of me freezes. I shiver in response to his hand trailing upward. He's always had the power to reduce me to a bumbling mess with one touch, one kiss, one glorious orgasm at a time. It's why, despite my aversion to commitment, I kept coming back for more. Why I could never tell him *no* when he asked to see me before deploying or while on leave. It's why no matter how I felt about relationships, I had to have him. He was and still is my greatest weakness.

His dark blond hair springs through the opening before his forehead. I drag the shirt down over his eyes, regretting it the moment they reopen and find mine. The deep color captivates me. How have I never noticed the specs of copper in his irises, floating like fall leaves on the darkest, purest oceans? And why did it take almost losing him forever to appreciate the qualities that make him special? Not just his handsome appearance, but his heart, his compassion, and the way he accepts everyone for who they are. Me, in particular, flaws and all.

Not that it changes anything. I still can't give him what he wants, and soon he'll remember how he feels about me. My only job is to not make it worse in the meantime.

I do what I can to get his arms inside the shirt without causing too much discomfort. He grimaces only a few times, and I call that a win as I pull it down over his torso.

This is torture. How am I going to dress and undress him daily and survive it?

My heart revs at the thought of our next task—removing his shorts. He must sense my unease, interpreting it as caged lust, and locks me in a one-arm embrace. He isn't entirely wrong. The man is sexy as hell, and I wish I could enjoy this. I wish the feel of his arm wrapped lovingly around me didn't feel like betrayal.

"You're going to have to wear the shorts you have on," I say to break the tension, my voice sounding airier than intended.

"Can't control yourself around me, can you?"

"No," I answer honestly and stand to escape this little entrapment before he can advance it further. "Let's get you to the bathroom, and while you finish getting ready, I'll pack breakfast."

I insert his arm into the sling and get him to his feet, but once he's upright, his eyes glass over. Panic engulfs me when he wobbles. He'll be too heavy to hold if he passes out.

I frame his face with my hands. "Jordan, look at me."

His eyes roll back as his eyelids flutter closed. The one good leg holding him up trembles, flaring my fear.

"Jordan," I try louder, and he responds, except his gaze is distant. "Focus on my voice. I won't let you go. I've got you."

Tears spring to the corner of his eyes, but don't fall.

"I know, babe. I know it doesn't feel like it, but you'll get a little better every day. Every activity will make you stronger. Think about the fun adventure we're taking today."

He blinks hard and his hand balls into a fist.

"That's it. Come back to me. We'll use that list of yours and find something to take your mind off this."

His hand presses into my hip—the crutch he needs while his energy surges. When he leans over and rests his forehead on mine, relief pours over my body like water, and I give into it.

"You're the best distraction I could ever ask for," he whispers, his voice thick and raspy. "I need to kiss you again."

"Jordan." I breathe in, unable to find the words to deny him. How could I when he needs me? When that's what his girlfriend would do? When my body longs to feel him?

His head tilts and his lips take mine before I have a chance to pull away. Not that I could when he's melting every ounce of control I thought I had. My heart aches for the fear he must experience every time his healing takes a step backward. My body yearns to feel him again. My brain sends conflicting messages the more we're together.

Giving in to any of what I'm feeling seems too dangerous for us both. I draw back before my hands go rogue and drop his shorts, after all.

"Wow. For someone who almost passed out, you seem plenty alert," I tease, trying to settle my pulse and reset my thoughts on the task instead of my urges.

"That's what your body and scent do to me."

"My scent?"

He leans closer to sniff my hair. "Vanilla and honey. It makes me very hor…hungry," he corrects, making me grin. *Join the club*.

"Well, the bagel and cream cheese will take care of that problem. The rest is impossible."

"I thoroughly disagree. Sex with my gorgeous girlfriend might surcharge my recovery."

"Or make it worse." I'm thinking about his fragile heart when I say it. Giving in to our urges will only hurt him more when he discovers the lies. "Come on. Let's get you ready."

Thankfully, the one and only bathroom is a few wobbles away.

"I'll wait out here in case you need me." I grab the doorknob, but before I can close it, his hand covers mine.

"I will always need you with or without injuries."

All I can do is flash a grin, hoping it looks more like a gesture of appreciation than guilt, and shut him inside. After retrieving the wheelchair, I wait and listen outside the bathroom. As long as I hear movement—a flush, running water, toothbrush over teeth—there's no need to worry about his safety. Everything else is a different story, but I'll have plenty of time to fret over it all later.

Soon, he reappears in the doorway with a broad smile. "I'm ready for that adventure you promised me."

I motion a hand over the wheelchair. "Your chariot awaits, sir."

Chapter Nine

Jordan

It took just one touch of Nora's soft skin to make me forget about the disturbing vision I had at the restaurant two days ago. Feeling how her body reacts to me, seeing the desire in her eyes, tasting her soft lips, I no longer care about the pictures my sick mind conjures up. She's in my arms and all mine.

Any trepidation I saw in her before must have been from fear. The same would happen whenever we'd reconnect before my deployments. We'd have fun and give in to each other's desires until my departure loomed closer. Then, the notion that I might never return would cross her mind, causing her to shut down. She'd let the unknown consume her even when we were keeping our relationship casual, and especially when it was more.

I almost died in the car crash, and I'm sure her reaction to that involved more than fear—anger, hurt, guilt—and I can't blame her. Dating someone in the military is terrifying. The one at home can go months without hearing from the other, especially if they're deployed. And there's no guarantee they'll return the same person they were when they left—physically or mentally. If they return at all.

For those reasons and because she witnessed the horrors of losing someone to war through Sydney, she fought against us becoming a couple for years. Frankly, I'm surprised she's acting as normal as she is right now. Must be the pity she feels for my situation. Her closing off will creep in as I heal and my return to the base grows near.

"We're here," she announces and turns off the car engine.

I take in the large stone building and grounds within view outside my window. Fall is abundant in the surrounding trees. Red, orange, and yellow leaves litter the ground underneath, but I see nothing to tell me where she's taken me.

"Your first bucket list trip is about to be crossed off," she says, tossing open her door and climbing out before I can investigate further. Soon, she's beside my door with the wheelchair, motioning for me to join her.

My body is still screaming at me for moving when I see the sign by the entrance: Blue Sky Winery. "Are you planning to get me tipsy so we can party right tonight?"

"Not exactly. The restrictions on your prescriptions said you can have up to two glasses of wine occasionally. I doubt you'll get a buzz from that."

"Party pooper."

"Come on," she says, pushing me toward the entrance. "Partying may not be in the plan today, but we *can* have a little fun."

"How is a winery fun if I can't get drunk?" I ask to get a rise out of her.

"We're getting out of the apartment and creatively crossing something off your bucket list. Stop complaining."

"I was really enjoying where things were heading at the apartment." I lean back to see her reaction as the wheels roll over the uneven lip of the ramp, shaking the chair. I groan at the impeccable timing and resulting electric current now shooting through my torso. "Oww."

She activates the automatic door and addresses the hostess, who seats us at a table by windows overlooking the vineyard out back. The rows of grapevines seem to go on for miles over rolling hills, untouched by the season. Mountains I've seen my entire life whenever I leave the city but never appreciated line the horizon in the distance. The sun shines only on them, casting shadows over the vines.

"Beautiful, isn't it?" she asks, ending my observation of our destination.

I nod and return to my favorite view. "So, sexy tour guide, what do you have planned for us?"

"You'll find out soon enough."

The waitress brings us two glasses of ice water and menus, the latter Nora declines.

"We'll have the special," she declares, sending the waitress off to place the order with the kitchen.

"What's the special?"

"Not telling you. Just sit back and enjoy the surprise."

To show my appreciation for the effort, I place my hand on the table and wait for hers to slide into it. She hesitates, transporting me back to the moment the vision sliced me in two at the restaurant. It shines another light on everything that's been different about her lately—the deer in the headlights look she has when I touch her, the distance she keeps, the constant distractions, the delayed time between texts. Other than that mind-numbing kiss this morning, her reactions to me have been off.

Then again, she's never liked displaying our couple's status in public. Frankly, I'm shocked her first suggestion was to go out to a very popular, crowded winery…even if it is located over sixty miles northwest of Richmond. But that also means no one should know us here. So, the question stands. Why is my hand empty without the warmth of her touch?

Disappointed that nothing's changed in the PDA department, my hand falls back into my lap.

"Jordan, I…"

The waitress interrupts her excuse (or lack thereof, I'm predicting) by dropping off a sampling of four wines. Each kind, displayed in a dainty decanter on a wooden tray, is a different hue. Then, she adds a set of eight even tinier wine glasses beside it.

"Enjoy the Italian experience," she says with forced enthusiasm, unaware of the brittle tension between us. "Your charcuterie board will be here shortly."

"Italian experience?" I ask, muscling up the motivation to climb the wall she's rebuilt with staggering reinforcement.

"You wanted to drink authentic Italian wine in Italy. This is as close as you're going to get in Virginia."

"I appreciate it."

Her lips roll into a self-aware grin before she selects a decanter and pours a sampling into two glasses.

I follow her lead as she swirls the shot-sized portion of wine and holds her nose to the rim to sniff the fragrance. The deep burgundy liquid smells of sour dirt and my face revolts.

"Come on," she teases. "It can't be worse than warm, cheap beer that you've happily drunk over the years."

"Nothing is better than beer…warm or cold."

"This is your wish, remember?"

"Touché." Draining the glass, the smooth liquid coats my throat. To my delight, it tastes better than it smells.

"I thought we could check off another item on the way home," she says, reaching for the next decanter.

"Please tell me it's number six."

"How am I supposed to know which number it is? I can only recall a few of them." Her eyes grow wide, accurately guessing I'm up to no good.

"That's a shame. You would know if you saw it and based on how innocently you said that…you don't." I wink and secretly wish for number six to be checked off the list sooner than later.

"Hmm," is all she says to dignify my comment. "Ready for the next taste test?"

"Sure."

She moves the used glasses—more like shot glasses on blue twisted stems—aside and pulls two yellow ones out of the box set. "Which flavor would you like to try next?"

"How about the gold one to match our glasses?"

"Perfect."

While she fills each glass, I'm reminded of the night we met. The three girls—Nora, Sydney, and Denise—had ordered a bottle of champagne to share. Us guys—me, Will, and Benji—ordered the cheapest beer on the menu. Like today, I couldn't take my eyes off Nora while she expertly opened the bottle and filled the glasses for everyone. She knew exactly how to hold the glass for a smooth pour and when to stop to prevent the bubbles from spilling over. Her tongue trailed over her lips in concentration, sending blood gushing to my other brain.

"I forgot how good you were at that. It only makes me want you more," I venture, causing her to pause on the way to passing me a glass.

"You think pouring liquids into a glass is sexy?"

"Oh, yeah. But only when you do it. Nothing stands at attention for anyone else." I nod to the aforementioned, easily influenced brain for emphasis.

"Is that so?"

"Is there anything I do that turns you on?" I'm phishing, but desperate times call for equally desperate questions.

She gave me a long, searching look, and for a moment, I wonder what she's trying to figure out. It's not like my feelings for her are a secret, but unfortunately, hers are. After all this time, is she still unsure about her own heart? About me?

"If I told you," she begins, dropping her eyes, "it would take out all the fun and mystery."

"Indulge me with one."

She set those devastating dark eyes on me and grinned. "Your new body turns me on."

"You like scars, bruises, and broken bones?" Of course, I know what she meant, but I'm curious about what she'll say next.

"No. Those break my heart."

Her eyes drift to the wine she'd yet to drink. I miss them on me. I miss the sparkle they had just moments ago before something I said or she thought cloaked them in sadness.

"What then?" I urge, bringing her back to me.

"Your Italian cheese, meat, and fruit board has arrived," someone, other than our disinterested waitress with a drawn-out southern accent, asks. "I bet you two darlings are ready for some yummy food. Am I right?"

Neither of us darlings jump to answer. Nora's gaze drops first, and after a long pause, she speaks up.

"Can we get this boxed up instead? We'd like to go enjoy the view and fresh air." She said it without looking at me, spiking my wandering curiosity.

"Why, of course. The vineyard this time of year is so romantic. Be sure to take the east trail. It has the best mountain views." She frames the side of her mouth as if the next thing she says is a secret. "And with the surrounding grove, it's the most private. If you know what I mean." She elbows Nora and sashays away with the tray.

"The most private, huh? Now, I'm intrigued." It's a risk to bring up intimacy, but I can't help myself. Despite my injuries, there's nothing I'd rather have than Nora's naked body on mine…in broad daylight, where I can appreciate every inch of her again.

Her gaze cuts to mine with slight irritation and a sliver of amusement. She enjoys my dick as much as I do, if not more, and I know she's suppressing the urge to jump me. She had to work extra hard at it this morning. It's only a matter of time before we both get what we want.

I lean in, ready to get this ball rolling. "Did you know that number six involves a tree? Sounds like fate to me."

"A tree? Seriously? You're in—Jordan. Jordan," she says again. In my head, I'm responding, but hear nothing. She's right here, but it sounds as if she's shouting at me from across the room. Is she trying to warn me about something? Am I sitting on an ant hill? With the way my body tingles and stings, maybe I am. Maybe I'm already covered in the little shits. I'd swat them away if my arms would move.

A chair scrapes against the hardwood floor, and that's where my attention falls, thanks to my muscles letting me down. My head slumps, and then my shoulders. All I can see is four feet, the light of the room fading in and out around us. Her hands land on my shoulders, propping me up.

"This isn't happening," Nora complains, missing her usual sass. Fear soaks every letter. "Jordan, listen to my voice.

Focus on me, a knot in the floorboard, something. Focus, Jordan, on something outside the darkness."

There's a small scar on the ankle bone, parallel to the sandal strap circling her right foot. Three freckles in a line turn the scar into a T. Adorable.

"T fer Taylor," I slur.

"What?"

Resting my head on her shoulder, I relax for a bit while section by section my body is reconnected to my brain. It's dizzying, but better. Energy follows sensation in my feet, legs, arms, and finally torso, allowing me to sit up.

"You have a natural tattoo on your ankle."

Thanks to a host of reasons I don't care to rehash, Nora and I do not cross number six off the bucket list during our stroll. But that's okay. I'm still upright and able to experience something new with my girl. A moment worth capturing for a lifetime.

Retrieving my phone from my pocket, I wave her over for a photo. She must feel sorry for me since it takes only two pleas to get her to agree, begrudgingly, of course. The woman hates selfies more than PDA and making her step out of her comfort zone when it comes to us is my favorite pastime.

As we make our way back to the car, I swipe through the photos of her leaning over my shoulder and smiling. The sun's rays highlight her face and hair like the angel she is to me. I hold up the phone to show her my favorite shot.

"You're so beautiful," I tell her, in case I haven't already said it today. The brain is a little foggy these days.

We load into the car minutes later, and I dig into the charcuterie sitting on my lap in a to-go container before we back out of the parking space.

"How is it?" she asks, eyeing me with interest. We both skipped lunch—*thank you embarrassing episode*—and the lot of salty meats, crackers, and flavorful cheeses is calling to us both.

"Heaven," I answer with a moan. Snagging a piece of smoked gouda from the lot, I hold it in front of her mouth. She takes it with her teeth and merges onto Interstate 81.

"To where are we heading next, my beautiful tour guide?"

"What number, obviously *not* number six, is climbing a mountain?"

I stare at her like she said something ridiculous, which she did.

"What?" she asks with an indignant smirk.

"Have you looked at me lately?"

"I got a pretty close view this morning."

"What makes you think my ailing body can climb a mountain?" I toss a grape into the air, catch it in my mouth, and chew while she continues to revel in her grand scheme.

"I didn't say we'd need your body for this task."

"That's a shame. But how else are we—" And then I see it—the wayfinding sign for a scenic mountain drive.

"There are about a dozen different places we can stop along the *climb* to the top to look out at the valley below."

"Clever."

Halfway up, we pull into a parking spot at an overlook. Since we can see everything through the windshield, we don't bother dragging my heavy ass out of the car. In this area and time of day, it's the valley's turn to be in the sun's spotlight. The nearby trees showcasing their fall colors and the bluish-gray rolling mountain chain in the distance, is so breathtaking I can't take it in fast enough.

"Do you know why the Blue Ridge Mountains have that bluish hue?" she asks.

I take another look at them. Surely, I've heard the reason, yet it doesn't populate. "I don't remember. Why are they blue, beautiful tour guide?"

She swallows and looks away before answering. And when she does, her voice is oddly guarded, "They look blue because of a chemical the native trees release. It scatters blue light from the sun and makes them look like a kindergartner painted them."

"That's right. It's all coming back to me." It wasn't. But who's keeping track? "What other trivia do you have in there?" I nod toward her head, and my right hand begs to run its fingers through her silky hair. She curled it this morning, and knowing she fixed her hair for today contradicts the retreat I felt from her at the winery.

"Well, did you know that the Blue Ridge Mountain chain is one of the oldest in the world?"

"I didn't."

"Yep. They started forming millions of years ago, before dinosaurs."

"Well, I guess I should have paid closer attention in Virginia History class."

She smiles. "Yes, you should have, but I didn't learn that in history class."

"Whew. I was regretting all the time I spent ogling at Marsha Blakely across the aisle."

"Marsha, huh?"

"Red hair, blue eyes, sweet, popular, the kind of girl who volunteers for school events. She was homecoming queen our senior year."

"Hmm. Sounds like the exact opposite of your current type."

"Oh, yeah? What's my current type?" I ask, then raise a hand to prevent her from answering. "Let me describe her. She's strong. Takes no shit from anyone, especially me. She has the softest skin—the kind I can't keep from touching to make sure she's real. Her eyes are like melted chocolate. I could lose myself in their depths all day. Her smile lights up any room. But when that smile is because of me, I feel like the luckiest man in the world. This girl is my past, present, and future. The only one I will ever love."

She stares at me, her mouth dropping open in shock or to say something that won't form. I've never hidden how I feel at any point in either our friends with benefits or exclusive relationships. How can any of what I just said be a surprise? I'm not one to hold back. I go after what I want, and like her, usually, I say what's on my mind.

I shift as much as I can in my seat, expecting her to collapse into me to hide how much my words affect her.

Instead, she throws open the door and stalks to the edge of the overlook.

Speechless, I watch her lean over the railing, her head down as she breathes deep. I'd give anything to go to her, hold her, and take back whatever I said to upset her. But for the life of me, I can't figure out what that is. Her commitment issue is old news. But shouldn't hearing someone confess their love be a happy moment? It made me happy to say it.

She'll come around. I'm not worried. You don't throw away a connection like ours—something that strong, that electric, that all-consuming. And when I'm healed, I'll start working on convincing her of that forever part.

Chapter Ten

Nora

Guilt, fear, and regret collide like dysfunctional fireworks inside me, suffocating and choking me the more I replay the day's events. Kissing Jordan. Feeling my system burn for him again. Hearing him pour his sweet, forgetful heart out to me. If I can't hold my shit together for the next five days, this lie will be my undoing.

I despise the mixed signals I'm dishing out—pretending to be his girlfriend while freaking out every time he acts like my boyfriend—making him question us both. In my defense, it's not like I have experience with fake dating ex-boyfriends with amnesia. It's maddening. It's sad and so alarmingly confusing.

My heart fluttered unexpectedly when he said he'll always love me. I've never had someone put me first and love me like I matter. Half of that is my fault. I push men away when they get too close. But the other is my sick, twisted childhood.

No one, no matter how strong they may be, could come away from that knowing how to deal with relationships in a healthy way. I've been to therapy. I know I'm fucked up, but change is hard. Accepting love is near impossible when I'm so used to everyone I care about leaving, as if I meant nothing to them.

My father left me alone with my lunatic mother when I was an impressionable second grader. My best friend chose popularity and boys over standing by my side in front of school bullies. The person I thought would always stand by me through life after high school broke up with me because suddenly, I wasn't good enough for his family and future. My first stepfather, who treated me like his own, protecting me and earning my trust, left without even a glance over his shoulder when my mother showed her true colors and kicked him out.

Then, there's Jordan. He left for three tours, and each time, I resigned to never seeing him again. To never seeing him again. It happens all too often, shattering hearts, families, and hope, and I had to protect myself.

And now? That fear is no longer relevant. He's here to stay, and the more time I spend with him, the more I question why I fight it. Why I don't let him see all of me—the stuff below the surface and locked away behind titanium walls. But after telling him everything, would he still want me? The nature of our predicament may render that question null and void in the end. Being honest about my past may be too late once he learns I lied to him in the worst possible way.

I can't worry about that now. I'm already neck deep on a sinking boat with no island in sight to be my saving grace. All I can do is focus on one moment at a time. I don't know what I want beyond today, yet I'm tired of swimming. If I give this relationship all I have until it's stripped away, maybe a shred of who we once were will survive after this boat sinks to the bottom.

Summoning the fierce badass he thinks I am, I stalk back to the car and drop into the driver's seat. His eyes question me, and I answer by taking his face in my hands and kissing him. Our teeth clash in a demand for more, passion flaring between us as if no time has passed and no secrets loom over us. My fingers dig into his hair, and it's appalling how much I want him. While my body has always been his, my brain is the stubborn one, usually talking me out of doing anything that could hurt later. But in giving myself to him in this rebellious detour, I can't figure out where my heart stands on the matter.

Pulling back, almost too fast not to cause alarm, I suggest, "We should keep going."

"Agreed." His hand reaches for my shirt, and as much as I want him to fist it and yank it over my head, I place a hand on his chest.

"I meant we need to keep climbing this mountain."

"If you insist." A defeated look drops his longing eyes to my mouth as he resettles in his seat. "You never said where you learned those facts about said mountain."

Grateful for the switch to an innocent topic, I nod toward the windshield and put the car in reverse. His eyes soon land on a large sign with **Blue Ridge Mountain Facts** printed in bold letters at the top. A family stands in front of it reading the information.

"Really? You read that sign as we sat here?"

I shake my head in mock disappointment before backing the car into the road. "Just like a man. Can't see what's right in front of him."

———

The rest of the trip up the mountain then back to Richmond went by without tough conversations or confusing freak outs. We settle into the roles of two people comfortable in each other's space.

But the long day also weakened Jordan and his overworked body. He didn't try to start something we couldn't finish with adventurous hands. He didn't ask why I escaped the car earlier and looked as though I considered hurling myself over the railing. He didn't bring us up once over the last several hours.

While it is easier on me to ignore things, he prefers to face concerns like the enemy—assess, address, and neutralize. The fact that he isn't addressing what happened on that mountain has me assessing every word, glance, body movement, and murmur.

What if another side effect of his injuries is taking hold? What if he remembered something? What if he's waiting to see how far I'll take it before he calls me out?

For a distraction, I put a pot of water on the stove for tea before pulling his wallet out of my purse. "Is that famous bucket list in here?"

"Since you're holding it, I assume you're going to check."

"With your permission, of course." He nods, and I unfold the worn leather. "Did you have fun today?"

"I did. I'd choose to spend time with you over anything."

My heart squeezes as relief consumes and relaxes my muscles. I roll my shoulders, realizing how on edge I'd been, waiting for something to drop and ruin our easy flow. "Especially over sitting in the quiet apartment."

"Especially over that...at least until you're willing to remove my chastity belt."

And just like that, flirty Jordan is back. Thank goodness. This side I know how to handle. "You're not ready for that," I inform him.

"I beg to differ."

"Anyway." I pinch a yellowing piece of paper that looks to have been folded and refolded until its creases are tearing and hold it up. "Got it."

"Go ahead." He waves a hand. "Read all my desires."

My eyes narrow with suspicion. "I thought this was a trip bucket list, not a—"

"It is," he says a little too quick, cutting me off.

"Hmm. We'll just see, won't we?"

I unfold the list, which I soon realize is an old, faded store flyer with his scribbles on the back. Most of the ink on the front has worn off. Only a few random words and shapes remain. Turning it over, I begin reading the list aloud.

"Drink wine and squish grapes in Italy. Check." With a grin, I lean my elbows on the counter.

"Sort of."

"It's checked for now. Next, climb a mountain. Check."

"I could go for another climb so long as you kiss me like that again."

It had been a kiss I won't soon forget, and a piece of my resolve was left on that mountain alongside part of my heart. Damn him.

"Next," I continue, ignoring the heat rising from my core into my cheeks. "Cave exploring, skydiving, gambling in Las Vegas. Oh."

I look up from the list and find him smirking.

"Number six," he says in a confident, you-know-it-would-be-amazing rasp. It's a look I adore on him.

Clearing my throat, I skip that sexy little number to something safer. "Swim with dolphins, learn to paint. That's sweet."

He shrugs. "It's important to her."

"And what's important to your sister is important to you." He truly had the purest of hearts. Returning to the list, I squint to read the next entry. Am I seeing this right? Ride a steam engine?"

"I loved trains as a kid."

"How are we going to find a steam engine around here?" I stare at him in dismay.

"You said you wanted to get creative…you'll figure something out."

"You're impossible."

"You mean impossibly charming?"

My gaze holds his because yeah, I could get behind that statement. The wind gusting through the open windows on the drive home mussed his blond hair, giving off a carefree, surfer charm. The eyes that can soften even my sharpest edges bore into mine, revealing a side of him I've never truly witnessed until this moment. He's more than charming, and I wish I hadn't damaged everything beyond repair.

"Yeah," I agree, my voice wearing my regret. "You're impossibly charming." And a lot of other memorable adjectives.

"What's next on the list, Nora?"

He must have felt the shift between us and needed a diversion or knew I did. I look at the list, but my eyes are unfocused, reeling from the revelation that I regret destroying what we had. A regret stemmed not only from hurting him but accepting his love and not returning it. From never telling him how sweet and thoughtful and amazing he is. And mainly from pushing away and shattering the best thing that's ever happened to me.

"Nora."

"Right." I suck in a breath and blink to clear the fog. "Skiing in Vale, Niagara Falls, something about a camel, rafting, camping in the Grand Canyon, and…"

"And what?"

Holding the list closer to my face, I squint for a better view. "The last one is missing."

"Missing?"

"You erased it."

"That's weird. I don't remember erasing anything or even the last time I looked at that list."

"I can make out an M at the start and an L and E. Sorry." I shrug and stuff the list into his wallet. "You'll have to remember or come up with a new one."

Speaking of remembering something forgotten, I drop the wallet and add two tea bags to the boiling water on the stove. Half the water has evaporated thanks to the list distraction, but I focus on the simple task to keep my thoughts off my regretful heart. Locate the sugar and a large pitcher for making sweet tea—Jordan's favorite. Consider measuring the sugar, forget how much to add, pour in what looks like an unhealthy amount, and hope. Stir in the hot water from the pot and cold from the tap. Collect a glass from the cabinet and fill it with ice and tea.

I glance over at him. "Feeling okay?"

"Sort of. Bruises are throbbing." He checks the time on the microwave. "Mind grabbing my meds?"

"Sure. Think we did too much today?"

I place three prescription bottles in his lap, hand over the glass of tea, then push him to an empty spot beside the couch.

"No. Well, maybe, but I don't care. It was worth it."

"Not used to retirement life yet?" I joke, not realizing the slip until it was out of my mouth.

"Hell, no," he continues without a beat. "And never will be. Other than the cost of losing all this time with you, I can't wait to get back to work."

"Want to watch a movie?" I blurt. It was an awkward transition, one he could chalk up to my reluctance to talk about our relationship, but it had to be done. The conversation had taken a dangerous right turn, thanks to my unfortunate slip, and I'm not prepared to handle the aftermath if it stays off track.

"Sure, but pick something you like." He nods at the prescription bottles. "This concoction usually knocks me out."

"In that case, we should get you into bed," I suggest, knowing I won't be able to move him if he falls asleep on the couch.

"Hmm. I like that idea. Will you join me? I can't stomach the idea of having you so close but not with me."

"Jordan."

"Nora," he says in the same exasperated tone, taking my hand. "You're my girl, and I miss holding you. Please."

How could I resist that plea? How did I ever before?

With a nod, I move to stand in front of him and kick off my ankle boots. His eyes stay on mine as I kneel to remove the sneaker from his uninjured leg and push all three out of the way with my foot.

Rising again, I peel off my sweatshirt, unbutton my jeans, and wiggle out of them. I take a step toward my suitcase to retrieve a pair of shorts, freezing at the sound of his deep voice. It wraps around me like velvet and a soothing warmth fills the void inside me.

"Don't. I want you just like that."

"What about my bra? I was thinking I'd be more comfortable without it, but if you prefer—"

"Good point. No bra. I wouldn't want you to be uncomfortable."

"How thoughtful of you."

Pinching back a grin, I reach both hands around to unhook the bra. All amusement leaves his face as desire and primal need have him fidgeting in his seat. His gaze trails from my lips to my breasts, pushing against the tight cotton. I hook the strap inside my right sleeve and pull it down my arm, repeating the feat on the other side. For the last step, the one I can tell is making his mouth water in anticipation, I bunch my shirt above my waist to pull out the garment underneath. With a flick of my arm, I toss it onto the couch behind him.

"Your turn." After two unforgettable kisses from him today, all I can think about is doing it again while trailing my fingers over the ridges of muscles and smooth skin.

I help him out of his layers, amazed by how sensual it is to undress him with careful precision. His breath heats my cheek, teasing me with how close he is. If I turn my head, my body will have what it craves.

Him.

I want him, even though I shouldn't. Even though it's wrong, and potentially destroying this sinking ship with a relentless thunderstorm. I need his hands and lips on my skin. I need him to unravel me and take me under.

"Bed. Now," he whispers through gritted teeth, his control shredded and faltering.

Straddling his legs, I set aside the glass and medication to wrap my arms around his waist. "Hold on to me."

"Gladly," he says and grips my left shoulder.

Unable to resist, I place a kiss on his cheek and start the countdown. On one, he pushes up, instantly smashing our bodies together—shoulders, chest, hips. I can feel the cold metal of his dog tags through the fabric as he leans on me, his hand sliding down my back to cup my ass. Stunned, I look up in time for his mouth to cover mine, possessive, greedy, and hot. Holding him closer, I realize how much I missed our connection and the surge of electricity we invoke in each other.

"What are you thinking?" he asks, moving to my neck.

"I…can't think…when you do that." I also can't stop myself from leaning back to allow more space for him to continue whatever he's doing to me. My knees quiver, but since I'm the one holding up this pleasure party, I steady myself. "I don't think you should do extracurricular—"

He takes possession of my lips with his before I can finish drawing a line in the ever-changing quicksand that is our current relationship. If I had been wavering on whether to give in, this kiss would have been convincing enough. Consequences be damned.

A low moan flutters in my throat as his hand finds its way inside my shirt, and a rough, calloused palm embraces my breast.

"What do you think now?" he asks, clear on his intentions.

"I think you're my weakness, and when you touch me like that, you can have anything you want."

"That's what I like to hear."

"But," I manage through the haze of my own unmet needs, "you haven't taken your meds yet."

"Forget them. I want to be fully present for every minute."

"We must be careful. You're injured in places easy to make worse with what you're offering."

His posture deflates, making me smile.

"Don't worry. It just means we have another opportunity to get creative."

"I love how you think."

Chapter Eleven

Jordan

I can't remember the last time I felt this incredible. Probably the last time I was with this woman. When Nora mentioned being creative, holy shit, she meant it. We've always kept things interesting, spontaneous, spicy, but last night fell into its own category. It felt as though we were exploring each other for the first time all over again. It was tricky with the whole arm sling and cast problem, but we pulled it off and then some.

I also told her exactly how much she means to me. Again, a little reassurance never hurts, and with our history, it's warranted. I bared all, fearless and unconcerned about causing another retreat, and she took it with surprising grace.

Although she stayed silent, she didn't retreat as I expected. Instead, she burrowed closer to me, love radiating from her body more than words ever could. That surrender alone tells me she feels something, if not the same as I do. That she's leaning into her feelings and no longer pushing them away. It's all I've ever asked and needed from her.

She stirs beside me, and I shift to give her space, but there isn't much to give. Last night, we crashed on the small mattress tucked in the corner of the living room. If the neighbors had been out, they may have gotten an X-rated show.

Thinking about the memories we made and suddenly ready for more, I brush her hair off her shoulder and kiss the soft skin I adore. She groans. Not exactly the response I hoped for, but early mornings rival selfies in her book.

With a chuckle, I ask, "Do you feel as amazing as I do?"

"Mmm. Better."

"Impossible. You haven't had coffee yet."

"Maybe you're my new morning boost."

Groggy, she rolls over and wraps a leg around me, accidentally jamming a knee into my cast. I wince on reflex, and she shoots up to an elbow, pressing a hand to my sore ribcage, fully awake with sheer terror on her face.

"Oh. I'm so sorry."

After a long inhale, I let the burning air out slowly while the knives jamming into my muscles and bones slow their assault. "Now, I believe you feel better than me," I tease through gritted teeth.

"Not funny," she scoffs and continues her survey. "How are the ribs?"

"Same."

"Is that good?"

A chuckle rumbles and escapes with an exhale. "Sore but manageable."

"Okay. Head?"

"Thank you for worrying, but I'm fine," I say, hoping conviction will steady the words, scratching my throat on the way out. "Didn't you hear me say how amazing I feel?"

"Your face says otherwise. What can I do?"

"You're doing it already."

"What am I doing?"

I bring her hand to my lips. "Looking at me like that." *With love in your eyes.* But I avoid mentioning a topic of friction between us and settle on something safe. "Like you want to jump me again."

"I didn't jump you…far from it."

"But you would have if my injuries hadn't prevented it."

"Of course," she says to placate me, but I know better. She *so* would have ridden me like a bull.

"Are we staying in today or hitting the road again? If I had a vote, I'd say we—" She intercepts my lips on the way to her neck with a finger. Her eyes travel down my torso to my good morning greeting.

"We definitely need to get out of here."

"I had other ideas."

"So, I see. It would be in your…"

Her voice sounds hollow as it floats in the air. While I try to focus on her and the light she brings into my life, her beauty and the soothing sound of her voice drifts away into darkness.

Nora

"Jordan." I tap his cheek to get his attention and freeze when his eyes roll back. As he trembles, I line the wall with pillows from the couch and keep a close watch over him.

A quick check of the time: 7:34 a.m.

Each second that passes feels like an hour. I check again. 7:38 a.m.

The backs of my eyes burn at the implications of this moment. This seizure has already lasted longer than his first, and he shows no sign of calming.

7:41 a.m.

Tears pool and fall unnoticed, leaving glistening streaks down my bare skin.

"Please, Jordan. I can't take this much longer."

7:44 a.m.

I'm reaching for my phone to call an ambulance when the tremors cease, and I reach for him instead.

"Jordan, can you hear me? Jordan." I hold his hand to my chest.

He groans and turns his head, crushing his eyes closed to the light, the pain, me. In the silence, I let out the dueling tension that had compounded since waking in his arms. He's all right, and we can reclaim a normalcy…until the next crisis at least.

I trail my other hand over his hair before I shift to the couch to give him space. Watching his chest rise and fall with each labored breath, I realize I have zero control over this situation. There's nothing I can do to prevent Jordan's seizures or the pain I'll cause when he remembers. For now, he looks at me with those mind-numbing eyes, and I lose myself. It's not like me. I'm always in control.

But for the past several days, I've been anything but the master of my domain. At some point in the night, my heart told my brain to go fuck itself, and I don't know what to make of it. Jordan, Sydney, Emily—these are the people who follow their every whim and heart's desire. Not me. I don't throw caution out the window and have...*emotions*. I don't cry or lead with my heart first. I don't allow myself to dabble in vulnerability. Nothing good ever comes from that.

UGH. In. All. Caps.

Who am I? I don't recognize the woman I became the second Jordan showed up at VETS. I'm spiraling, and can only wonder: Where's *my* rescuer? The one who shows up without being asked when my world is crumbling. Like when I scrape my mother off the floor, comfort Sydney during moments of uncertainty, and shelter Jordan. Where's my person, waiting in the wings to talk some sense into me and pull *me* off the ledge?

Again, with the self-pity. It's time to suck it up and get back to the only version of me I can understand in this alarming and muddled mess I've gotten myself into.

Glancing around, I look for something to consume my attention and cushion the walls of my wavering sanity. As if in answer, my phone alights, delivering the distraction I needed. I snatch it up and read the message.

> **Josie:** I tried to call Jordan, but he didn't answer. Everything OK?
>
> **Me:** It was until about 10 minutes ago. Seizure. Longer than the first.
>
> **Josie:** Oh no. Can you talk?
>
> **Me:** Better not. He's sleeping again, and I don't want to leave or wake him.
>
> **Josie:** Good idea. How was yesterday?

Last night jumps into my thoughts and my cheeks burn hot. I look down at my nude body, grateful this conversation is not a video call. I wonder how Josie would feel about Jordan and I reconnecting physically. Scratch that. I don't have to guess. She'd be as furious as I feel guilty.

Slowly, I type out an answer to her question.

> **Me:** We had fun getting out of the apartment, and he seemed to be feeling better.
>
> **Josie:** Did anything happen to trigger it?

If he had any nightmares, I slept through them thanks to Jordan cleaning out the cobwebs and destroying my sex ban like a military attack—unrelenting explosion after explosion until nothing remained. Sleep came quickly after that, and I expected us both to wake up satisfied and relaxed. Not more troubled than before.

> **Me:** Not that I saw. Hope it wasn't from all the activity.

> **Josie:** What did you do?

Drank a little wine, took a long adventure, and enjoyed a lot of sex. My body is spent from that last one since most of the effort was on me. But I had no qualms, and Jordan certainly couldn't muster any. I settle on relaying *most* of the truth.

> **Me:** Just took a drive and had some wine.

> **Josie:** Wine + medication. That might have done it.

> **Me:** I checked the recommendations. [frown emoji]

> **Josie:** Don't beat yourself up. It could be anything or nothing. I hate not being there.

> **Me:** How's the set up going?

> **Josie:** Amazing. I've met so many people and remembered why I love NYC.

Me: Glad you have this opportunity. So is Jordan.

Josie: Thanks. Have any plans today?

Me: I thought we would go out again but probably shouldn't now.

Josie: Please have him call me when he's feeling better.

Me: Will do.

For the two hours that follow, I try to keep busy while he sleeps. After getting dressed and starting a pot of coffee, I settle on the couch to check my work email and research post-concussion syndrome. Apparently, his symptoms could last months. With a sigh, I close the laptop and wonder how Josie will manage on her own after his memory returns.

The thought of it makes me sick. To keep fear at bay, I pull up Netflix on my phone and tap on the first non-romantic show I see. It takes five minutes to realize the main character is a healing veteran.

"Nope." Turning off the phone, I toss it to the other side of the colorful antique loveseat. "Now what?"

To not wake Jordan, I decide to eat a leftover bagel for breakfast instead of cooking something more sustenative. The selection and prep wastes all of two minutes. If he doesn't wake up soon, this day will not only test my sanity but destroy it.

As I make it back to the living room with hot coffee and a bagel, he stirs.

"Hi," I greet, setting down the mug and plate on the coffee table and kneeling beside the mattress. Blood stops gushing through my veins with the icy way he stares me down. It's the same cold indifference he had when he walked out of my apartment for the last time nearly ten months ago.

"Hi," he finally responds, but remains still under the blankets.

"How do you feel?"

"Tired."

"Do you remember what happened?"

"What?"

"Do you remember waking up…and the seizure?"

"Oh. No." His eyes crush closed for a moment. "I'm sorry you had to deal with that."

"Jordan." I place a hand on his stomach, and his muscles tense. "Never apologize."

He takes me in for a moment. "You seem different."

My hand slides into my lap before he feels my nerves. "I do?"

He nods slowly, his eyes still studying, his frown more pronounced.

"It's probably because you gave me four orgasms last night. A record for us." I push to my knees to place a gentle kiss to his lips, but he doesn't respond. Sitting back, I reach for the bagel and try not to focus on his icy gaze. "Are you hungry?"

"Yes."

"You can have this after we get you up." I set the plate on the mattress for incentive and hope it lifts his mood. Without thinking, I remove the blankets, revealing his nakedness I somehow forgot about. My eyes travel over him. At least part of him is happy to see me, I joke to myself.

I feel him watching me, waiting to see what I'll do next. My mouth waters for another taste of him until his shiver in response to the cool room recalls my caregiver responsibility—the helpless feeling of seeing him disconnected and trembling is still too fresh to get the juices flowing. I toss the blankets back over him.

"You've had a difficult morning."

"Feels like it."

"We'll take it easy today, and if all goes well, we can resume our travel itinerary tomorrow."

He doesn't protest. Instead, he sits up, using his good arm for leverage, and leans against the pillowed wall without my help. I watch him closely, searching for signs of an impending seizure, new pain, or reason for the sharp decline in his mood. His eyes close as he breathes deep and shuts me out.

Passing over the bagel, I rise to collect his clothes, the medication, and a glass of water. The plate is empty by the time I return.

"Well, you did say you were hungry," I joke, expecting him to join in the banter, but he stays stoic, distant.

I drop to my knees in front of him and work the sweatshirt, boxers, and shorts into place. Unlike yesterday, there are no longing eyes meeting mine. No advances to touch me. No smiles, teases, or words of affirmation. Only heavy tension and disturbing emptiness until I reach for the prescriptions.

"I'm done with those."

"Why?" I ask, still holding the three small bottles. "They're prescribed for a reason."

"Mainly pain, and I don't like how they make me feel."

"You wanted them yesterday." Many things were different yesterday.

"It's my body."

"Fine." I set them aside and shudder from the unyielding agitation in his tone. "Is there anything else I can get you?"

"My phone. Please," he adds, recognizing his answer sounded more ungrateful than he intended. My usual colorful response tickles my throat but doesn't form. He's been through a lot, and his head injury is undoubtedly affecting him more than either of us realizes.

I snatch his phone from the kitchen counter and hand it to him. "I'm going to freshen up. Are you sure you're okay?"

"Yeah." He raises his gaze to me, but it quickly falls back to the phone.

"I'll help you to the bathroom when I get back. Don't forget your PT appointment is later this morning."

He nods but gives me nothing further to tell me he isn't upset or falling apart inside. In a matter of hours, he's gone from sweet, adoring boyfriend to tolerating my presence.

The love I saw in his eyes the last few days has disappeared completely and since nothing happened to trigger it—quite the opposite, in fact—that could mean only one thing.

He knows.

―――――

Jordan

> **Me:** Would you have time to talk after my appointment today?
>
> **Jackson:** Of course. Everything all right?
>
> **Me:** I'm not sure.
>
> **Jackson:** I'm here for you, buddy. Text me when you're finished, and we can meet in my office.

Chapter Twelve

Jordan

My stint in the military has been anything but uneventful. While I may not have found myself at the other end of a rifle, grenade, or handmade explosives like Jackson and Sergeant Montgomery have, trouble seems to find me on every mission and seemingly with little searching.

During this morning's seizure, my fucked-up brain ran through those near misses—the dozen or so situations that threatened to end my life. The fear I felt in those final moments, crawling up my spine and rolling in my gut. I don't make a habit of thinking about those times. Facing my mortality isn't a favorite pastime, and nothing good comes of it. I prefer to focus on the present, making the most of every day I'm blessed with.

But when the wreck played on repeat through the chaos and in full technicolor like I was there, everything changed. I've been living in the past since I woke up.

I remember feeling free the minutes leading up to the truck T-boning my pristine, antique, Ford Mustang. Not borrowed. Not a rental car. *Mine.* I remember buying it the day before, giving a good chunk of the cash I saved over the last eight years to the pretty, gray-haired lady excited for her vacation. I remember driving to Richmond to celebrate my discharge with friends.

Discharge.

After my body heals, I'm not going back to the base, and I'm unsure how to feel about that. I'd been excited to experience life when I left. Now, it feels like I'm mourning the loss of a best friend, my only constant (other than Josie), and life as I've always known it.

My entire adult existence, I've been a Marine. I don't know how to be or do anything else. I don't even know if any of my combat skills translate to a job without serious threats, war, terrorism, or combat. *Civilian life.*

Before the crash, I planned to travel the world. But facing this new chapter seems like a blinding neon sign with arrows pointing in every direction. Where do I go next? Which direction is the right one? How do I even start when I have no intel?

I hadn't realized my life is an unfinished puzzle until a few missing pieces slid into place while I slept. I'm a veteran with no real-world skills, no job, and no prospects. If I hadn't had Josie to take me in after the accident, I don't know where I'd be. A charity case for my friends or VETS?

I awoke after the seizure with so many unanswered questions about the future on my mind and wondering how Nora fits into it.

Last night reminded me of how much I love her. How I've loved her since we met at the marathon. She's tattooed herself onto my soul, and I'll never be me without her. And with the way she held me in the moonlit shadows, I thought she finally felt the same.

Then, the seizure and subsequent puzzle-building memories told me more than Josie or Nora have since the wreck. Nora and I are not together. Not in the way she's pretending. Far from it.

Some of the details of our history are missing or frayed at the edges, but the truth is as undeniable as the bullet now lodged in my chest. Waking up this morning, the pain of losing my brothers, my career, and the love of my life all over again ripped me in two.

It took everything I had to fight the urge to lash out. Looking at her and feeling her hands on my skin sent a surge of anger through me I never experienced before. She was wearing my sweatshirt and looking at me as if the last year hadn't happened. As if the lies are no trouble at all.

I can't tell Nora I know. Not until I figure out the missing details and remember how we got here. Why we're not together and why I still love her. Although, I have the sinking feeling that will never change, no matter what she does. And I need to decide how to handle that.

Am I comfortable taking the chance on her when whatever broke us up could happen again? Or would it be best to move on? Then, there's the service…the only job I know. Do I go on with my life alone as I planned when I retired, or do I re-enlist and drown out my heartbreak with something bigger than myself? But none of those questions matter until I answer the most important question of all: Can I trust her again?

Under normal circumstances, last night's activities could have convinced me of just about anything, but some things are more important than unforgettable sex. For a relationship to thrive, loyalty, love, and trust must be present, and each is non-negotiable.

———

After a quick shower by her standards, I retreat to the bathroom and run the faucet, pretending to be washing up. I stare at my unfamiliar reflection and comb my short hair for ten painstaking minutes, delaying the inevitable for as long as I can. My appointment at VETS isn't for another hour, and it takes only twenty to walk there. That means forty minutes left to go on hiding. It's cowardly, but I can see no other option.

Sitting on the closed toilet seat, I read through my missed text messages and voicemails. Josie called three times and left one brief message, asking me to call her back. That's not going to happen.

She sent several updates on her art show set up and mentioned a few people she'd met like I have a clue who they are. Normal everyday shit as if she has no secrets, schemes, or remorse. Convinced she is the writer and producer of the farce that has been my life for the last month, I ignore her messages and pull up Sergeant Montgomery's contact.

My fingers hover over the tiny keyboard as I decide how to begin.

Me: Did you know?

I tap the delete key until the abrupt question disappears. Of course, he knows. He signed my damn discharge papers. He witnessed the crash and stayed with me at the hospital until Josie arrived. When he came to visit me shortly after leaving the hospital, he also seemed surprised at my mention of returning to work. He wanted to ask something, confusion wrinkling the skin around his eyes, before Josie interrupted. I remember finding it odd that she cut his goodbye short and walked him outside.

She must have informed him of the plot to control my life that night. And when we went out with Jackson soon after, he said nothing. Why? Whatever the reason she'd given him, it must have been convincing.

Me: I thought brothers had each other's

Delete. This conversation is better had in person.

"Jordan, are you okay?" Nora calls from the other side of the door. Her voice is like a poison-laced drink to my system—revolting, scandalous, wounding.

"Yeah. Just getting ready."

"Need any help?"

"No," I say adamantly and all too quickly. "I'm almost finished."

"Okay. The chair is in the hallway when you're ready. We need to leave in ten."

Give me fifty terrorists poised to tear my head off, and I'll run toward the threat. But faced with having to look at the woman in the process of breaking my heart, and I want to hide away in a bathroom the size of a closet. I hate confined spaces. Hated crawling through pipes, being pushed together like sardines in planes with crates of supplies, and camping under vehicles or inside thick brush in the dark for hours on missions. But I did it for my country and for the safety of my brothers. I did it because each activity had a purpose.

Hiding from my so-called girlfriend in a tiny apartment bathroom serves no purpose other than showcasing my cowardice. And no Marine is weak. Grasping the doorknob with fervor, I swing open the door. The abrupt motion startles Nora, who had been waiting with the chair, into gasping audibly.

I hop twice, spin, and drop into the wheelchair without a word or a glance in her direction. Not exactly man-of-honor behavior, but it is all I can muster.

"I guess this means you're ready to go?"

"Yes."

She attempts to make conversation during our walk but gives up somewhere around the halfway mark. Once we enter VETS, I check in and she deposits me in the physical therapy suite.

"I'll meet you in the lobby in an hour."

"Actually, I'm meeting with Jackson afterward."

"For how long?" she asks, perturbed that I hadn't told her before now.

"Not sure."

"That's fine. I can check in with Sydney and get caught up on a few things around here. Take your time, and text me when you're finished."

She stalks out, taking with her the elephant that had been sitting on my chest for the past two hours. Air finally enters my lungs as every muscle relaxes.

"Hi, Jordan," Avery, a physical therapist volunteer, says as she enters the PT lobby.

"Hi. I thought you were only here on Tuesdays and Thursdays."

"I had today off from work and your therapist called in sick." She shrugs and takes hold of the chair handles. "You're in my hands today."

"I can live with that."

"Such the charmer."

We enter the dedicated fitness room for PT patients. Unlike the main fitness room in the center of the two-story VETS facility, it's a fraction of the size and peaceful. Other veterans and therapists are working in hushed tones, and a clank of metal weights coming together occasionally rings over the calming music playing through the PA system. It's a welcoming atmosphere, designed to prevent triggers and soothe fragile veteran psyches while focusing on healing their bodies.

"I love it here," I whisper.

"Me, too. It's why I'm here on my day off instead of gallivanting around the city."

"Surprising. Every time I see you, you're drinking, dancing, or letting loose in some way. The very definition of gallivanting." I smile at my joke, and her fists find her hips in mock disapproval.

"Well, you should thank your lucky stars I'm not. You could be stuck with Gary instead of me." She glances over her shoulder at the aforementioned therapist, encouraging another patient in that drill instructor way of his, then comes back to me with a sympathetic wince. "He's a former Navy Seal and wouldn't let you skip the last rep when your legs give out. So…"

"I'm thanking those stars as we speak."

"Smart." She reaches for a chair, slides it closer, and sits before opening my chart. "How much longer until the cast comes off?"

"You tell me. What does it say in there?" I motion toward the folder she's scanning. She checks the calendar, hanging on the wall beside us.

"You're over half-way there, depending on how fast you're healing. We'll continue to focus on circulation and improving the strength of the muscles around your injuries. How's the shoulder feel?"

"Okay until I try to move my arm."

"Putting on that sweatshirt didn't feel too good, huh?"

"Not particularly, but I didn't think anyone would appreciate me coming in here shirtless."

"You'd be wrong about that. Seventy-five percent of the volunteers and employees here are females with eyes."

I laugh, enjoying our easy banter. Avery and I don't know each other well, but through mutual acquaintances, our paths have crossed on multiple occasions over the last few years. She's always been flirtatious and bold, and today is no different.

"Let's get to work, shall we?"

Over the next hour, she tortures me with muscle stretches and joint exercises, but by the time she's finished, I feel better than when I arrived. Our light and friendly conversation keeps my thoughts distracted, and I am grateful for the opportunity to get to know her better. She walks me out while we're in the middle of an animated debate about which is better with beer: steak or burgers, when my cast nearly trips Nora on her way by.

"You two look like you're having fun," she says, breathless from her hurried trek across the fitness room.

Avery seems to notice my discomfort, and I wonder how much she knows about my current and past situation with Nora. I should have prodded her for information while I had her undivided attention. She comes to my rescue by responding.

"Yep," Avery says. "I didn't realize Jordan here was so entertaining."

"That's because you're usually…*occupied* when we're at the same location."

She swats me on my good shoulder. "You're just jealous."

Guess that answers my question. There's no way she would flirt if she knew Nora and I were quote, unquote *together*. She thinks we are still distant exes who rarely speak to each other.

Nora stares at us, silent and dumbfounded. I can't tell if she's upset or just surprised by the familiarity and casualness between Avery and me. Either way, I'm not in the mood to find out. Her feelings, hurt or not, don't enter my realm of concern yet. Not until I have all the facts.

"Hey, aren't you supposed to be off this week?" Avery asks Nora. "I thought you were on vacation or something."

"Staycation," Nora corrects, apparently wanting to keep things between us a secret. Convenient. "I just came in to take care of a few things."

"Avery, do you have a minute to take me to Jackson's office?" I ask, ignoring Nora, who would be expected to transport me as my designated caregiver for the week. But since she doesn't want anyone to know, I'm happy to oblige.

"Sure. I'd be happy to."

To give me something other than Nora's betrayal to think about, I text Jackson to let him know I'm on the way to his office. We arrive at the same time.

"Hi, buddy. How are you feeling?" he asks and takes over control of my chair.

"Feeling great right now, thanks to Avery," I say as she turns to leave. She sends me an appreciative wave before Jackson pushes me inside.

"She is one of the best. Got me walking again."

"That's right. And you had *two* broken legs. Not an easy feat."

"Amen to that. So, what did you want to talk about?" Jackson set the brake and takes the seat across from me beside his large mahogany stained desk.

My hand combs through my hair when I realize I don't know how to start without sounding insane. But if anyone can understand, it's Jackson. He's been through more trauma than my entire unit—former unit, I remind myself—combined. He is the best person to talk me through the visions and memories and unreconciled feelings.

"This may sound crazy…"

"Just say it. I'm used to crazy," he says easily.

"Fair enough. I think Nora is pretending to be my girlfriend because she thinks I can't remember us breaking up. Some moments of our relationship are clear, like they happened yesterday, and some are blurry. Why would she do that? And why would Josie go along with it? She hates Nora."

"Wow." Jackson's light blue eyes darken before he rises and paces to the window, his fingers gripping his chin. With his long hair tied up into a loose bun, I have a clear view of the tension that popped into his jaw and shoulders at the mention of my predicament.

"You knew, didn't you?"

How could everyone I know be in on this deceit? Everyone but Avery, who may be the only person I can trust right now.

Jackson spins around. "The doctors recommended that we not correct you. That you be allowed to remember on your own to reduce stress. They didn't know the implications of that advice. No one was thrilled about it, but we all had your best interest in mind."

"Who asked you to play along?"

"Jordan. That doesn't—"

"It was Josie, right?"

"She loves you so much. She didn't want to see you get hurt again. At least, not until you were stronger."

"But she's not here, having to see or deal with any of it."

My pulse drums in my ears, and if Jackson said anything further, I didn't process it. Josie left when I needed her most. She's usually the one I go to when I need to talk through any dilemma. Nora lied and led me to believe she was falling for me. After last night, how could I not think that? She touched me with more desire and love than I've ever felt from her, and my own grew over the hours we spent in each other's arms.

Then there's Sergeant Montgomery and Jackson, who are some of my closest friends. Marines are supposed to have each other's back. Not go along with pointless charades that will only blow up at the first opportunity. Guess we stepped on that landmine today and there can be no putting any of it back in the proverbial ground.

Poor injured, fragile Jordan. Is that what they all think of me? Is that what drew them all to deceive me? Did they expect me to roll over and accept it? Screw them. Fuck that.

Feeling capable and strong after my workout with Avery, I rise from the chair. Angry bolts of lightning shoot through my left hip and leg, but I hold steady and bite back a grimace in response.

"Jordan. What are you doing?" Jackson asks, rushing toward me.

"I need some air."

"Sit down. Let me take you," he offers, but the last thing I want to do is talk about this with anyone involved.

"No. You've done enough." Ignoring the resulting pain, I plant my weight on my casted leg long enough to move the other toward the door. I continue to wobble toward the front desk where I find Avery talking to the receptionist.

With a confused glance behind me, presumably at Jackson, she rushes to lift my right arm and sets her shoulders under it for support.

"What are you doing?" she asks, panic grating her voice.

"Getting out of here."

"Why? Are you okay?" She places a hand on my chest, and her eyes widen at the rapid thumping inside.

"I'm fine."

"Where's your ride?"

"Busy. Are you free?" Since my pride has been trampled to an irrevocably low level, I take no issue with exploiting her friendly compassion.

"I am. I just had the morning shift today."

"Mind taking me somewhere?"

"Sure, but you'll have to get back into the wheelchair. I can't carry you to the car."

Chapter Thirteen

Jordan

"Mind telling me what's going on?" Avery asks after we're on the road.

"Nora and I broke up."

"I know. Last summer."

I turn to her, ignoring the stings rippling through my thigh. "Last summer?"

"Jordan, I know you've been through something awful, but what's—"

"I lost some of my memory in the crash."

"Oh." She keeps her eyes focused on the road, her knuckles turning white around the steering wheel. "You remembered your breakup today, didn't you?"

My silence is enough to fill her in.

"I'm sorry, Jordan. That sucks."

"Thanks." A weary chuckle escapes. I'm grateful she isn't trying to placate or pity me. "You don't know the half of it."

"How about we have lunch, and you can tell me all about it? Or," she backtracks when I sigh out my hesitation, "we can eat in silence. Whichever works for you, but I can see you need a break from it all."

"You are a smart one. Who knew?"

She glares at me over her shoulder before laughing. The carefree sound is intoxicating and a far cry from what I expect to encounter when I'm forced to face Nora again.

She glances my way again. "Do you have someone to talk to at home? Who's staying with you?"

"Nora."

"Ouch. But why would she—"

"Fake girlfriend in-home care set up by my sister. She's been pretending we're still together since I left the hospital. I was blissfully happy for all of one week."

She pulls into a parking lot, and I don't bother to check which restaurant she picked. All I need is cold beer, hot food, and someone on my side.

"Well, it's a good thing you found out now and not a month from now," she says to offer consolation, even if it is a weak and embarrassing one.

"I guess."

After getting me in the wheelchair, over the sidewalk, and up the entry ramp, we soon settle at a table in the corner by the front windows. The natural light, Avery suggests, will help my grumpiness.

"Funny."

The waiter soon stops by, and we both order a beer, burger, and fries. Hers with bacon and cheese. Mine with barbeque sauce.

"Seems like our debate earlier was a bit pointless," she says after we're alone.

"What do you mean?"

"You argued that steak was better with beer, yet here you are ordering a burger at the first opportunity. That must mean I won the argument."

"No. That means eating a burger is easier than steak when you have only one hand." I wave my right hand for emphasis.

"Sure. Great excuse, but I'm still taking the win."

"Whatever." A smile tickles my lips as she sits back and crosses her arms with finality.

"So, tell me. How in the world did Nora become in charge of your care?"

"Diving in headfirst, are we?" I snatch up the beer as the waiter sets it on the table. "I can't even get five minutes of warm up first?"

"Like ripping off the bandage. Easier to not think about it too much before yanking."

I wince at the analogy. I've ripped off plenty of bandages in my lifetime as a reckless boy and later in the military. It's never pleasant when arm or leg hair is involved. This conversation will be no different, and I suspect I'll be bald and exposed in no time.

"I've gathered that Josie...my sister," I clarify when she tilts her head in question, "asked her to play along. Jackson said he was asked, for my well-being, and she would be the only one with details about my injuries and the balls to set all this up."

"Sounds like she was just looking out for you."

"I thought you were on my side."

"I am. One hundred percent, but I don't think she did it to hurt you. I assume you two are close?"

"She's the only family I have, and she's been taking care of me since I was a kid." I think back to the dozen other times she's made decisions to protect me or prevent me from getting hurt. All I've appreciated until now. "But this one cut deep. Imagine loving someone with your entire being and waking up one day to find the future you thought you had with them was a lie."

Avery's gaze fell to the table as her thoughts drifted. "I don't have to imagine. I know intimately what that feels like."

"You do? What happened?"

"I thought I'd be with Jackson for all my days, but he felt differently."

"What?" I sit back in my chair, my hand dropping to my lap. Jackson is a disgustingly happy married man, and I didn't know there had been someone before Emily. When we all served together, the guys would joke about Jackson being married to the Marines because it had been his life's purpose and he never dated. I assumed he met Emily during his rehab with Avery since she's also a physical therapist. Dumbfounded, I ask, "You and Jackson dated? When?"

"Shortly after he returned to Richmond. It only lasted a few months, but I've loved him my entire life."

"I don't...I don't know what to say."

"It's fine." She waves a hand in the air. "We're not here to talk about me. Did something happen to bring back your memories?"

"I had a seizure."

"Oh, my god."

"As you put it, it's fine. Not my first. Probably not my last. Side effect of the concussion from hell."

"Jordan. That's terrible."

"Yeah. But not as terrible as remembering the morning after you had the best sex of your life with the person you love. The same person you thought was with you because they cared about you. Now, I'm wondering if she was just using me for my dick."

"Hmm." She hides her amusement behind her glass as she takes a sip.

"What?"

"For her to fake date you in your condition and with your history...it can't be *that* magnificent."

"What can't be *that* magnificent?" I ask, setting down the beer I picked up before the odd question left her mouth.

"Your..." She wiggles a finger at my lap.

I look down, solve the mystery, then return her gaze with a smug grin. "She always seemed to think so. Seemed to think so last night with each of her four orgasms."

Her jaw goes lax before she slowly closes it. "You're exaggerating. Who has four orgasms?"

"She does, apparently."

Avery tosses the straw from her glass and gulps down half the liquid inside. It dribbles down her chin before she catches it with a napkin.

"You're blushing."

"I don't blush." She sets the napkin over her thighs and crosses them.

"And you're fidgeting. Whatever is the matter, Avery?" I tease, enjoying the carefree conversation. Nora and I used to have the same before…

"What is it?" Avery asked, leaning on the table. "Did you remember something else? You've gone pale."

Ignoring her, my thoughts dive deeper into the past. To a wedding reception.

---

10 Months Ago

"Are you going to go talk to her or just stand here, gawking at her like a jackass?" Mark asks. We've been friends since Basic, both serving under Jackson before transferring to Sergeant Montgomery's unit together. He doesn't know my history with the most beautiful woman to grace my presence. I save that for my closest confidants. But any fool can read my face and follow my eyes. They've been laser-focused on Nora since she walked in.

In a crowded room at Jackson and Emily's estate, even through the dim light, commotion, and music, there's no denying how much I need my hands on her. Need to hear her sexy voice and get lost in her gaze. Both are beyond tempting. More than dangerous. I've never been able to resist her, and at this moment, I don't want to.

Two months ago, I saw her for the first time after a long separation. We'd both gone to the same restaurant with friends—she's sitting with some of them now. At that run-in, we didn't talk much beyond an awkward greeting. For some reason, she seemed embarrassed to know me, but then again, that's normal Nora behavior when it comes to me.

I brushed it off after several unsuccessful attempts to get her alone so we could catch up, but that one interaction was enough to replant her firmly in my thoughts. I haven't been able to dig her out of my mind since. No matter how she treats me, it's like I'm addicted to her, willing to endure whatever for one glance, one touch, one moment of her attention. And after seeing her in the tight, green dress tonight, hugging her hips and dropping off her silky shoulders, I need to touch her before I implode.

I take a step in her direction, ignoring the crude encouragement Mark's spouting behind me. My resolve is dialed in, my target selected. There's no escaping. I will have what I want this time.

Halfway to the contact point, she notices me. My hand casually slides into my pocket, over-confidence and four beers fueling my swagger. Our eyes lock and some sputtering nonsense flutters in my chest as she watches me approach. The other women turn in my direction when she disengages from their conversation. They scatter like mice when the cat struts into the room. Yeah, that's me—a cat on the prowl for his next meal. And that delicious meal is Nora Jean Taylor.

Once she's in my arms, I will devour her. Inch by inch, I will taste and savor and—

Within touching distance now, her scent washes over me, and I freeze. The combination of lavender and something else I've never encountered before is different than I remember. Stronger, sexier. It's enough to knock my confidence down three notches and reduce me to a pile of mush at her feet. Then again, she could rub on dirt from the garden and dress in a paper bag, and I'd still find her irresistible.

"Hi," I say with all the suave I can muster from the slivers that remain.

"Hi. I didn't know you were coming."

"Wouldn't miss it. You look beautiful as always."

"Thank you."

Enveloped in her calming scent, I stare through the haze, trying to capture a clear memory of her in this moment. How the overhead string lights sparkle in her eyes. The soft wave of her long hair, spilling over her right shoulder. The sultry way she's holding my gaze with intrigue and challenge.

Is she glad to see me? Her welcoming posture, shoulders open toward me instead of curved away as she was at the restaurant, eyes bright, and crooked smile, tells me she's not retreating or hiding tonight. She's inviting me to take a shot at seducing her and in front of all these people. She brings her wine glass to her lips and sips while holding eye contact. Damn, I hope alcohol isn't what's fueling this change in her.

"Do you want to sit?" she asks, resting the base of the glass on her shoulder. But the question only shocks me into another stupor. Based on our last interaction, it's the exact opposite response I expect, quadrupling my already crippling desire for her.

"Actually, I rather dance." I reach out a hand and count the heart beats drumming in my ears until her palm slides over mine. It's warm and velvet soft and bringing back memories of the hours I spent exploring every inch of her skin.

Lacing our fingers together, I lead the way through the intermingling couples to the dance floor. Spinning her around, I take in the view before pulling her close. We sway to the beat while the lead singer of Journey belts the lyrics of *Separate Ways*. How ironic this song should play now.

Here we stand
Worlds apart, hearts broken in two

Someday love will find you
True love won't desert you

You know I still love you
Though we touched and went our separate ways

It might as well be our theme song. I've always loved this girl, yet I walk away over and over. Why? Is it because that's what she wants? What about what I want? Having her back in my arms and feeling her melt into me breathes life and a new resolve into me. My life had been empty without her, and I didn't know.

This is what I want. Her with me always. I can't let her go this time. I won't.

———

The waiter returns with our orders, snapping me back to the present.

"Jordan," Avery says cautiously, setting a hand on mine. "Give me the bottle."

"What?"

"Give it to me before you crush it."

Still caught between the past and present, my gaze shifts to her touch. She gently peels my aching fingers from around the glass, then sets it aside, watching me closely.

"Shake it out and breathe," she instructs.

Too confused to think for myself, I flex my hand to relieve the stiffness as instructed. I inhale, but instead of filling me with calm, all the emotions I kept bottled up since leaving VETS burn hot and sprint through my body, erupting at the same time.

"Jordan, breathe," she says with more sharpness this time and demonstrates. Inhale. Exhale. Repeat. I focus on her, doing as she encourages. It wouldn't seem so impossible if my world wasn't in the process of crashing down around me.

I continue to mimic the motion until I crawl through the wreckage. The air in my lungs feels thin and lacking life-sustaining quality, but at least I can breathe normally again.

"You zoned out for a few minutes before panic took over."

"Yeah. Reliving the buried past will do that."

"Where'd you go?"

My throat feels like I swallowed a spoonful of powder. I reach for her water and gulp half of it to keep my throat from closing. "Back ten months," I finally answer.

She counts on her fingers. "December? What happened in—Oh, Jackson and Emily's wedding. I remember you and Nora that night at the reception. You looked so happy. I hated you something fierce."

A rumble in my chest ignites a chuckle, and it feels good. "You hated us?"

"Oh yeah. I'd never been more miserable than I was that day."

"I get it."

She bites a fry and my stomach churns. Food no longer appeals. I rather drown my frustrations, sorrow, anger in a keg of beer. Reaching across the table, I retrieve the bottle Avery took away from me and drink.

"What happened after the reception? I shot dagger eyes at your back as you two drunken lovebirds left together. I thought you were going to undress right there in the foyer."

"We made it to the car first…barely."

"Was she unable to resist that magnificent dick of yours?"

"Precisely."

Her easy laughter settles me until my phone vibrates in my front pocket. I react with a jolt, and she follows my gaze.

"Everything okay down there?" A sensual nibble on the fry steals my attention, and I roll my eyes in response before reading the text message.

Nora: Where are you?
Nora: I'm worried sick.

"You've lost your sexy glow again. Is that from Nora?"

"Yes. She's wondering where I am." I stare at the screen, debating on responding or tossing the phone into the mop bucket I see within range. I played basketball in high school. I could totally make it.

"You should respond."

"Why?" I ask, meeting her watchful gaze.

"Because she wouldn't be faking it with you if she didn't care."

"Do you know how ridiculous that sounds?"

"Yes. But hear me out." She interprets my long, audible exhale as consent. "She could have easily told Josie to deal with you herself. Instead…" Her voice projects slightly louder when I scoff. "Instead, she drops everything to be by your side. There's no way that was a simple decision for her."

"Avery, she fucked me like I meant something to her."

"Maybe you do. Have you considered that?"

A young couple walking by the window catches my attention, and I ponder that new idea. I can't get far enough past my shock to consider it a real contender. There are too many hurtful actions and words left unsaid, poking holes in the theory.

My gaze follows the happy couple until they pass a group of people entering a store. Next to the store, a woman with long brown hair sits on a bench. She's staring at her phone, her legs crossed and bouncing nervously. She drops the device onto the wooden seat with frustration and glances across the street, her arms folding over her chest.

"Shit."

"What?" Avery leans on the empty chair next to her to look out at the city beyond the restaurant. "Is that…"

"Nora."

"You should be there, talking with her. Not me."

"But I'm enjoying your company, and you're the only one who hasn't screwed me."

"Not yet." She wiggles her eyebrows. "Your magical dick has me intrigued."

"Shut up. That's not what I meant, and I know you're taken."

She puffs. "How do you know that? I haven't mentioned dating anyone."

"You flirt differently than I remember witnessing with others. Innocent, in a way."

"Maybe you just don't do it for me."

A dismissive snicker escapes my throat. "Right. I believed you when you said my competence intrigued you, but not enough to believe you'd go for it if offered."

"You think you're so smart."

"And right." My attention drifts back to Nora outside. The woman I love. The woman who ripped out my heart and stomped on it at least twice. Who knows how many more there are that I don't remember?

"You should go to her or let me bring her to you," Avery suggests.

"No. She should have to suffer a little while longer." I take a swig of beer. "Plus, I'm not ready to hear her excuses yet."

"Suit yourself." She picks up her massive burger with two hands and takes a bite, moaning as she chews. "Oh, my god, this is so delicious."

"Yeah?" Her tongue swipes the juice and sauce from her lips, and my mouth waters. Not from the sensual motion and sounds she's making while she enjoys the flavors, but because I'm hungry again. Picking up the large slippery sandwich with one hand isn't as easy as it sounded when I ordered. "Is there anything I can do to entice you to cut mine so I can join you?"

Incredulous, she stops chewing and stares at me for a bit. "That's Nora's job," she says with a full mouth. "I'm just the chauffeur slash commiserating buddy."

"Come on. I'll starve."

She bats her lashes at me, seemingly unconcerned with my plight, then drops her burger on the plate with a sigh. "Apparently, sexy blue eyes are my weakness. Pass it over."

Chapter Fourteen

Nora

Jordan knows. I saw the change in him this morning, and despite understanding the consequences, I still allowed myself to hope the pin in that damn truth grenade hadn't been pulled while he slept.

But the second he awoke, I felt it coming.

"I need a break," I announce, interrupting Jackson and Sydney's discussion. Their heads whip to me in unison, startled by my voice. I'd been stuck in my head since Jackson recounted his conversation with Jordan to us, but I can't listen to their concerns anymore. I've already got all of them covered. "Thank you for your help."

"Nora," Sydney calls to my back as I storm out of VETS. When I reach the street, I keep going, turning onto the sidewalk with the sole purpose of walking until I can confidently hold my shit together.

What I did warrants being left behind. I shouldn't be rescued by a phone call and given a chance at forgiveness. I thrusted us both into a destructive situation that could have been avoided. Thinking about the endless emotions he must be experiencing, I'm grateful he's at least with someone who can help if they trigger another blackout or seizure.

At that disturbing vision, panic rises into my throat, making the busy street blur and coil around me. I lower to the first bench I see and wait for the maddening merry-go-round my life has become to slow to a stop.

Talking to him and hearing he's safe would go a long way in hitting the brakes on this carnival ride. Then again, are there adequate words to express my regret? To help him hate me less than I hate myself?

Glaring at my silent phone again, I plead with the universe to make him respond. I never should have gotten involved, and I hadn't been thinking when I let my guard down. Letting him in and sleeping together only made things so much harder than they needed to be. Endless black hole kind of complicated.

There are no good explanations for why I did what I did. Sydney would say something about my heart getting in the way, and she'd be right. That whole fuck-it conversation my heart had with my good judgment on the mountain is to blame, along with dangerous and stupid wishful thinking.

Wishful thinking had me anticipating a buildup before an explosive ending to our arrangement—casual hints, fragments of history coming up randomly in conversations, and a meandering situation that eventually led him to the truth. A gentle lead-in to a confession and subsequent breakup. A loud, messy one because what I did doesn't deserve careful control.

I never expected all the horrible ways I've hurt him to come crashing down at once, snapping our mending connection and me into a million jagged and irreconcilable pieces.

I shouldn't have let Josie and Sydney talk me into this.

Shit. Josie. I need to tell her.

Opening the contacts app on my phone, I search for her number. Hurried footsteps sound on the concrete nearby, but I'm too distracted, frantically pulling words together in my jumbled brain that might prepare Josie for her brother's wrath, to pay attention.

The determined heels stop by the bench. "Are you okay?" Sydney asks, sitting beside me.

"No." My voice strains under the pressure of the honest answer as hot air burns in my lungs.

I grasp at my slippery control, begging for something to ground me, and that's when it hits me. I'm tired of lying. Tired of running from my feelings. And so damn tired of pretending—for Jordan, for Sydney, for the world. I'm not who they think I am, and I can't go another minute cloaked by this fake persona.

"You look like you could use a friend," she says, placing a hand on my back. She means to comfort me, but her friendly touch sends a tangible reminder that I don't deserve her sympathy. I've been lying to her, too.

"I need more than a friend. I need therapy."

"All right. You've offered me that service for years. Let me return the favor. What's got you upset? Other than the obvious," she adds.

When I don't answer, she continues. "But don't forget why you entered this arrangement. You did it for his wellbeing. Don't be so hard on yourself."

"Easier said than done."

"We're always hardest on ourselves. Women are strong but notorious for taking the blame, soaking in everyone else's emotions as our own, and apologizing when we've done nothing wrong."

I puff out a breath and check my phone for messages. Still nothing. "I've done plenty wrong. This is just the latest."

"What are you talking about? I know you, Nora Jean, and you—"

"You don't know everything about me, Sydney." I shake my head, disgusted that it's taken this long to tell her. "No one does."

"Then, tell me."

Dropping the phone to the weathered bench, I lean my elbows on my thighs and attempt to ignore how exposed I feel. My entire adult life, I've run from the hopelessness the truth always invokes.

"My real name is Roan. I changed it to Nora after high school graduation when I escaped the hell my life had become."

Sydney sat motionless, stunned into silence, but her hand still rests on my back, providing the encouragement I need to continue.

"The summer after tenth grade, I discovered my mother's boyfriend of the month was drugging her. He'd sneak a little cocaine into her food or drink, more and more until she got addicted. Once that happened, she would give him whatever he wanted. It was like he ripped her soul from her body. She'd never been perfect—fickle, scatter-brained, and disorganized with backwards judgment, especially with men. But nothing I said or did brought her back from that. All her focus was on keeping him happy and getting her next hit." Lost in the terrifying past, tears fall undetected. "While she was passed out one day, he chained me to my bed."

"Nora, no." Her other hand flies to her mouth as tears pool on her eyelids, afraid for me. But shame and embarrassment turn my focus to the pavement below.

"He intended to do some terrible things, but my boyfriend Tristan had suspected something was up when I didn't respond to his texts. The police arrived before the first customer did. When Tristan came over the next day, he admitted to knowing what that asshole was doing to my mother, even though I tried to hide it." Story of my life.

"Thank goodness."

"After that, my mother entered rehab in Pennsylvania, and she stayed clean for the next two years. Guilt from having to look at me every day after she got me back from the system kept the demons at bay for a while. But she eventually turned to other things to make her happy. Booze, gambling, men—her main vice. She really knew how to pick 'em. My senior year, the guy she was sleeping with moved in. As man of the house, he enjoyed displaying his dominance.

He was verbally and physically abusive toward my mother, even though she did everything for him. He didn't lay a hand on me until I cracked and tried to stop him from touching her."

Sydney sucks in a sharp breath. "What happened?"

"Guess it was more fun to manipulate my mother by using me as his punching bag. And when that wasn't satisfying enough, he added weapons." Emotion lodges in my throat, choking me until I have no other option but to let it out. It burst from my chest with such force, several people slow their pace to stare.

Wrapping me in a hug, she soaks in my pain as if it's her own. Her tears wet the back of my shirt, but I can't reach for her. My body, my heart, it all hurts too fucking much.

"This is why I can't be with Jordan."

"What?" she asks, straightening. "I don't understand. He'd do anything to keep you safe or help you heal. Nothing in your past could make him not love you. If anything, he'd love you more for how you've overcome it."

My head shakes, spilling more tears over my cheeks. "I can't have kids, Sydney."

"Because of the…of the…" she stutters, struggling to put a label on the abuse I survived.

I sniff, falling back against the bench to face her. "Plastic surgery fixed most of the external evidence. But the internal damage to my uterus was too extensive. He wants a big family, Sydney. A picket fence, a big yard, the fairy tale. I can't give him that."

"You haven't told him, have you?"

"I haven't told anyone. Everyone knows me as Nora—the confident, carefree, sassy persona I adopted when I changed my name. Pretending to be someone I'm not helped me cope and forget. It's like jumping into a book and becoming that character. I'm a damn good actress."

"Had me convinced." She meant it as a joke to lighten the mood, but it made the guilt weighing me down sting even more. I've been lying to her the longest.

We met our sophomore year in college when she answered my ad for a roommate. I wasn't the easiest person to live with at first. While I didn't want to let anyone in, lack of money created a need. I'd grown accustomed to keeping my distance, but over time, I found a kindred spirit in Sydney and came to trust, love, and lean on her. We'd drop anything to be by each other's side whenever required—as she is doing now.

"What will you do now that he knows?" she asks, taking my hand.

"No clue. Josie won't be back for several days. I doubt he'll want me anywhere near him, but he needs constant observation."

"Do you want to continue helping him?"

Considering the question, it doesn't take long to decide where I stand. "Yes."

"I have to say, I didn't expect that. Did something change your mind about all this?"

"I still don't like the deception involved, but at least it removed my blinders. He's amazing. How did I not realize?"

My eyes plead with Sydney, who smiles, smug in the all-knowing answer she's about to deliver. "I remember telling you on multiple occasions how good you two were together—how good you could have it with him again—but you were too stubborn to listen."

"Yeah, yeah. I remember."

"After the marathon," she continues. "After that crazy girls' night last fall. And many other times in between. You should listen to your best friend occasionally. She's quite brilliant."

"You still want to keep that title? Even after I lied to you all this time?"

"Nora, you were doing what you thought you had to do to protect yourself. I don't blame you. I'd have done the same."

Feeling the metaphorical multi-ton truck lift off my shoulders, I tug her into an embrace. "Thank you. I don't know what I'd do without you."

"You, Nora Jean slash Roan…" She pulls back to meet my gaze. "What was your old middle name?"

"Nope." Shaking my head, I draw a proverbial line in the sand between us. Some things are better left in the twisted past.

"Come on," she urges. "Best friends are good at keeping each other's secrets. It's in the code."

I study her, wondering if I can even mutter it. It's a part of me I despise and have fought so hard to bury. But she's right. After hiding the real me from her for so long, everything needs to be dug out and exposed. Even if it is ridiculous.

She watches me expectantly, and I sigh, resigning to enduring further embarrassment.

"Jolene."

"Jolene? Like in Dolly Parton's song?"

I can't help the cringe that wrinkles my face. "Yeah."

"What's wrong with that? It's a pretty name."

"Not when it was the dog's name first, thanks to my mother's classic country music obsession and lack of creativity."

"Yikes. Okay. You're right."

"Thank you."

We sit in silence for a moment, Sydney's arm around my shoulders, our heads tipped and resting together. As the city goes on around us, memories play out in front of me like home movie clips. The sweet, loving way Jordan's gaze blazes into mine and burrows within my soul. His unwavering acceptance of my growing list of flaws. The way he's always been there, waiting for me to come to my senses. Well, at least he was before the rude, heartless way I discarded his second marriage proposal. And now this. His laugh, which is always at the ready. His goofy jokes, and over-the-top reactions to plays and referee calls during football games. I don't understand half of it, but his intensity is adorable. The sly way he takes care of me without my noticing, because he knows I'll stubbornly protest. The sexy V shape of his torso and the ridges of muscle filling every inch as though an artist sculpted them into his skin. How he can make just about any place, any moment into something hot and sexy. His glorious pride in being mine.

"I love him," I blurt out, causing Sydney to sit up and toss up her arms in celebration.

"Hallelujah."

"I love him," I say again, laughing. It feels good to admit my heart's full for the first time in my life.

"Great. So, what are you going to do about it?"

A wave of excitement rolls through me, and I shoot off the bench, only to lower again as trepidation sinks back in. "Nothing."

"What? Why?"

"Because nothing's changed."

"What are you talking about? Of course, it has. You've finally come to your senses, and—"

"Sydney." I let out a long breath, as exasperated with myself as she is. "I still can't give him the family he wants. Hell, I'm not even sure I want to be a parent. I didn't exactly have the best role models growing up." I hold up a hand when I notice her pulling together a protest. "I need to do some soul-searching in that department first."

"Fair enough."

"And there's the matter of me breaking his heart three separate times and lying to him. That's hard to come back from."

"But—"

"No, buts. I need to figure out my life—come to terms with the things I've kept locked away and the decisions I've made. In the meantime, while he's stuck with me, I'll do what

I can to give him back his life. He deserves that and so much more. But if I give myself to him and he doesn't want me, then I'll make sure he's free of me with his heart intact when this ordeal is over."

"What about you and *your* heart?" she asks carefully. "You matter, too."

"I'll be fine, so long as he is."

Chapter Fifteen

Jordan

I've never seen Nora cry before, and I can't tear my eyes from the wreckage. She's crumpled in Sydney's arms, her shoulders shaking. Anger and hurt rumbles inside me while I ache to be the one comforting her.

"Do you think that's about you?" Avery asks, pushing her nearly empty plate aside. Since seeing Nora hunched over, drowning in her own pain, I've barely had the energy to pick up the fork.

"Part of me says no."

"And the other part?"

"Remembers the new side she laid bare last night." My system has yet to recover, not only from the seizure and memories, but from the love that poured from her touch.

"You need to talk to her."

"I will."

"When?"

"I don't know." Snatching up the fork, I stab a piece of neatly sliced burger with more force than necessary, making a clanking sound against the rustic metal plate underneath.

"Well, I can't sit here all night while you figure it out. After you eat, I'm taking you home. Or here's an idea: You can ride with your *girlfriend*, who happens to be sitting less than thirty yards away. Save me the trip."

"You're right. I'm sorry for wasting so much of your time."

Her head tilts with a sympathetic smile. "I'm happy to help, but if you don't mind me saying…"

"You don't strike me as someone who bites their tongue for the sake of others."

She shrugs and sips her water, wetting her throat for whatever mind-blowing point she's about to make. "Delaying the inevitable only makes it harder. Take it from me. I've had more than my share of the waiting game when it comes to matters of the heart. It's not fun."

"Okay. You've convinced me."

"Good. Text her."

"Right now?" My heartbeat doubles in speed as it does when I'm standing at the base of a chopper, preparing to jump. Facing Nora again, knowing what I know, feels just as daunting.

"Delay equals hard, remember?"

"You and your dirty talk. All right, all right," I surrender as her brow dips into a scowl. "I'll text her. But I can't promise the conversation will happen without items or curse words being thrown."

"That's fine. Do what you have to do, but make sure you miss."

The corners of my mouth turn down into a pronounced frown. "Do you really think that lowly of me? I would never—"

"Stop stalling. I'm tired of entertaining your ass."

———

Me: Hi.

Nora: Where are you?

Me: Benny's Pizza with Avery.

I watch Nora turn around in her seat on the bench and locate the familiar restaurant. The wind picks up her long waves, blowing them off her shoulders and exposing her red, splotchy face.

Nora: Do you want to talk?

Me: Yes. Not here.

Nora: Home?

Calling the apartment *home*, like we made one there together, stings now that I know everything that happened inside those walls had been fake.

Nora: I'll go get my car and come pick you up.

Me: No need. I'll meet you there.

Nora: OK.

"Still willing to give me that ride?" I ask Avery. "I need a little more time to think."

"Sure." She motions for the waiter to bring the check and a box. "I'm proud of you."

Oddly, the sentiment soothes the smoldering edges of my nerves. "Thanks."

"Get out your wallet. You owe me."

———

Avery continues to provide unsolicited advice on the short drive. I appreciate the attempt to walk me through the upcoming uncharted territory, but I still feel lost without a map or a flashlight or a damn clue where to begin.

I'm unprepared. Frankly, I rather pretend nothing happened to warrant the advice—as if Nora never came back to me. Never kissed me. Never made me believe I could have all of her.

If I had anyone else to call, I would release Nora from her obligation and somehow summon myself to move on.

But how does one move past a betrayal so deep and so goddamn delusional and somehow retain a belief that true love exists? She isn't stupid enough to think this arrangement would have had a happy ending. So why attempt it? What good could come of it?

I'm drowning in a what-the-fuck conversation with myself when Avery pulls up to the apartment building. Nora is sitting on the small stoop, her arms circling her knees, shielding herself against the chilly fall afternoon. Storm clouds gather in the distance, a symbol of what's to come.

"You can do this," Avery says before popping the trunk and exiting.

She greets Nora at the back of the car, and together, they unload the wheelchair, whispering to each other as they work. I don't care to hear what they're saying. It's easy enough to figure out without the embarrassment of hearing it spoken aloud. Like a shift change at the command post, Avery's giving Nora a rundown of our lunch and what to look out for. A status update in the pathetic and unfortunate life of Jordan Jones.

Avery soon appears at the door and opens it, while Nora holds the wheelchair steady. It takes every ounce of strength and energy I have left to rise from the car on my own and plop down into the chair. My body screams in protest not only from the movement, but at the first scent of Nora behind me. I close my eyes against the pang in my chest sent there by the memorable combination of vanilla and lavender.

I don't hear if Avery says goodbye or if Nora provides instructions before pushing me to the courtyard and through the sliding glass doors of the apartment. Despite what I promised to both of them, I can't do this. I can't look at her, much less talk about how she's destroyed my trust. I don't want to hear her excuses or if she wants to jump ship—her typical response. I need to sleep and forget this day ever happened.

She parks me beside the couch, expecting to start the conversation I agreed to. It's not happening.

With my head down, I'm the first to break the silence. "I can't do this right now," I croak, too weak to put anything other than frankness behind the words and shake my head. "I need…"

"What do you need, Jordan? Just tell me and you'll have it."

"I need to be alone."

"That's not a good—"

"Please," I bark, interrupting her protest about my condition. I don't care. I'm suffocating in her proximity and need space.

"Okay." Her hands fly up in surrender before running down the tight jeans covering her thighs. "I'll get the other bed made."

She hurries to the bedroom, giving me a chance to breathe. In the quiet, my thoughts reel. How am I going to survive until Josie returns? Not sure being around my sister will be any easier. But being angry with your sister is different. A different pain.

"I understand you don't want to talk right now," Nora says, walking back into the living room. "But I'm leaving the door open so I can—"

"Why did you do it?" I blurt out. She's right. I don't want to talk about it, but that one question keeps gnawing at me. And if I'm going to get any rest, I need an explanation whether I'll believe it or not. "And I want the truth."

"No more lies, Jordan. I promise."

"Not sure if I can trust your promises but go on."

"I deserve that." She takes a timid step closer. "Josie asked me to pretend. She feared what the truth would do to you in your condition."

"That doesn't answer the question. Why? Why did you say yes?"

Her trembling hand combs through her hair as she sits. "Because when it comes to us, I've been selfish. It's always been about what I want and don't want. I never considered what you needed or tried to give it to you."

"Is that why you offered yourself to me last night? You thought I needed sex?"

She spins to face me sharply, the deep intensity in her eyes surprising me. "I was with you because I wanted to be."

"Your needs, then?"

"Jordan, no." Her breath comes out all at once in a frustrated huff. "Well, sort of, but only because I wanted *you*. I haven't been with anyone since…" she trails off.

"Since when?"

"Since we were together at Jackson and Emily's wedding." Her eyes find me, and the truth is there.

"Why?"

"Because you broke me."

My blood pressure spikes at the accusation. "How did I—"

"Do you remember that night?"

"Only fragments. Beautiful ones." Dropping my gaze to my lap, I wonder if she's about to ruin the few incredible memories I have of the evening. Of her wrapped around me for hours in public and private, and my love for her growing beyond my comprehension.

"Then, maybe we should talk about that when you do."

"No. Everything else I believed to be true and good has been destroyed today. What happened?"

She picks at a nail and sighs. "You proposed…again."

"Again?" I don't remember proposing either time. Shit. What had come over me? Why in the world would I cross that line, let alone *twice*?

The boundary she set on day one was drawn in permanent ink. Of course, she wouldn't agree to marry me. She's the casual relationship, unattached type, and I've been wasting my life. I've been chasing a woman who will never choose me. How could I not see that before? "Holy shit."

"Jordan, I—"

"Don't bother. I can guess how it went down after that. I've never been more to you than a good fuck."

"That's not true."

Angry fire gushes through my veins at her denial, preventing the gentleman in me from emerging. From hurting her as she's hurt me. "I loved you with everything I had. I gave you what you wanted on your timeline and on your terms. It would have destroyed me to hurt you, but that wasn't enough. I'm realizing now that *I'll* never be enough for you, and all of this, us, was a waste of time." I look away from the tears welling in her eyes, unable to face the evidence of the hurt I'm causing. "When Josie comes back, I never want to see you again."

A breath hitches. I hear it choking her, but I can't care about that. She ruined what we could have been. *She* deceived *me*. She used and tossed me aside over and over. The reality of that hits me square in the chest.

"I'd like to go to bed now."

Heavy silence grows between us as she remains planted. She wants to say something, but there are no words to make this hellish situation less painful, and she knows better than to try right now. With a resigned sniff, she rises to grip the handles of the chair and pushes me into the bedroom.

"I can handle it from here," I say when the chair stops beside the bed.

"Okay. I'll be right back with some water and your toothbrush."

Before I can protest, she rushes out, soon returning with a handful of items to get me ready and through the night. By then, I'd pulled myself onto the mattress to release her from any obligation she may feel to help and turned my back to the door.

A sense of mourning washes over me as she walks out without a word, symbolizing the end of our relationship. The end of my willingness to fight for something I could never have. The end of a dream. Just yesterday, I thought she would be in my life forever. That even though she was distant at times, she still wanted me. Still wanted *us*.

That fantasy was attached to me like a cancer until the truth set me free. I don't remember my proposals or the aftershocks that surely followed. Some part of my twisted brain must be protecting me from reliving that agony. But no matter what's happened since then, I'd be an idiot to continue believing she could ever wholly be mine. If handing over my heart, giving her the best sex of her life, and asking for the opportunity to love her forever (twice) doesn't make her choose me, then nothing will.

And I'm over it.

Chapter Sixteen

Nora

Somehow, after leaving Jordan in the bedroom, I drag my exhausted body to the living room and fall face first onto the couch. I can't bring myself to lie on the corner mattress—to be surrounded by his scent and the memories of how happy we were there.

I've never felt that content before. This morning, I would have been happy to snuggle in his arms for the rest of the day and forget about the responsibilities waiting for us both.

It didn't use to be that way between us. Even when we officially dated last year, I couldn't turn off the fears and doubts. He never held *all* of me. Only the parts I knew I could control.

Our relationship started because of sex—both of us craving a release. That night, I would have accepted it from anyone who could turn me on. But he surprised me and ruined my chance of enjoying sex with anyone else. No one makes me writhe like he does, and after a while, I stopped trying to replace him. He became my beautiful release, and in the beginning, he seemed to enjoy being my chosen fix.

That utopia ended the first time he brought up commitment and feelings and God-forbid marriage. I panicked, tossed him out like he meant nothing to me. But he stayed in touch. After that, he gave me enough to keep the withdrawals at bay, and before long, the cycle repeated itself.

Holy shit. I'd acted like my mother.

And isn't it fitting and annoyingly ironic that I should finally come to my senses when he comes to his? When I acknowledge what I've been fighting all these years, he decides he can't stomach fighting for me any longer. I'd laugh at the absurdity if every ounce of me didn't ache from missing him already.

My phone lights the dark room with an incoming call, but I ignore it. It's either Sydney checking on me or Josie doing the same about Jordan. Poor Josie. She's oblivious to the one-hundred-and-eighty-degree turn the day has taken. She deserves to be warned, but I'm not sure it's my place to tell her. Although Jordan doesn't need the added stress of explaining it all to her, either. Not that he's interested in talking to her any more than he is to me, I'd imagine.

I grab the phone and check the Caller ID. It's Josie. Since she'd be concerned if no one responded, causing more questions, I wait for the phone to stop ringing and send her a text. I don't want Jordan to overhear me recount the mess our arrangement has become. And I don't want to hear the hurt and frustration in my voice because of it.

Me: Jordan's sleeping. This is quieter.

Josie: It's early. Everything OK?

Me: He's fine. I think. But you should know, he remembers.

A long pause. She's freaking out on the other end.

Josie: Guess that means he also knows what we've done.

Me: Yes.

Josie: Is he upset?

Me: More like pissed.

Josie: Fair. I knew he would be, but I did what I thought was best. How are you holding up?

Me: Not good.

Josie: I'm sorry I roped you into this. Truly.

Me: You didn't force me to do it.

Josie: No. Just guilt tripped you.

I don't have a response that wouldn't make her feel worse, so I type nothing.

Josie: I doubt he wants to be with either of us right now. But are you still able to help until I get back?

Me: Correct. Yes, I can stay.

Josie: Thank you. I'll come home ASAP.

Me: The show is this weekend, right?

Josie: Yes. Three more days, and it will all be over. There will be no enjoying it now.

Me: He needs time to cool off. He'll be better by the time you return…hopefully. It's good you have somewhere else to be.

Josie: I hate dumping this on you. I assumed he'd remember everything well after I got back, allowing me to take the brunt of it.

Me: Me too. But it's fine. Customer service with a smile is where I excel.

I want to laugh, but that comment also shines a spotlight on all the things I'm terrible at handling. Unfortunately, most of those things involve a man who's as perfect as they come. If he hadn't been so damned set on waiting for me, he'd probably already be married to a deserving woman with enough babies to fill a basketball team.

For the first time, imagining Jordan with someone else cuts to the core. It's a wound I'll have to bear after what I've done. I don't blame him for giving up on us. Hell, I would have given up on me long ago. But he's loyal.

From what I can tell, he hasn't strayed since we met. Although, I can't account for the months between our breaking up and coming back together. Maybe he sowed a few oats, dipping his toes into the sea of beautiful women who would love and appreciate a thoughtful, kind, and sexy man.

My stomach churns at my loss.

> **Josie:** I'll try to reach out to him tomorrow. See if he'll answer.
>
> **Me:** Good luck.
>
> **Josie:** You, too. And thanks. You're more selfless and caring than I gave you credit for.
>
> **Me:** No. You were right all along.

Tears sting and threaten to pool and spill, and I don't wait for her response. Shutting off the phone, I toss it onto the mattress beyond and let the sorrow I've been harboring over the last twenty years wreak havoc on my system.

For hours, I sob into the warm cushion. Although my body is heavy with fatigue, sleep doesn't come easily. The few moments my thoughts silence long enough to drift off, they're dreamless—just dark nothingness. And perhaps that is exactly what I need.

Opening my eyes to the sun, streaming in through the curtainless windows, I go to toss my arm over my head to find that blissful state of numbness. But I still when I see Jordan leaning against the doorway of the bathroom, watching me. There's nothing in his stare to help me discern what he's thinking or feeling. His expression is blank, almost as if he's resolved to feel nothing for me.

"Hi," I say, sitting up without breaking eye contact. "Can I get you anything? Some breakfast?"

"No. I've got it."

I shoot up in a surge of nerves when he takes an awkward step toward the kitchen, then another.

"Jordan, you don't have to do this. I want to help."

"I'm fully capable of making my own fucking breakfast." His voice is hoarse, like he spent the night screaming, and I wish he had. At least then we'd be talking through what's happened between us. "I'm sorry," he says with a long exhale.

"Don't apologize. I deserve it."

"Yes, you do, but that's not how I handle things. I'm just…hurting."

"I know." My voice is barely a whisper. "Do you think we could talk for a few minutes this morning?"

He looks down the short corridor between him and the kitchen as if to consider which would be worse, hobbling down the hall or listening to me. "All right."

"Please let me bring you something to eat." I motion for him to sit. "And coffee."

Without answering, he limps to the living room and drops onto the couch in obvious discomfort, overwhelmed by the effort it takes to walk.

"Thank you," I say and hurry to the kitchen.

Busying myself with making coffee, scrambled eggs and bacon, I try not to think myself into a panic before we even start.

With two eggs and three slices of microwavable bacon plated, I grab the steaming pot of coffee and fill two mugs. After adding three sugars and a dash of creamer to each, I deliver the hot meal, grateful for the opportunity to get a few things off my chest, yet terrified what I have to say won't matter.

"You're not eating?" he asks, accepting the plate.

"I'm not hungry."

Seemingly unconcerned, he lifts the fork and stabs at the eggs. "What did you want to say?" he says without looking up.

It's probably better that way. Seeing the pain and bitter disconnect in his eyes won't help me get through this.

Folding my legs under me, I grasp the warm mug for comfort and begin.

"I'm not sure, actually." I swallow down the nerves creeping in and remind myself that I asked for this conversation. "I guess I wanted to say I'm sorry."

"For which part?" He doesn't stop eating to grace me with a glance.

"The parts that hurt you."

"Which ones? Because there seem to be many."

"All of them."

His hand pauses over the plate as he considers the implications of my answer. "What does that mean?" His eyes cut to me for a moment before returning to the plate on his lap.

Years of flimsy excuses and regrets flood my thoughts, making my explanation spill out faster than I can process it. "It means I regret the way I've put your needs behind my own. I hate that it took almost losing you to recognize what I had. I'm sorry for lying to you. Although I was convinced it would help you recover, it was wrong. But I'd do it again if it is necessary to learn what I now know. You fell in love with someone who doesn't deserve you." Emotion fills the void in my chest, and I inhale sharply. "It took me longer than it should to realize how truly special you are."

The tension is so thick in the air I can almost taste it. I want to reach out, but the rigid shape of his shoulders and the tick in his jaw keep me planted in fear. Maybe it's too late for an apology or too soon. Either way, the words would have eaten me alive if I didn't say them. Now, at least, he knows how I feel.

He moves the plate from his lap to the table and rubs the back of his neck. "I need a moment."

"Of course." I rise on unsteady knees and retreat to the kitchen to give him space.

My hands tremble as I wash dishes and keep a watchful eye over him. The last thing he needs is more stress. I'm the person assigned to his care with the sole responsibility of making his life easier. And what have I done? Shackle his recovery with pain, anger, and an agonizing reminder of what could have been and how I destroyed it.

Chapter Seventeen

Jordan

My mind can't focus on any one thing Nora said. It's all too shocking to process. How many times have I wished for her to care for me as I do for her…or used to. Fury and confusion are blocking my ability to determine if I feel the same as I once did.

Do I still love her? Can I trust that her confession is from the heart and not from guilt?

She's kept me at arm's length for five years, never letting me in, and it feels that way today. Even after admitting her regrets, it seems like there's more she's holding back. Although, at this point, I can't imagine what that could be.

While she's upset about hurting me, I can't tell if love is behind it. Anyone can have empathy. Love is something else entirely, and she's never seemed to have any for me.

"I need to know," I say without turning around, but loud enough for her to hear. "Did I ever mean anything to you? More than someone you liked to sleep with?"

When she doesn't respond immediately, I twist to find her in the kitchen, her expression frozen in shock—eyes wide and lips slightly parted. Recovering, she dries her hands on a towel and crosses the room to sit beside me. She takes a moment to gather herself, staring into her clasped hands on her lap. I've never seen her like this—introspective, insecure, vulnerable. Her armor is cracked and faltering, and I'm intrigued.

"For a long time, no. But there's a lot about my past you don't know," she adds quickly when I puff out a breath and shake my head at the confirmation of my suspicions. "Things that stripped me of seeing love as a possibility for me."

"Like what?"

Her lips roll into a tip-lipped grin. "Can we save that for another day?"

"No," I snap, not meaning to, but I'm tired of everyone tiptoeing around issues. "I deserve to know why you treated me like your whore for the last half-decade."

"Jordan," she tries to calm my raging temper, but answers are the only thing that can help with that. And even then, there's no guarantee getting them won't make it worse.

"Nora, you've never given me the real you. For just once, I beg you, be honest with me."

"I've given you everything I could until this point."

"Really? Everything?"

"Yes. It isn't much, I realize, but until I told my story yesterday, I didn't think my past affected me as much as it has."

"Who did you tell?" I ask, anger boiling inside me at being the last to know again. Then, the memory of her crying on the bench outside the restaurant reminds me. "Sydney."

"Yes. Even my best friend didn't know, and I realized something else in that moment."

"What?"

"I have two best friends. Two amazing people I couldn't imagine living without."

I search her face for answers, confused about what she's trying to say.

"You, Jordan. You are someone I don't want to live without. But after all I've done, I resign to that being my fate."

What in the hell? My heart is throwing itself against my ribcage, the thumping sound deafening. My voice rises above it. "Why is that your fate? Because you think I won't want you after your lies?"

"Yes, partly." Her tone remains controlled, and I wonder how she's doing it. How is she not losing her shit as I am? She wrings her hands together before pushing them through her hair and pacing to the sliding glass door. She looks out, her eyes clouded and distant. And again, I'm confronted with a new side of her I've never seen. A side created from suffering and trauma.

"What happened, Nora?" In the silence, my body begs to take hold of her shoulders and gently shake her attention back to the conversation.

Last night, I vowed to protect my heart, no matter what she said or did until she was out of my life forever. But these awkward pauses, her detached stare, her confession, and the agony in her eyes, they're all chipping away at that resolve like it's made of glass.

"I can't have children," she says so softly I'm not sure I hear her correctly. "Courtesy of my mother's stellar partner choices."

She doesn't look at me, and the frustration fluttering around inside me ignites into fury. "What did they do to you?"

My hand clenches the edge of the cushion under me while I wait. I need her answer to stop my imagination from letting in murderous thoughts. "Nora."

Cautiously, she tells me about being abused and assaulted by cowards claiming to be men, recounting the decision to change her name and leave it all behind when she went to college. A scream boils in my chest, and I'd give anything to bang my fist against the wall or kick and stomp on the coffee table until it's a pile of shards on the rug. But the only emotion that comes out of me is a bucket of tears.

She rushes to my side and holds me as I cry on her shoulder. I can't fathom the trauma she must have gone through and continues to experience, but I can feel it. Every inch of me aches down to my bones as waves of sobs rip through me.

After a while, I straighten, feeling drained, puzzled, and embarrassed. My gaze rises to find her eyes red and puffy. Tears glisten on her cheeks, and I steal them away with my thumb.

"I'm sorry," she whispers and leans against my palm.

There are so many things I want to ask and say, but nothing will stop her from feeling responsible for all our issues. She's taking the blame for it as if I haven't made mistakes. As if she's the only one with flaws. Not having the words to articulate what I'm thinking, I say the only thing I can. "I'm sorry, too."

"I want you to know," she begins, taking my hand. "The day we spent together at the winery, the drive up the mountain, and that night, all of it was real." Holding my hand to her chest, she kisses my knuckles. "I'd never felt closer to you."

"Nora…"

"I'm not asking you to forgive me. Although, I hope you can one day. I just want to help you get back on your feet, so when you're healed, you can experience life the way you planned. The way you deserve." She swallows hard and closes her eyes for a few seconds.

"Without you, you mean."

The feel of her skin burns against mine, making me draw my hand away. I don't remember imagining a life without her before yesterday. And even then, it seemed impossible. Maybe I had after her last refusal, but I doubt the picture fully formed. Surely, I assumed we'd find a way back to each other over time. She's been a part of me and my dreams for too long to just erase her completely. Fulfilling the bucket list is as close as I've come to trying to move on when—

I pat my shorts for my wallet, but, of course, it's not there.

"What is it?" she asks, concern leaking into her tone.

"I remember something. Where's my wallet?"

"In the kitchen, I think."

"Can you grab it?"

Her eyes narrow at me before rising and retrieving the wallet. Returning to her seat, she hands it to me and watches me closely. I locate the worn list among the bills and receipts inside and unfold it.

"What do you remember?" she asks, looking over my hand at the list.

"The last one." I stare at the paper, specifically the space where I erased the last entry, not believing I gave up on that dream.

"Great. Why does that seem like a bad thing?"

"It's surprising that I erased it."

"What was it? Maybe we can add it back in and keep working on the list."

My head shakes slowly. "I don't know if it's possible anymore."

She places a hand on my leg, shooting an electric current through my already charged system.

"We'll have to get creative, of course, until you're back to normal, but I'm willing to try if you are," she says, and the implications of her words are not lost on me.

"You don't even know what it is," I say lamely.

"No, but if you're not ready, I'm hoping you'll tell me when we get to it. We can accomplish everything else and leave that one for the grand finale."

She begins laying out plans for us to spend more time together, checking off each activity. I watch her talk through the list and explain her ideas without hearing a word. It's her smile, and the way her eyes, now dry and bright, sparkle with excitement. I hate how that surprises me. Not because I learned just yesterday that we're not actually together. It's because the only time she's ever shown joy or excitement about being with me is when she's dragging me to bed.

After everything I learned and with the remaining pieces of my past still missing, can I handle being around her more, knowing I can never have her forever? She said it herself. She's planning on leaving me for the last time at the end of her obligation. She thinks the future I deserve doesn't include her. That she's not good enough for me after her betrayal, because of the way she's treated me over the years, and because of her inability to have children. Do I believe that, too?

"What do you think?" she asks, bringing my thoughts back to her.

"About what?"

She grins, seemingly undeterred by my distraction. "Can we start over?"

"What?" Shock robs my ability to hold back that gut reaction. "Start over how?"

"Pretend the last five years never happened. It would be nice to start again from the beginning."

"Beginning of what? We jumped straight over the get-to-know-you part of any relationship, friends or otherwise."

Her back straightens at the sharpness in my tone. We had a one-night stand that evolved into many nights scattered across years. Even when we were exclusive, our relationship consisted of very little outside of sex. Thinking more clearly on it, I barely know her.

"That's the problem I'd like to correct."

"Why? Aren't you planning to walk away when your obligation is over?"

"You're not an obligation, Jordan."

"A regret, then? A conquest? A fuck buddy? We sure as hell have never been friends or true partners. Set aside your unfounded belief that you're not good enough for me. What am I to you?"

Her eyes lock on mine in shock, her answer dissolving on her tongue.

"That's what I thought. No wonder I erased the last thing on my stupid list. It's unattainable."

"What is?" she manages, and I glare at her.

"Making you love me."

"Jordan," she says on an exhale as her fingers press to her lips. "I—"

"Don't. Whatever you're about to say, I doubt I'll believe you." I drag my hands down my face, trying to calm the fickle emotions, popping up like summer storms inside me. "But despite that and everything that's happened, I don't want to be angry at you anymore. If starting over will take some of the hurt away, I want to try."

Turning her face to the window, she blinks quickly before closing her eyes. "You're incredible."

A scoff bursts from my chest. I don't feel incredible. I feel like a jackass—a gullible, glutton for punishment jackass who refuses to tell the woman who's broken my heart more times than I remember to leave me alone. A woman who's made a mark so deep on my soul, I may never love another.

Yep, jackass me is still holding onto hope. Still wanting to change her mind. Still fucking in love with her.

Chapter Eighteen

Nora

That afternoon, after much convincing, I got Jordan out of the apartment. We spent most of the day staying out of each other's way, speaking only when required for his care. He's angry with me, and I can't blame him. I'm angry with myself. But I can't sit in this silent box a minute longer. The best way to start over, or at least attempt to get past this animosity, is to have a little fun. And I have the perfect idea.

"Ziplining?" Jordan asks as I pull into a parking spot at Great Escape Adventure Park.

It isn't the best zipline near Richmond, but it's the closest with an accessible line—safe fun for those with limitations. Maybe a little fresh air and adventure will squeeze the sour mood out of us both by day's end.

I cut the engine and turn in my seat to face him. "We're crossing skydiving off the list."

"With ziplining fifty feet off the ground?" he says skeptically.

"This mimicked skydiving better than a hot air balloon ride, which was the other option. It's just a slower, steadier pace while being securely fastened to a harness on a wire. No uncontrollable freefalls, no clouds, or fear of falling to your death. I thought you'd enjoy this more. But if you're scared, I can call the hot air ba—"

"Who said I'm scared?" he quips.

"Your complaints and stalling tactics."

"I'm not stalling. Just gathering information."

"Okay." I wave a hand in his direction. "What other questions do you have?"

"Aren't there rules against riding with casts?"

"Not here. They have a line with a seat, or you can choose the wheelchair accessible contraption, if you prefer that. The accessible line is motorized. Instead of sliding down a wire with gravity, your speed is controlled by a motor or something. I didn't exactly examine the engineering of the system. Just know it's safe for riding with casts or wheelchairs."

He glances out the window. "Ramps instead of stairs?"

"Yep. Are you done?"

"I was done a long time ago," he says without looking my way.

Uninterested in contemplating any hidden meaning behind that loaded comment, I throw open the door and retrieve the wheelchair. Since the area schools haven't let out yet, there are no lines or delays to wade through. After paying, signing our lives away in waiver forms, and sitting through the required safety briefing, we travel a short distance to the first platform. Finally, we're allowed into our harnesses, the last step before the fun begins.

When presented with options, Jordan chooses to forego his wheelchair for a little added adventure.

"I can handle it," he says to the female attendant, who quickly volunteered to help strap him in. "My body feels good today."

To that, she mumbles, "I bet it does," while reaching around his waist to buckle the first strap.

Good lord. Rolling my eyes to the older and far more disinterested male attendant, I watch him get to work on the clasps on my apparatus. He must be more experienced than the girl helping Jordan, since I'm suited up in all of thirty seconds. His assistant, however, can't stop giggling and gawking long enough to do her job. She's nauseatingly adorable—big green eyes, long silky hair the color of whiskey flowing down her back, toned legs, and smooth, unblemished skin—and staring up at Jordan like he makes the moon glow.

None of that bothers me. I get it. He's an attractive man. Stunning if I'm shooting for accuracy. Heads are bound to turn. Women are sure to swoon. I get it. It's the smile she's invoked from him that has my lunch churning in my stomach. I haven't seen his sweet brand of joy for two days and watching him give it so freely to someone else, rattles me more than I care to admit.

"Ready?" I ask to break up the flirting session. Both heads snap to me, all smiles gone.

"You go first," he says, giving his attention to the small hands hovering over his abs. Only a few straps and his cotton shirt are separating her skin from his.

Is this what jealousy feels like? Rage bubbling like a geyser about to erupt at an innocent person, all because they notice something in a matter of seconds that you've disregarded for years? Because they can invoke your favorite smile with minimal effort?

With a huff, I stalk past and jump off the ledge, letting the harness take me away to the next platform. Hopefully, each layover on our way down the wooded hill won't offer the same distraction. This is supposed to be fun for me and Jordan to help repair our relationship. Not fun for Jordan and every random model who works here.

Landing on the platform, I scold myself for acting like a jealous teenager and turn to wait for him to join me. After a few minutes, he appears through the trees in his modified Adventure Seat, the bright white cast on his left leg standing out among the evergreens and matching his toothy smile.

"He seems to be going faster than I did," I say to the young male attendant behind me, sitting on a stool and watching TikTok videos on his phone.

"Mmm hmm," he mumbles.

With a sigh, I train my eyes on Jordan. His pace slows slightly as he approaches the platform, but it doesn't seem to be enough. I brace for impact.

"Nora!" he yells, a touch of concern leaching into his excitement.

"It will stop," the attendant offers without lifting his eyes. He lifts a lazy hand to push a button on the control board I didn't notice until now.

The wheels on Jordan's apparatus screech to a soft halt several feet inside the platform.

"Watch out," the attendant's monotone voice says to me. As I back away, Jordan is transported along the ceiling rails to the exit on the other side.

I join him at the edge, grateful to see him smiling again.

"I can't believe you found this place. It's amazing." He glances up at all the gears and parts, working seamlessly together, and follows the line out into the wooded area beyond. "There should be more adaptive activities like this."

Wonder and serenity take over his face, and I hope the peaceful feeling holds for the rest of our outing. It's quite the view, and I find myself lost in it.

Uncomfortable with the sudden skip in my heart's rhythmic beating, I run both hands through my wind-swept hair.

"Would you like to go first?" I ask gently, and the side of his mouth tips up in a crooked grin.

"I'd love to." His eyes lock on mine, the amusement I enjoyed in them moments ago, fading quickly. "See you on the other side."

He gives the attendant the go-ahead, and as the trees envelop him, it occurs to me how much I want this do-over to work. I'm all in on Jordan Jones, friend or boyfriend. I'll take either at this point to secure his presence in my life. But if he chooses the former, deciding my baggage is too heavy to carry, I'll be the one nursing a broken heart soon.

The next three stops go smoothly. At each break, he smiles more and jokes not only with the park employees, but with me. Seeing him happy and carefree helps me feel the same.

"What's your favorite color?" Jordan asks the attendant on the last jumping off point in our descent.

"Ugh, green."

"Perfect. Why was the color green notoriously single?"

"He likes to tell dad jokes," I explain, but it doesn't make the young guy any more interested.

"Why?" he asks cautiously.

"It was always so jaded."

I' snicker behind my hand as the attendant stares at Jordan like he said something incomprehensible.

"Get it? Jade is a shade of green."

"Kids these days," I joke when he gives up and joins me at the edge of the platform.

"No sense of humor whatsoever."

"None." Looking up at him, his pinky brushes against mine and he doesn't recoil. After our last two conversations, that one tiny development felt as significant as a kiss.

On the final platform, we return our harnesses and purchase hot cocoa on the way to rest our legs by the fire pit behind the lodge. The sun has dipped below the tree line, casting the sky in orange and pink strokes. This section of the park is somewhat deserted with the after-school action taking place in the trees. The privacy by the fire, the swaying trees, and sunset, it's incredibly romantic and a new boldness fuels my next action.

I reach across to place a hand on Jordan's forearm, resting on the chair, and he jolts. He'd closed his eyes to enjoy the quiet peace of our surroundings, and I give him no warning before touching him. "I had fun today."

He studies my face for a bit before responding. "Me, too. It was nice getting out of the apartment. Thank you."

"You're welcome."

Sliding my hand back to my hot mug, I take a sip and fold a leg under me to face him. "Tell me something I don't know about you."

"Seriously?"

"Yes. I know all your sexual desires like the back of my hand, but very little about your other likes and dislikes, your childhood, your dreams."

"Nora, I don't know…" He sets his mug on the browning grass beside the chair.

"Come on. We said we were starting over. Pretend we're just two new friends getting to know each other, or this is a first date."

"Must be a new friendship since I don't remember asking you out."

I look him over, wondering if he's about to stomp on the idea. Although his eyes stay trained on the fire, his lips tip up into a smirk.

"I believe today was my suggestion, and I drove and paid. Sounds like I subtly asked you out."

"Fine," he says, turning those gorgeous eyes on me. "But an end of date kiss isn't allowed. We barely know each other, and I deserve to be wooed first."

"Wooed?" I ask, laughing.

"Courted. Pursued. Wooed."

"Whatever. I can woo with the best of them."

His smile drops into a pensive frown like he wants to say something but opts not to ruin the mood. He's taking me in, surely wondering if I mean it. Time to set the record straight.

"Jordan—"

His gaze turns to the fire. "I hate sushi."

"What?" My spine straightens in disbelief. "We ate sushi like every other time we were together."

"I know. It's your favorite." He cuts his eyes to me, grins, then goes back to watching the fire. The flames light his face and the lack of anger in his features. He's not upset, but I feel all the guilt, anyway. It's just another example of him compromising for my happiness.

"I had no idea."

"How can you like raw fish so much? It's disgusting."

A chuckle burst out of me, shaking my body. I hold my mug over the grass when the hot liquid threatens to splash on my clothes.

"I don't know. It tastes good to me. What's your favorite food?"

"Hamburgers."

"Typical."

"Shut up," he teases. "Your turn."

"All right. My favorite color is purple."

His eyes take a slow, exaggerated tumble. "I thought we were saying things no one knew."

"I don't know your favorite color." More guilt rushes over me like a cold shower.

"Red."

"Oh. Well, it *is* your color."

"My color?" he asks, his brow rising.

Lifting the mug to my lips, I say, "You look hot in red," before sipping.

"Hmm." He smiles, satisfied with the compliment. And it's all I need for the rest of the evening.

"Do you not have a joke for my color?"

"I have a joke for just about anything."

"Well, let's hear it." I prop an elbow on the chair's arm, resting my chin on a fist.

"I'd love to, but it's your turn again." He gives me a sorry-not-sorry shrug. "And I want something a little harder to know this time. Your favorite color was a copout."

"All right. Geez." I giggle, but the euphoria doesn't last. He wants something deeper. Something he hadn't already figured out on his own. There's only one direction to go to satisfy that request and it's back in time. Nothing is as deep and depressing as my childhood. "Did you know I also spent time in foster care?"

"No. When?"

"Early high school After the asshole—"

"Got it. No need to rehash that."

"Thank you. My mother went to rehab for a bit, and I stayed with a couple on a farm. They were the quintessential wholesome duo. The wife cooked three meals from scratch each day—none of that box shit I was used to—and loved to bake. I think I gained ten pounds while I was there. The husband, along with a few part-time farmhands, took care of all the chores and the business side of things. They had cows, horses, chickens, goats, fields of various vegetables, the whole Old McDonald set up."

He leans closer, giving me his full attention, and my swoon mimics the bubbly girl from earlier. Recovering, I get to the point. "Anyway, they always had music playing while she cooked or he worked. I could never escape it, and turns out, I like country music. Now, when I hear it, I think of the only people in my childhood who never hurt me."

"I've never heard you play country music before," he says softly, touched by the story.

"I don't. Sometimes it's unavoidable, but the nuances, the lyrics, and the memories are so…"

"Bittersweet?"

"Exactly. Even though I felt safe and cared for there, I knew it was only a matter of time before they tossed me back to the wolves. And I wasn't very kind to them. I thought it was in my best interest not to get attached. After all, I was going to lose them, too."

"Too? Who else did you lose?"

I stare at him, wondering if I should continue. This part of me has been locked away my entire adult life. But looking into Jordan's thoughtful, sympathetic eyes, it's easy to see that strategy was wrong on so many levels. The past has driven every aspect of my life despite my efforts to control it, hide it, ignore it. And it's time to let it go.

"My father left when I was six, and I haven't heard from him since. My first stepfather, Tom, left when I was nine. He treated me like his daughter, and I trusted him. Loved him. One day, he'd had enough of dealing with my mother's shit and just left…like I meant nothing to him. The house had a revolving door of stepfathers after that, the next one more horrific than the last."

Needing something to coat my dry throat, I take a few gulps of cocoa. It had cooled to the temperature of warm chocolate milk thanks to the chilly evening. "My boyfriend broke up with me after high school graduation. His family convinced him I would weigh him down, preventing his life goals from becoming reality."

"That's ridiculous," Jordan says sharply, and I appreciate the conviction.

"Thank you, but looking back, they were right. He was there for me through it all, but as a steadfast family man, he needed someone who fit in with the rest of them. Give him the large family he eventually wanted. He's best friends with his five siblings, and they're all raising their children together."

"Nora."

"It's fine." I wave off his concern and get lost in the intoxicating waves of red and orange rising from the stone pit. I wish for it to soothe me. To change how I feel about the past—about myself. But I learned at an early age that wishes never come true. If you want something to happen, you *make* it happen. No invisible being or magical universe is going to give you anything.

The fire cracks, sending sparks into the air and awakening me from my thoughts. Closing my eyes, I take a deep breath. "So sorry for that mood dampener. Today was about having fun."

"I had fun," he says sweetly, holding my gaze. The flames light only part of his face, just enough to see the tender way he's taking me in. Oh, how I've missed that look. "Did you?"

"Of course. So much that I don't want it to end."

He smiles, and my body temperature kicks up a few notches. "I have an idea."

"What is it?"

He points to something behind me, and I twist to see it. A sign directing patrons to…I squint to read it through the haze of dusk.

"Ax throwing?" Turning back to him, his kind smile has evolved into smug assurance.

"Yep. We're going to imagine the target is anyone who has ever hurt you. You'll name each one and say goodbye, never again, or fuck you. Whatever makes you feel better."

Not meaning to, my shoulders slump in a physical display of my first thought: It's never that easy. But I straighten and intentionally adopt Jordan's positive thinking. Besides, with him by my side, anything is possible.

In case the stars are aligning above us and something magical is happening in this moment, I toss up a wish. A simple one for sweet, tender-hearted Jordan Jones to forgive me.

Chapter Nineteen

Jordan

"You're doing great," I encourage Nora from my stool at the corner table. She's on a roll, landing the sharp edge of the hatchet on the target three times in a row, after the first six smacked against the wall with a resounding thud. "Who are we saying F U to next?"

Her eyes brighten as she plucks a name from her mental list of wrongdoers—the sources of her pain and reasons for her always settling for less than she deserves. "Tristan."

"Okay. Who's that?"

After crossing the booth to collect the last two hatchets she threw, she strolls back to the starting position beside me. "High school boyfriend."

She sets one hatchet on the wall hook and raises the handle of another, adjusting her grip. "Whoa. Wait a second."

"What?" The hatchet falls to her side as her arm and shoulder relax.

"Does that mean you dated only one guy in high school?"

"I thought we discussed this," she says, not grasping my confusion.

"One guy."

She studies me as she puts the pieces of my questions together. "Yes," she says with conviction and a touch of exasperation. "I was committed to one guy for three years. He was the only one to stand up for me until he didn't. He broke my heart…hence the start of my disdain for relationships."

She raises her arm and flings the hatchet toward the target. Bullseye.

"Yikes. Guess you meant that one."

"He was the total package and concluded someone with a few dents and scratches wasn't good enough for him." She shrugs and removes a bottle of water from the small bucket on the tall bar table, holding me up. "I've accepted it, but he confirms the theory."

"For the record," I begin and wait for her big brown eyes to give me their full attention. "Not all boyfriends leave."

She hands me a bottle. "No, but some leave even when they don't want to, and that's worse."

"Nora." I remove her hand from around the water bottle and warm it in mine. Our eyes meet. "You can't let the tragedies of others control your life. What happened to Sydney and countless others who lost someone they love won't happen to you."

"You don't know that. It could have happened every time you deployed."

Tiny hairs on the back of my neck rise in response. "You worried about that?"

Her gaze drops to our hands before she nods.

"I thought..."

"That I didn't care? That if you died, I'd go about my life like we never met?"

I swallow hard. "Yeah. I had no reason to believe otherwise."

A sudden tear pooling on her thick lashes surprises me, but I can do nothing but watch it glisten in the light as it leaves a trail down her cheek.

"Although I didn't like to admit it then, you were important to me. I cared about you."

"And now?" I ask, not giving two shits if it's too soon or too bold. I need to know.

Her face is unreadable when her gaze rises to mine. I wonder what she's thinking, what she'll say, or if she'll do what she always does and evade the question. I don't notice her inching closer until she's standing between my legs and placing my hand on her waist. My heart takes off as she frames my face and lowers her head. Her breath is hot on my lips, and I want nothing more than to taste her again. Feel her pressed against me in sweet surrender. I want her.

"Does this answer your question?" she purrs into my ear, her fingers combing through my hair and down to cup the back of my neck. My hand tightens around her thin waist.

"I think I need more information."

A soft moan flutters in her throat, pushing me over the edge.

"God, I—"

With a peck to my forehead, she steps back and collects the remaining ax from the floor. "Sorry." Her shoulders pop up in fake sympathy. "You said no to first date kisses, and friends don't do that."

I watch her, my mouth gaping open, as she aims the ax at the target and sends it flying. It lands just to the right of the red center mark.

"That was for me."

The comment snaps me out of my trance. "You?"

"For all the times I stood in my own way."

"You are good at that," I tease, missing her warmth against me. "You hit the target. Does that mean you're going to stop? Getting in your own way, I mean."

"I want to."

"And I want to help."

Her eyes shimmer with wetness again, and I'm mesmerized by this new vulnerable side. "Are you sure? Even after—"

"Even then. That's what friends are for, right?"

Her lips pucker slightly as she considers the question, and it takes no time at all for me to decide that I fuckin' hate the friend zone.

―――

Later that night, we go our separate ways. Nora to the couch and me to the bedroom. But ever since the living room lamp switched off hours ago, I haven't been able to get what happened between us out of my mind. The feel of her body close to mine. Her warm breath on my skin. The unexpected tears and confessions. Her request to start anew.

There's no doubt I want that more than anything. I don't care that she can't have my children. I don't care about her lies or past. She's mine. Always will be. But she'll need to this conclusion on her own.

The more I press, the more bricks she'll install around that stubborn heart of hers. And that's okay. She can construct all the fortresses she thinks she needs to protect herself. I know her tactics and weaknesses better than she does, and I'm not afraid to fight for what I want. With unlimited artillery and close proximity on my side, I'll be sitting in the shadows, waiting for the right opportunity to destroy her walls once and for all.

———

"What are you doing?" Nora asks, sitting up, still half asleep, with pillow creases bright red on her face.

"Making breakfast. What's it look like I'm doing?"

"Moving around on your own, and potentially hurting yourself again." She rises to stretch and the long sleeve pajama top rises above her navel, exposing more skin than I can handle.

All night I tried to get that flat stomach out of my thoughts to no avail. And now, she's taunting me with it. The spatula tumbles out of my hand and rattles against the skillet.

"Case in point," she mumbles, snatching the plastic kitchen utensil from the appliance. "You're going to burn your one good arm."

"I can disassemble, reassemble, and accurately shoot a rifle," I protest. "I believe I can handle a simple skillet."

"Not today, apparently."

"That's because you—"

She pivots to face me, and I realize I'm within touching range. If I engage a few muscles, her body could be on mine at last—my lips pressed against her neck.

I hobble to the other side of the counter since my body can't be trusted.

"Because I what?" she asks, raking her sexy lazy eyes over me.

"You had to wear that." My finger waves over her body, gaze following, and she looks down.

"You like old and…"

Thin and hugging every delicious curve. Her bare nipples are poking through the soft white fabric with pink and purple polka dots. If I'm not mistaken, she's not wearing any underwear, either. Sweet mother of Jesus.

"Stop with the distractions. The pancakes need flipping," I demand before my lower half explodes.

"Alright." Her lips pinch to hide her amusement, but I don't miss the subtle way she arches her back and rolls her head while she turns over each pancake tantalizingly slow. A stretch she could blame on morning stiffness, but I know what she's doing. She's flaunting her curves to draw my attention. Exposing her kissable neckline to make my mouth water. Oh, it's a river in there, but she'll never know. This is her go-to war strategy, and I'm already two steps ahead.

"Let me know when they're ready. I'm going to wash off." A long, cold, burn-off-the-sting-of-unfulfilled-desire kind of sponge bath.

"Okay," she says, drawing out each letter almost as a question.

It took everything I had to keep my hands and lips to myself. But I'm focused on the primary mission. Something bigger than what I may want and need in this one small moment. Resisting the urge to give in too soon will not only make accomplishing the mission easier but also incredibly more satisfying.

―――

"So, what are we calling yesterday?" she asks before taking a bite of pancake dripping with syrup. She's sitting on the floor opposite me on the couch, our plates touching on the small coffee table.

"Can you even taste that pancake?"

"What do you mean?"

"There's so much syrup it's no longer a pancake." My upper lip creases like I taste something sour. "It's soggy mush."

"What's the problem? I like it wet," she says with a mischievous grin, making my bite clog in my throat. "Don't you?"

Damn. So much for having the leg up. I'd like to yank *her* leg—

"Anyway, I asked you a question before you ignored me and criticized my breakfast."

"You did?" I wash down the dry mound of pancake with orange juice, wishing it had come with more gooey syrup. But I can never admit that and add another leg to her advantage. She's knocked me down with her sexy strategy enough this morning.

She lets out a long exhale. "I asked what you wanted to label yesterday. First date or friend outing?"

"Oh. Since when do you into label anything between us?"

Her eyes narrow playfully. "Since yesterday, obviously."

I consider the best answer for the mission and settle on, "Friends." But add, "For now."

That seems to satisfy her curiosity.

"After your PT and therapy appointments today, I thought we could go on another adventure. Up for a long drive?"

"Depends." I take a bite and stare into her beautiful, dark chocolate eyes.

"On?"

"What we're crossing off the list."

"I thought we could cross off Las Vegas."

My fork drops, and I sit back in shock. "You want to drive to Las Vegas?"

"What? Of course, not. We don't have that kind of time, and you have appointments scheduled."

"I would have gone," I mutter, returning to breakfast.

"Me, too."

Smiling, I'm intrigued about where she wants to escape today. "Where do you want to go?"

"Ever been to the horse track and casino in Charlestown?"

"No. Let's do it."

"That was easy."

"I already told you. I'll go anywhere, do anything with you."

Based on her lack of come back, I'd say the advantage has tilted back to my side.

"It's a few hours from here," she continues, recovering faster than I like. "But since your appointment is early today, we can make it before the races start."

Eyeing her, I sip on my juice. "Want to make a wager before we go?"

"You know it. What are we betting and what are the stakes?"

"I bet you dinner I win more times than you—horses, casino, slots, whatever."

"You're on." She takes the last bite of pancake left on her plate, her eyes never leaving my face. "And when I win, I want a dinner on the river."

My jaw goes slack. Restaurants on the river are swanky, expensive, and you go there to be seen. Or, you have money to burn like there's an endless flow into your bank account. "Okay. Will you be wearing that dress I love so much?"

"The one you always talk about peeling off me?"

"That's the one."

"Maybe." She smiles into her glass before taking a long, teasing sip. "Maybe I'll buy something new with all my winnings."

"Mmm. I have half a mind to let you win, but there's the whole male pride thing."

"That's fine." She waves a hand and gathers my empty plate. "When I win, I want it to be because I beat your ass. Not because you let me."

"I can't wait. When's my appointment?"

She checks the clock. "In about an hour. That gives me enough time to get ready…" She stops when something on the counter catches her attention. "And you enough time to talk to your sister."

"What?"

She holds up the phone, lit with Josie's photo, highlighting an incoming call from her.

"I guess it's time," I concede and take the phone when she passes it to me on her way to the bathroom.

"You've got this." She kisses my hair, and I tuck the significance of the subtle gesture of affection away to dwell on later.

I wait until she closes the door and turns on the shower before hitting the *Call Back* button.

"Hi, little brother," Josie says after the first ring, her voice timid and uncertain.

"Hi, Jo Jo." I use her nickname to settle her nerves.

"How are you?"

"Better."

"That's good. I'm sure you got my texts, but I wanted to call and apologize again. Please know that I never—"

"I know. You were just looking out for me like you always do."

She lets out an audible exhale. "You're not mad?"

"Not anymore. I've had time to think about it, and with the way things are working out, I'm grateful you made that decision."

"You are? What's worked out, exactly?" The caution in her tone makes me smile. She's never been a fan of Nora's, but after the sacrifices Nora's made recently, I expect that's changing.

I glance toward the closed bathroom door and lower my voice. "I think Nora and I have turned a page. She seems to finally be coming to terms with her feelings for me."

"Oh, Jordan. How many times are you going to let her hurt you?"

"As many times as it takes."

"Don't say that." The words come out on an exasperated exhale.

"I know you don't want to see me crushed again, but I don't think that will happen."

"Jordan, you never think that. That's the problem. You never see it coming."

"Even now you believe she'd turn her back on me?" Josie hasn't experienced Nora's transformation over the last two days, yet her opinion matters to me.

"What makes you think this time will have a different ending?"

"For starters, she stopped lying. She looks at me differently. We're going out in public together. We're no longer sleeping together, which—"

"No longer? Did you sleep with her before you remembered?" Her raised voice shrills through the tiny speaker. I recoil at the assault on my ear, holding it away from my face until she's finished.

"Josie, calm down. Isn't that what couples do? I thought we were together."

"But she knew. The little floozie."

"I'm not mad it happened. Why are you?" The question only fuels her fury, but it was too tempting to resist.

"Of course, you aren't, and you know why."

"Well, we were two consenting adults, and I'm not a child, so…"

"Yeah, yeah. I'll shut up now."

"Thank you."

She sighs into the phone again. "I'm happy to hear you're happy and not angry with me."

"Oh, I was furious."

"And I'm happy I missed that, too."

"When are you coming home?"

"Well, that's another reason I'm calling. It might be a few more days than expected. Grant is working on getting media interviews after the show, and if all goes well, I might even be on *The Today Show*." Her voice squeaks with excitement.

"Josie, that's amazing."

"It's not guaranteed, of course, but if my art catches the attention of a few collectors, there's a chance this could be the start of something."

"In that case, I hope I don't see you for another week."

"Aww. Thank you. But it's just not the same without you."

Wanderlust fills me, and I open my mouth before considering the consequences. "Maybe I can make it after all. I haven't had any seizures since…you know…and Nora and I are taking a trip to—"

"Where are you going?"

"I was about to tell you before you interrupted."

"Right. Sorry. I'm a little scatter brained today."

"It's not just today, Josie." I laugh, but the other side of the phone is silent. "Anyway, as I was saying, we're going to Charlestown."

"Where's that?"

"West Virginia. If I handle that well, a trip to New York shouldn't be too much."

"Oh, I'd love that so much. But talk to your doctors first. I miss you so much."

"Miss you, too."

A sniffle comes through and another. Damn it. I've made her cry.

"Josie. Don't do that."

"I'm sorry," she says on a loud, snot-filled inhale. "I'm just so relieved. It's been hard not talking to you, wondering if you're okay and if you'll forgive me. There's too much to do here and not enough time. They wanted three new pieces to match the theme, and I've hardly had a moment to think. I had to pretend to go to the restroom at the restaurant we're at to get away from Grant long enough to call you. And you know how much I hate public restrooms. Every time the door opens, I expect it to be him coming in to scold me."

"He *is* overbearing."

"Ugh. He's stressed, too, and making mine worse. But he wants this as badly as I do."

"It will all be worth it in the end."

I look over as Nora exits the bathroom—hair wet, cheeks flushed, skin moist, and wearing nothing but a towel. She grins over her shoulder as she bends to sort through her suitcase, exposing more of her long legs. Josie's voice continues to carry through the phone, but I comprehend none of it as Nora straightens to hold a shirt out in front of her. Without her arms holding the towel in place, it slides down her breasts to the tops of her nipples. A touch of those alluring dark circles peek out above the blue towel, and I—

"Jordan, can you hear me?" Josie asks. I hear her but can form zero words in response when Nora bends over again.

Cleavage and more cleavage glistens in the sunlight as if she rubbed glitter lotion all over her body. Maybe she had, or maybe her skin is just that perfect. Either way, this sexy little display of hers has torched my war strategy as if it never existed. It's a new game now. If this is how she's going to play it, all chances of a friendly game is also going up in smoke.

All's fair in love and war, baby, and it will be fun to remind Nora of my competitive side. I'm not afraid to play dirty and—

"Jordan!"

"What? I'm here. Jeez, sis."

Nora looks over and bites back a smile as I run my jittery fingers over my hair. She tosses some garments she chose from the suitcase over her shoulder and struts back to the bathroom. Disappointed the show is over, but glad to have a moment to get blood circulating through the brain inside my skull again, I give my full attention to my sister.

"Sorry, something was distracting me."

"Nora walking around naked or something?"

Caught, I shake my head at how predictable and simple-minded the women in my life must think I am. "Not exactly."

"Close enough, I bet. I'll let you go deal with that. Grant will send out the calvary for me if I'm not back soon."

"Okay. Knock 'em dead, Jo Jo, and remember to enjoy it."

"I will. Hope to see you soon. I love you."

"Love you, too."

Tossing the phone onto the cushion, I let my head drop back while thoughts of Nora and our recent conversations spin out of control. Why did I ever say Nora and I should work on being friends first? It's clear she desires more than just friendship. Right? Isn't that why she's teasing me with the towel bit and smiling when I react the way she knew I would? Or am I manifesting again?

Reading her is near impossible these days. She's different than I remember, and I've learned things about her that amaze me. It's bringing us closer, yet it feels like there's more she's not telling me.

No. I made the right choice. We need to get to know each other without sex complicating our do-over. If I'm going to make Nora mine forever, we must build a stronger foundation. One built on trust, friendship, and admiration. Sex can come after that. The icing on the cake. A finale worth waiting for. Making love instead of reacting on our lust.

That's what I want.

End of story.

Now, can someone please tell that to my dick?

Chapter Twenty

Nora

"Hi, Nora," Sydney greets when I step into her office unannounced. "I've been thinking about you." She rises from her seat to wrap me in a hug.

"Thank you for your texts the other day. They helped me get through."

"That bad?" she asks.

"At first."

Sydney leads me to the window seat, and we sit with our legs crossed, facing each other.

"I have to say, I didn't expect to see you looking so…chipper."

"Thanks?" I say with a laugh. "But I agree. I never thought he'd let me back in this quickly, if ever."

"That's great. Says a lot about his heart."

"And another example of why he's much too good for me." A car leaving the parking lot in the distance catches my attention. I watch it for a moment, ignoring the argument Sydney's making on my behalf. I love her for it, but I'm still reeling from the rollercoaster of the past forty-eight hours and don't have the energy to think about myself.

"So," she says, shaking my arm. "What happened?"

I chuckle. "You won't believe me."

"Oh. That sounds juicy." Her hands slap together, fingers wiggling with excitement under her chin.

My thoughts jump to our intimate night together without good reason, and I shake it away. It's the last place my brain should be going. "I asked if we could start over. Forget the last five years ever happened."

"Perfect idea. I take it he agreed."

"Without hesitation."

"Because he still loves you?" Hope brightens her eyes. She really needs to stop reading so many romance novels. It causes unruly and unattainable expectations.

"I can't speak to his feelings. We've been all over the place since he remembered. Whenever we make some headway, we circle back to another pain point. It's excruciating."

Sydney takes my hand. "What changed?"

"We got out of the house and had some fun. Ziplining," I add. "Then, we just talked. I opened up about my past and told him as much as I could."

"How did he react?"

"The way he does with everything. He was supportive and empathetic. Sweet and understanding. What?" I ask when I notice Sydney's playful smile.

"I love seeing you in love."

"Yeah, well, I don't know what I'm supposed to do with it. There's still so much to figure out." I toss up my hands in annoyance and let them fall into my lap.

"You're not still preparing to let him go, are you?"

"I have to." With a huff, I pace to the other side of the room.

"I'm so confused."

"I told him we'd never have a traditional family. He hasn't told me yet if he can live with that. Right now, it's not a big deal because there's no commitment, and children are nowhere near the conversation. But what about a few years from now when he's ready to settle down?"

"What about a surrogate?"

My arms cross defensively. This conversation took a hard left turn, and I'm struggling to keep up. "I don't know. I've never considered having kids, so there was no point in looking into the whole egg thing."

"And now?"

I shrug. "I wonder about it…occasionally…for tiny little seconds here or there when I allow myself to look deep into his eyes."

With a few heavy steps, I drop onto the window seat and fall into Sydney's embrace.

"What am I going to do?"

"Exactly what you're doing. Take care of him, show him how you feel, and see what happens."

"Sounds simple enough. But it is anything but simple."

"Rarely is following your heart easy or a black and white endeavor."

"You would know." Sitting up, I collect the hands that have caught more tears than I'll ever shed. Sydney's heart has been through a meat grinder, yet her belief in the power of love holds true. If she believes my hollow heart can be warmed by and filled with love, then maybe I should believe it, too.

"And you know what?" she asks with an unsteady smile and a wink. "It's always worth it."

A knock sounds on the door before it opens.

"I thought I'd find you in here," Lori, one of VETS' front desk receptionists, says to me.

I shoot to my feet. "Is Jordan okay?"

"Jordan Jones? Oh, yeah. He just started his therapy appointment."

"Good." My hand, which had found my neck when my heart leapt into my throat, slid to my side in relief. "What's up?"

"The temporary yoga instructor didn't show."

"Again? That'll be the third class we've had to cancel. The temps are so unreliable," Sydney complains.

I check the time on my phone. The next class starts in three minutes. "I'll look into another company when I get back, but I can fill in today. Please tell the class I'm on my way."

Lori nods, and I turn to Sydney, eyeing her ponytail. "Got an extra hair tie I can borrow?"

"Nope. But you can have this one." She pulls the scrunchie from her hair, her long red waves falling over her shoulders.

"You really are the bestest friend ever."

"I know."

I give her a quick hug. "If you see Jordan before I'm finished—"

"I'll let him know you're busy melting hearts."

"What are you talking about?" I ask with a little too much virtue to be believable. "It's not hot yoga."

"Ha. Maybe not, but I've seen the guys in your class. In a matter of minutes, they melt into puddles at your feet."

"What can I say?" I shrug. "I'm good at my job. Glad I wore my good yoga pants today." I wink as we walk out together, Sydney's arm linking with mine.

"Ha. In that outfit, I worry about our sensitive grumps."

I look down at the window of the baby blue V-neck specifically chosen to stir something inside Jordan. "It's impossible not to show cleavage in V-necks, and if I'm going to do something, I'm going to give it one hundred percent effort."

"Well, you, at full effort, is everyone else's two hundred. So, go easy on them."

"Never," I declare, and duck into the classroom to greet my unsuspecting students.

Jordan

"Stop. Please," I ask of the therapy assistant, pushing my chair toward the lobby. We pause at the door of a small classroom beside the main fitness room.

I see Nora in the mirror talking with a man and laughing. He slides on a long, white coat before settling his hand on the small of her back as they make their way toward us. What is she doing in there with him?

"Hi," she says, stopping just outside the door frame when she sees me. "I was about to come find you. Thanks, Liv," she says to dismiss my guide.

"Saved you the trip." My eyes dart to the Clark Kent double standing protectively tall beside her. Glasses, dark hair styled perfectly into place, sizable pecs protruding inside his T-shirt—royal blue, of course.

"Jordan," I greet, reaching out my right hand.

"Henry," he says casually in a subtle British accent as he shakes my hand. I smile at the irony, and he returns it, mistaking my amusement for friendliness. Nora, who knows me well enough to know the difference, is shooting laser eyes at me—the same kind Superman would use to slice cars in half. I flash her the same grin with a touch of *I caught you*, singeing the edges.

"See you next class," Henry says, touching her elbow before strutting away.

Nora waits until he disappears into the doctor's offices before whipping around to me. "What was that?"

"I was about to ask you the same thing." I smirk, and her eyes narrow as she surveys me. "He thinks you're hot."

"And I think he's a co-worker."

"A hot co-worker. Does he always dress like that?"

"Like what?" she says with a sigh, taking hold of the chair handles.

"Like Clark Kent."

"Who's—" She pauses to let the pieces fall into place. "I can't believe I didn't see it. And his name is Henry." A guilty giggle bubbles out, and it's the cutest sound. I'd like to record it to replay on cloudy days.

"I can't either. Bet he has an entire wardrobe of blue shirts to bring attention to it."

She pushes me out the door, stops on the sidewalk, and leans down to whisper in my ear, "Are you jealous of the Henry Cavill stunt double masquerading as a doctor so he can *woo* me into being his Lois Lane?"

"Great use of my word," I say before getting back to the issue. "You noticed him flirting?"

"Hard not to." She pushes the chair into motion. "He's never subtle about it."

"Never? This happens a lot?"

"Nearly every time I see him."

"And he hasn't asked you out?" Her silence provides all the answers I need. "Did you go?"

"No."

"Why not?"

"Jordan, why are we talking about this?"

"Because friends talk about these things." And I want to know if I have competition. Fitness model-like competition with several college degrees, investments, and a full wallet and passport. "Did you talk to Sydney about it when he asked you out?"

She let out a long breath. "Yes. But I don't want to talk about it with you."

"Why not?"

"Don't ask stupid questions. Are you excited about tonight?" she asks to change the subject, and now that I know this Superman isn't her kryptonite, I'm happy to let her.

"Yes. It sounds fun. Is this a place I need to dress appropriately for or is it casual?"

"According to pictures on social media, it looks casual."

"Good. A leg cast and shorts isn't very uptown."

After changing and grabbing a bite to eat, we hit the road. An hour into the trip when the comedy channel starts repeating skits, I switch it off and remove the sling from my left arm, tossing it into the back seat.

"What are you doing?" she asks, cutting her eyes at me for a moment.

"My therapist said I can remove it some each day to work the muscles more. And I plan to work it good tonight." I pump my fist like Tiger Woods after sinking a long curvy putt.

A grin alters her lips slightly, just enough for me to know my charm is wiggling its way under her skin.

"Is that your touchdown dance?" She laughs, sending tingles down my body and straight to my midsection.

"No, I'm Tiger—doesn't matter. The point is, I plan to be doing a lot of celebrating tonight."

"The only point I see is you think you'll need two hands to beat me at the tables tonight?" She graces me with another superior grin, and I'm glad her spunk is back. It's my second favorite side of hers.

"Not even close, but it will be easier to collect all my chips."

"Whatever."

"It won't be the same as our private card games, though."

"I hope not."

"We should play sometime," I suggest, curious to see what she'll say.

"Which game?"

"Any of them."

"Not going to happen."

"Why not?" I turn in my seat to see her better. Her brows are pointed inward, and she's frowning.

"They all involve getting naked or touching each other. Sorry, *buddy*, but I don't touch my friends in a sexual way."

She glances my way with a you-asked-for-this pout, and I want to kiss it right off her face.

"Good point," I say instead to throw her off. "We're starting over. New friends who know nothing about each other's body parts and urges. Getting naked at this point in our budding friendship would make things weird."

"Glad we cleared that up."

"Me, too." Giving my attention to the passing scenery outside my window, I shift to adjust the tightness in my shorts.

Damn mention of naked poker. What was I thinking? Now, I can't stop thinking about her sitting cross-legged and bare and looking at me with her sexy eyes over a hand of cards. Memories of our games flash in front of me like I'm on a sadistic merry-go-round. If I don't get off soon (pun intended), some parts of me might explode from the pent-up tension.

She turns off the highway, and I see a billboard for our destination, advertising it's only twenty miles away.

Hallelujah.

"We have a long list of bucket items to check off. What are your ideas again?" I ask for something less dangerous to think about.

Her eyes brighten again as she recalls the list. "Caverns for cave diving. For the crazy steam engine one, I found a scenic train ride nearby which would be beautiful this time of year. Snow tubing for skiing in Vale. Any water sports will have to wait. I'm not getting in freezing water, and neither should you."

"We'll see."

Her eyes circle to the ceiling and back. "We can go camping, maybe near a place with a waterfall for Niagara Falls."

"I actually had an idea for that."

"Yeah?"

Feeling brave, I take her hand and her gaze snaps to mine, holding there until the wheels drift over the road's rumble strips. She yanks the car back into the center of the lane and keeps her gaze forward.

"How do you feel about going to the actual falls?"

"In New York?" she asks, surprised and skeptical.

"I may have told Josie that I would try to make it to her show this weekend. I was hoping you'd be up for it. Then, we can head up north afterwards to take in the real thing."

"Shit, Jordan." Her hand slips from mine to play with her bottom lip while she mulls it over, making my pulse dance.

"Think about it," I say, letting her off the hook for now. "Use tonight as a trial run."

"Okay."

Chapter Twenty-One

Nora

"How much are you up?" Jordan asks, concern creeping in. There are two more horse races left, and his strategic way of selecting winners by reviewing stats and odds isn't working.

"I'm up 5-3. Maybe you should try my method." I bite my bottom lip to hold back a grin. His incredulous glare is so stinking adorable.

"I refuse to pick based on the horse's name."

"Suit yourself."

"Which one are you going with this time?" he asks, studying the information brochure for tonight's races.

The waiter drops off two more beers. "Thank you," I say before answering. "I like Harry Trotter."

"Seriously? His odds are twelve and one."

"I like an underdog." I snatch the pamphlet from his grasp and check the next race. "Let me guess. You're taking Gallant Fox, three and one odds."

Ignoring me, he scribbles our choices onto a napkin and holds it out for me. Since the betting booth is on the other side of the buffet, I'm tasked with submitting our bets on each race while he gets to relax and sip his beer.

"I think I can remember your boring horse's name. Five or ten dollars?"

"Five."

"Ah. Not so confident this time. Don't worry. Your plan is to strip me bare at the tables, remember?" I slink away, leaving him with that image to keep his blood and regret simmering.

By the time I return, his bottle is empty, and he's claimed mine. I motion to the one in his hand.

"What's this?" My other hand finds my hip in disapproval.

"Here you go, miss," the waiter says, handing me a beer.

"I know how much you loathe warm beer, so I asked the waiter to bring you another one when you returned."

"How kind of you. Was that before or after you stole my first one?"

"It was more of a simultaneous thing."

"Right."

The horses take off out of the gate, and he turns to watch through the wall of windows overlooking the track. The two candles in the center of the table light his handsome profile, and I can't look away. He's watching the track, eyes alive with excitement, and I'm taking in every detail of the stubble on his chin, the slight dimple in his cheek, and the long eyelashes framing his navy irises.

The horses cross the finish line, Gallant Fox three lengths before Harry Trotter, sealing his chance for a tie this round. He spins in his seat, a victory celebration poised on his tongue until his gaze lands on me. Elation melts into desire as our eyes linger. Without speaking a word, we both say the same thing. Both craving to touch, taste, and explore. Both deciding to ignore it.

"One more," he whispers, his voice strained. Breaking the hold he has over me.

"I need a restroom. Be right back." Weaving through the thinning crowd, I find the restroom at the entrance beyond the hostess stand.

Perched at the sink, I flip on the cold water and pat some on my neck and chest.

"Something got you all hot and bothered, dearie?" A woman—maybe in her eighties—says as she leans her cane on the counter to wash her hands.

I chuckle. "You could say that."

"He must be handsome. Or is it she? I'm not judging the ways of the youngins these days."

"You were right the first time."

She nods, turning off the water and shaking her hands. Since I'm standing between her and the paper towels, I snatch a couple and hand one over.

"Thank you." While she dries her hands, she analyzes me. "What has you in here pantin' instead of out there enjoying him?"

"You're a curious lady, you know that?"

"Heard that once or a hundred times in my life. When you get to be my age, there's not a lot to do. I like people. They're my entertainment. So, entertain me."

With a laugh, I regale her with my predicament, leaving no detail hidden. She listens to every word, soaking it in like a soap opera marathon, until I end the tale with tonight's outing.

"That's it?" she says finally, reaching for her cane.

"What do you mean?"

"You have a gorgeous man begging to love you, one you've admitted to loving in return, and you two are playing games? Pish Posh," she scoffs. "True love isn't a game, dearie. It's sacred. Every moment you get with the one you love should be savored."

"I know, but—"

"No buts. I want you to march out there right now, look him in the eye, and plant a hot one on his lips. Sounds like you both need the wake-up call."

Plant a kiss on Jordan after all the friends talk? I can't. It's too soon, and things are going so well. What if he pushes me away? What if a kiss makes things awkward for the rest of the night? "We're having fun, and I don't want to ruin it."

With a tsk, she shuffles past me and holds open the door. "Now," she demands, ignoring my hesitation. "Stop wasting time."

"Alright. I'm going. Thank you," I say with more force than necessary, but the old woman has me on edge. She's like a wise grandmother—warm and loving, tough and unwavering. One you don't dare defy. She could make the most stubborn of souls crumble with a finger wave or stern glare. I would have loved to have a grandmother like her. Maybe I did. I just never had an opportunity to find out.

"Show him your heart," she calls as I head back toward the restaurant. "And good luck."

I watch her rock back and forth between her good leg and the one requiring a cane and wish I'd gotten her name.

"You missed the last race," Jordan says as I approach the table. "And your beer's warm again."

"Don't care." Bending down, I take his face in my hands and plant a kiss on his lips before I could talk myself out of it. He surprises me by welcoming it instantly, parting our lips for more and squeezing the back of my thigh with a firm grip. I sigh into his mouth at his surrender before stepping back to lean against the adjacent rail. My legs are too weak to stand without support.

"What was that for?" he says breathlessly as he looks me over with wide, clouded eyes. God, I love it when he soaks me in like I'm the only woman in the world.

"I was following orders."

"I like this person. Who is it?"

Ignoring the question I can't answer and sound sane, I change the subject. "Did you win?"

He shakes his head, attempting to follow along with the incomprehensible conversation and new complication in our friends-only arrangement. "No. Tried your tactic. Didn't work."

"Darn. Ready to head to the casino?"

"Hell, yeah."

I wave for the waiter, and after paying the bill, we follow the signs to the attached casino. The combined noise of bells, music, conversation, and excitement is almost as loud as the gaudy carpet and flashing lights coming from every direction. I don't know which to shield first—my eyes or my ears. But I do neither since my hands are busy clutching the wheelchair handles and fighting the urge to run my hands down Jordan's chest. He's making me want things I can't have in his sexy, white button-down shirt and black shorts.

We opted for slightly more than casual, and he's pulling it off with minimum effort. I, in contrast, packed nothing to fit that description. After rummaging through my suitcase and trying on outfits for thirty minutes, I snagged a black, off the shoulder, cropped sweater from Josie's closet to wear with my ripped skinny jeans and ankle boots. It's giving off casual, sexy chic vibes and boosting my confidence whenever desirous male eyes glance my way. One set of navy eyes, in particular.

"Tables first?" I have to yell so Jordan can hear me.

"Sure."

We make our way to the blackjack tables and claim two stools. A waitress in a short miniskirt and low-cut top stops by to flirt with Jordan. He relishes in the attention before calmly ordering two drinks. *That's right*, my eyes say when she looks over his shoulder at me before stomping off.

"Did you order something she'll have to hand-squeeze?" I joke when he leans on the edge of the slick wooden table. "She looks perturbed."

"Nope. Just a beer and a glass of wine for you."

"Well, she looked as though she wanted you all to herself."

"Not tonight," he says with a wink. "I have a bet to win."

"I could have worn that dress tonight. All you had to do was ask."

He stares at me, agitated that he hadn't thought of that. "If I win, I plan to collect in New York and let the entire city know you're—"

Stopping himself, he frowns.

Mine. Say it, I urge silently, but he collects the chips and first draw from the dealer.

"Damn," he says after checking the cards.

With a smirk, I peek at mine and toss in a hefty bet.

Jordan folds immediately.

"Chicken," I accuse.

"Not chicken. Smart. I'm in this for the long haul."

Again, he stares me down, his eyes laying the meaning out on the table.

"So am I." I toss in a few more chips and flip over my cards without dropping his gaze.

"We have blackjack. The pot goes to the lady in black," the dealer adds amidst a chorus of groans and whines.

"Better get crackin', handsome. I'm up two."

Jordan wins the next two hands, bringing our friendly competition back to even. Three beers and four hands later, there's still no clear winner. Only a drunk ex-Marine and his *friend*. We cash in our chips and head to the slots to settle this bet once and for all.

Setting a timer, we decide the person with the most money when the bell chimes buys dinner. Somewhere along the way tonight between winning and losing and shots, I agree to go to Josie's show—as if I could resist the smile that accompanied the invitation.

Pulling the levers and pushing blinking buttons as fast as we can, bells and random noises sound off from both machines. It's obnoxious, but all I care about is racking up points and hearing Jordan's contagious laugh for the rest of the evening. It doesn't matter who wins at this point. Isn't a romantic dinner in either New York City or on the James River a win-win? We both want to go, but this last game is for bragging rights. And I never back down.

Happy tears blur my vision. I can't see who's winning. If it isn't me, it's not like I know enough about how to play this machine to change my fate. I'm just pushing and pulling when prompted, hoping to hoist an invisible trophy when the timer goes off. I check the clock and there's two minutes left.

Before the timer sounds, the large red light on top of his machine goes off, making me jump. He's either broken it or won the jackpot.

"Yes!" His arms fly up in celebration before he snatches me off my stool, pulls me into his lap, and dips me back with a kiss that fills me with primal desire all the way down to my toes. All ten of them curl inside my shoes, and I pull him closer, needing to feel more of him.

When he releases me, I'm not ready and equally unprepared for the tender way he brushes the hair from my face. He's about to kiss me again when casino staff join us to congratulate the grand winner.

Ten thousand dollars. He won ten frickin' thousand dollars at a slot machine in Charlestown, West Virginia.

"What will you do with your winnings?" the exuberant woman at the customer service counter asks, handing him a receipt to sign.

"I think my beautiful…friend and I will live it up in New York this weekend."

"Jordan, you should use that for your—"

"Come on. Let's go celebrate with a drink."

He drags me down into his lap again and rolls us to the bar. I giggle like a smitten teenager all the way there, my arms wrapped around his neck and my legs stretched out to the side. Either I'm drunk, or have untapped a side of me I never knew existed. A side that could be unabashedly happy.

Giving into the feels, I kiss his face all the way to the bar—his forehead, cheek, jawline, ear. That last one had him jumping to his feet and setting me on mine. A grimace scrunches his face.

"Is that from pain or something else?" My eyes fall to his shorts.

"Wouldn't you like to know?"

He hobbles closer to the bar, steps up to the stools, and offers his hand.

"Such a gentleman."

He waits for me to sit before sliding himself onto the stool beside mine with a long sigh. While we wait for the bartender to return with our drinks, I realize it's already after 10:00 p.m.

"Jordan." I place a hand on his arm. "I think we need to get a hotel room."

His eyes double in size as they travel over my body.

"No. Not for that." My hand slinks away, and I miss the feel of his skin under my palm. "It's getting late, and I've had too much to drink to drive back tonight."

"Works for me." He leans closer. "But we should get two beds. I can't have you traveling over to my side when you get—"

"Not a problem."

His shoulders dip with disappointment, but he recovers quickly and accepts our drinks from the bartender.

"What?" I ask, taking the glass of wine he slides down the sleek bar surface to me, his gaze lingering with a look I don't understand.

"Nothing. Except, I don't believe you. I seem to remember you not being able to keep your lips to yourself a few minutes ago."

"Yeah, well, a kiss is a lot different from what you were insinuating." And a lot less satisfying. Something flutters in my stomach, and I snuff it out with a sip of wine.

He looks over his shoulder and wiggles his brow. "Care to wager?"

"You're incorrigible." And too damn sexy for his own good. "What are we betting on now?"

"That you can't go the rest of the night without kissing me." He turns and leans an elbow on the bar. "And before you take the bet, you should know…" His voice lowers to a sultry growl as he waves me closer. I lean in without realizing it and let his sexy pine scent intoxicate me further. "I plan to do everything I can to make you lose."

I breathe him in a moment longer before sitting back to uncross and cross my legs, pausing in the middle with my knees wide. "If I didn't know any better, I'd think you were trying to push us into being more than friends."

A dumb look on his face tells me he hadn't thought through his challenge. That means, I'm winning…for now. Sulking, he reaches for his beer and gulps half of it.

Tonight will be a test of willpowers, and with alcohol involved, there's a high probability both of us will lose. Or win, depending on the perspective.

Chapter Twenty-Two

Nora

A bright light assaults my eyes, the pain radiating through my throbbing head like an oncoming freight train. I need to look away, but my head and body hurt too much to move.

Details of how our little Las Vegas night ended are blurry, but I can guarantee that whatever happened here will definitely not stay here. There will be repercussions and alterations to the norm that neither of us can predict.

It also didn't help that the hotel had only a few rooms remaining, all with one queen bed and a sleeper sofa. Apparently, Thursdays are a big gambling night, and we were lucky to get this room.

I glance at the sofa to find it empty and in its original shape. No transformation into a bed. No mussed sheets. No Jordan. A slight forest scent registers to my right and there's a void where my arm should be. It's dead weight from him lying on it and cutting off my circulation. If we're in the same bed...I lift the sheet and peer under with one eye. Holy hell. My leg is wrapped around him, and he's naked.

I'm naked.

Shit. Shit. Shit.

Sliding my tingling arm out from under him, I roll out of bed and search the floor on my hands and knees for my clothes. His and mine are strewn across the carpet and intermingled like we undressed in a hurricane.

Sitting on my knees, I yank on the black sweater—not bothering with a bra, mainly because I haven't found it yet—and snatch up my underwear. Rotating to my ass, I push my feet through the leg holes and realize there's only one. Yep. My underwear, the lacy pair I bought a few weeks ago, is ripped.

I kick my foot, sending the useless undergarment flying into the air. To my horror, it takes its time floating to the floor like a little parachute. What in the hell did we do last night? *Don't answer that brain.* My system is not recovered enough for the answer.

Tugging on my jeans, I'm thankful they're stretched out from wear, but I rather have a pair of yoga pants or pajamas. Doing the crawl of shame is nearly impossible with fitted jeans and sore muscles.

Damn, why is every inch of me screaming? And if I was active enough last night to be sore, I wish I could remember it. Must have been quite the—

My phone vibrates, and I race to snatch it off the bedside table, hoping not to wake Jordan. He had more to drink than I did. Maybe he won't remember either, saving me the embarrassment of having to admit I don't.

Turning toward the window, I check the message. Air catches in my lungs as I read.

> **Clark:** Missed you in class this morning. Barbie's whiny voice was anything but relaxing.

A snicker spurts out of my closed lips when I see the new contact label for Henry. Drunken creativity at its best. I wonder who else has a new nickname in my contacts list.

> **Me:** Sorry you had to endure that. I'm out of town.
>
> **Clark:** Will you be back tonight?
>
> **Me:** Yeah. Does VETS need something?
>
> **Clark:** No. Limping along without you. I meant for dinner.
> **Clark:** Interested?

"Who are you texting so early?" Jordan's groggy voice registers, and I plaster on a smile, though I don't feel it.

"No one. And it's nearly noon." I busy myself by picking up the remaining pieces of clothing, bottles, and wine glasses to make the place look less like a frat house after a party.

"What does Superman want?"

I straighten in surprise, an awkward load of clothes and dishes shifting in my arms.

"Why would you jump immediately to Henry?"

"Because you were smiling the same way as when you were with him yesterday. Did he ask you out again?"

After setting the glasses in the sink by the door, I dump the clothes on the desk nearby. "I'm not having this conversation."

"You should go."

The last thing I want to do is talk about Henry with the man I may or may not have feelings for and may or may not have slept with last night. The same guy who mended my heart with his tenderness only to ship me off to another man shortly after. What the hell?

"Who wouldn't want to go out with Superman, Clark Kent, or Henry Cavill's stunt double slash doctor?" he drones on. "He's the total package."

"Why are you doing this?" I ask, frustration weighing on every syllable. "Especially after last night?"

He pulls himself up to lean against the headboard, his hands folding calmly in his lap. "What happened last night, Nora?"

My head pounds with a new frustration as he stares me down. No emotion. No window into his thoughts. "I don't fucking know what happened. Everything after we left the bar is a blur. Are you happy?"

"Guess we both have gaps in our memories now. But I remember every detail. Want me to summarize it for you?"

"No. I just want to get out of here. I'm hungover, I feel out of control, and this thing with you…it's…"

"It's what, Nora?"

Wetness stinging my eyes is the final straw. Crumbling to the floor, I spin to drop my back to the foot of the bed and my face into my hands.

"Confusing," I finally say through the tears. "You're confusing."

The bed springs groan and squeak under his shifting weight. I hear him limp past me to the desk and slip on his shirt. The rustling sounds grow louder before his hands land on my legs. Opening my eyes, I find him wrapped in the sheet from the waist down, sitting with both his legs stretched out on either side of me.

"I asked you to go out with Henry because I don't want you to have regrets."

"Regrets?"

"Things feel different between us, Nora, and nothing makes me happier, whether we're friends or more." He grins but refuses to look at me. "If we grow into more from this do-over exercise, I need to be confident that you're choosing me over everyone else. That you won't be looking back and wondering what if."

"Jordan, are you going to do this every time a man pays me attention?"

"I don't know. We're not at a place yet where I can trust what you say you're feeling."

My legs drop to the side, weakened by his confession. He doesn't trust that I won't toss him aside when commitment knocks on the door again. And he has every right not to.

"Go out with him and see if you feel anything. If you don't, then we'll have crossed the first hurdle."

"Do you not want to be with me?" I ask, not meaning for those words to escape.

"I do. More than I want air to breathe. But it's not enough. We've tried a relationship, and it didn't work out. I don't want to make the same mistakes." He looks out the window, deep in thought.

He's done nothing wrong. It's all me. I pushed him away and forced him into doing the one thing I feared he'd eventually do on his own—leave.

"I need to feel and fully believe that when you choose to give your heart to me, you're handing over all of it. All of you."

With a sniff, I nod, and he swipes a tear from my cheek with his thumb.

"Will you go…for me?"

A long, burning exhale has my shoulders drooping. I drag my hands over my wet face before grabbing the phone. "This is insane."

"I like that you think hanging with boring ole me would be more fun."

"I don't just think it." I glance his way, soaking in the love in his eyes, then open the texting app. "Wait. I can't go." I set the device back on the floor.

"Why not?"

"He asked about tonight. We still need to drive back, and I'm not leaving you alone."

"I'll call the guys. They've been asking about getting together. We can have a poker night at the apartment. I'm still feeling lucky."

Exasperated by his endless index of answers, my eyes glance at the ceiling, and I wonder if he's talking about his gambling luck or what happened between us afterward.

"Which ones?" I ask, eyeing him with suspicion. "Guys I can trust, or guys who will want to find trouble?"

"Just Wes and Peter and maybe one more."

"Wes is a firefighter/EMT, right?"

"Yeah. See, he can help if something happens. Nothing to worry about."

"I guess."

He leans forward, propping his forehead against mine. Lost in his gaze, I didn't catch him stealing my phone until he places it into my hand.

"Text him."

"You're infuriating."

Me: When and where?

Clark: Marcello's 7 p.m.

Me: See you there.

I hold the screen up to show Jordan. "Happy?"

"Mostly."

"Great."

Jordan

"Nora, you remember Wes and Pete?" I ask when my friends enter the apartment.

"How could I forget?" She sets down a box of poker chips on the card table she borrowed from a neighbor and waves.

"And this is Q, short for Quinton. We went to Basic together."

"Nice to meet you, Quinton."

"You, too, ma'am."

"Ma'am? On that note, I'll leave you boys to your fun." She crosses the room to collect her purse, lowering her voice when she reaches me. "Tell him."

"I will," I whisper.

"And try to stay out of trouble," she instructs loud enough for all to hear.

"Hey, that's my line," I joke, hoping to get a rise out of her. She gave me nothing but a blank, agitated scowl.

"You don't want to join us?" Wes asks with a smirk.

"As enticing as that sounds, I have an appointment."

He frowns. "This late? What kind of appointment?"

"She has a date," I clarify.

"No kiddin'." Wes studies me, and I slowly shake my head, hoping to stop whatever he plans to say next. Of course, he ignores me. "What's on the agenda?"

"Just dinner."

"Where?"

She pushes the purse strap over her shoulder with a sigh and answers on her way toward the door. "Marcello's. I'm going to get ready at my apartment," she says to me. "See you later."

She flashes the group a tight-lipped grin as she escapes, and my so-called friends waste no time shifting their interrogation to me.

"What the hell, Jordan?" Wes asks with a sharpness I could do without. I've talked with him the most about my history with Nora over the years, and he's never hidden his disdain for the woman I love.

Pete and Q stop to watch us from the kitchen, the refrigerator door hanging open. All three guys are now staring at me like I grew a third arm since they arrived.

"What?"

"Why is she here? Strike that. A better question is, why is she going out with someone else if she's here?"

"Who is she?" Q asks.

"I've got this one," Wes says, holding up a hand to stop me from answering. "She's the girl he's been fucking for five years. And despite her refusing to date him publicly, he still asked her to marry him…twice. Which she declined both times."

"Shit, man," Peter empathizes, snapping open a beer.

Wes's assault continues. "Why is she here?"

"It's a long story."

"What did she want you to tell us?" he asks, accepting a beer from Peter. "I heard what she said to you."

"Come on. I'll fill you in while we set up the game."

We all sit around the tiny card table Nora borrowed from a neighbor with our drinks. While Q shuffles the cards and Peter distributes poker chips, I tell them about my injuries, the lingering seizures, and why Nora came back into my life.

"Since you're an EMT," I say to Wes, "she wanted to make sure you were aware and prepared."

"That's uncharacteristically kind of her, but she didn't seem to be in the caregiver mood when she left." Wes picks up his cards and tosses in a chip to start the game.

"She doesn't want to go on the date, and she's upset with me."

"What did you do?" Q asks, raising Wes's bet two chips.

"Asked her to go on the date." I flip three chips onto the pile.

"You're a dumbass." Wes shakes his head as he matches my bet.

"Agreed," Pete says, folding.

"Thanks a lot. You don't know everything, and this is how I make sure she's all in on our fake relationship before we make it real."

"You have to know how stupid that is. What if they have a connection? What if she fucks him, too?"

Well, that stung. "She won't."

"You said he's a doctor." Wes holds up a hand and starts ticking off all of Superman's appealing qualities. None of which I can meet. "Looks like a famous actor who plays one of the most beloved superheroes, has a limitless bank account, and volunteers his spare time to help injured veterans?"

"He also has a British accent," I add stupidly, living up to their opinion of me.

"You're right. He's got nothing on you," Pete chimes in, his sarcastic tone telling me precisely what he thinks of my decisions.

"You all can kiss my ass. And since you're obviously Team Kent, I will have no qualms taking your money tonight." I fan my cards out on the table, and revel in the groans of my less-than-supportive friends. "Royal flush."

Q and Wes toss their cards onto the table, and they slide across the chip pile I plan to rub in their faces.

"You're going to need it to compete with dates at Marcello's," Q jokes, dealing another hand. "That place is impossible to get into unless you're a local celebrity or rich as hell."

"Superman is both," Wes says before draining his beer.

"I hate every one of you."

Chapter Twenty-Three

Nora

Thirty minutes after I enter my apartment and change, the doorbell rings. Dropping my brush onto the counter, I jog to the door to see which neighbor needs something tonight.

Swinging it open, I tilt my head in mock disapproval at Sydney and her three-year-old son, William.

"I thought I might see you tonight." I welcome them inside, hug Sydney on her way by, then pick up William to give him a squeeze.

He lets out a loud squeal-laugh when I lift his sweatshirt and deliver noisy kisses to his belly, his deep red curls falling into his eyes as he wiggles. He's one of those kids with infinite energy and sweetness. It's impossible *not* to adore him.

"You can't be all weird on the phone and not expect me to come check on you," Sydney says, leading us to the living room couch. "Love the dress."

"Thanks." William's energy gets the better of him, and he squirms to get down. Once he's running about the apartment, I smooth the front of my black, white, and teal-striped, knee-length sweater dress before sitting. "I've had it for years, but it's too nice to wear to work or out at our usual places."

I glance over at William, examining the fake plant in the corner, to avoid Sydney's inquisitory eyes. Knowing her, she's shuffling through dozens of questions my recent behavior has invoked to select one that won't make me bolt. But she knows me too and my evading tactics. When I called her on the way home, any and all topics that involved or could lead to Jordan were sufficiently skirted. At the time, I needed my friend to take my mind off the chaos and distract me from losing my composure in the quiet car. I hadn't fully thought through the consequences before dialing her number.

"Where are you going all dressed up?" she settles on cautiously.

And that one weighted question is all it took to bring back the trepidation and confusion I felt leaving Jordan's earlier.

While I find the words to explain, William rushes over to us, looks up at me with his big, dark eyes, and hands me his plastic toy soldier—the one he goes nowhere without.

"He only shares that when he thinks someone's upset," Sydney explains.

"Well, aren't you perceptive?" I say, cupping his chubby, freckled cheeks in my hand and planting a kiss to his nose. "And the sweetest."

"I wasn't joking. You did sound off earlier. What's going on?"

In what feels like one strangling exhale, I summarize our trip, Henry's invitation, and Jordan's stance on the matter.

"Wow. There's a lot to unpack there," Sydney says, surveilling William's exploration of the unfamiliar room while she processes. "I can't believe you're going. Not only because you're not big on dating, but what about your feelings for Jordan?"

"He gave me no choice. He wants proof that I'm not going to push him away again…if we decide to be together."

"Can you give him that assurance?"

I've been avoiding doing that with any man since Sydney and I met, most of all Jordan. Still, hearing her skepticism stings more than it should. But she's right. Can I give Jordan the security he needs?

"I don't know," I answer honestly. "Everything about him and this situation is confusing. While I'm trying to wrap my head around how I feel, he's giving me whiplash with his ever-changing mind."

"What do you mean?"

"One minute, he's seducing me or saying the sweetest things that make me think he loves me. The next, he's insisting we stay in the friend's zone. If he has feelings for me, why in the he—heck," I correct for the young ears in the room, "am I going out with another man at his insistence?"

"It sounds like he's battling with his own heart and emotions the same way you are. William," she calls to him with a threat of a scold in her tone. He's reaching for the porcelain statue of a woman in a yoga pose Sydney gave me for my birthday. "Leave that be."

He stares at her, his arm stretching slightly closer with a mischievous smirk as if to test her sincerity, and I have to hide my amusement at my spirit child. I turn away before he takes my smile as encouragement. He soon moves on to something else, and Sydney praises his good decision.

"Sorry. Not exactly toddler-proof around here."

"No biggie. He spends a lot of time at Jackson's, so he's used to being told what he can and cannot touch."

"Goodness. How does that poor child keep his hands to himself with all the priceless and beautiful things in that mansion?" Laughing, I think of my own difficulties doing exactly that when I visited the historic Vane estate for the first time last year.

"It's an exercise in impulse control for him and patience for me." We laugh, and William's head turns to see what all the excitement is about. Unimpressed, he goes back to his inspection.

"We're going to New York tomorrow for Josie's show," I announce.

"That's exciting."

"I guess. I don't know how much more of this rollercoaster I can take. She's staying up there longer than originally planned, but I need to get back to work and my life."

"Doesn't that life include Jordan now?" Sydney asks, studying me.

"I'm not sure. I thought we were heading in that direction until he insisted on this." With a motion toward my pretty *date* dress, irritation takes root like an invasive vine. I hate everything it represents. Wearing it, I'm not myself, or more accurately, the person I've trained myself to be. That girl could enjoy Henry and not care about anyone's expectations or feelings. Her heart didn't get a say, and she lived by her own rules. She was free.

Since Jordan waltzed back into town, that way of life—that freedom I once relished—feels more like a noose with the other end attached to a ship adrift at sea.

"Will you tell Henry about Jordan?"

I consider the question. Is there anything to say at this point? My heart, the one vote I usually ignore, says there's plenty to talk about, and for once, my head agrees. "Yes," I decide. "It's another reason I'm anxious about going. I don't want to disappoint him. He's so sweet."

Sydney shakes her head. "I've never seen you like this."

"Like what?"

"For one, you're going out on a *date*." She emphasizes the word like it's something significant I've never experienced before.

Offended by her wonder, I think back, and nothing comes to mind to contradict her. Shit. Am I *that* woman? The one men take to bed but nowhere else? Is that what I've done to my life? Is Jordan the first man to want more and see me as worthy enough to have in his future?

What does Henry want? I haven't exactly painted myself in a wholesome light in the classes he attended. Quite the opposite, in fact, and it's been entertaining. Until now.

I sit up with a new revelation swirling inside me.

"Holy shhh—nitzel," I say, cutting off Sydney mid-sentence and shooting to my feet. William runs over to me, excited to start another tickle game, and holds his hands out to me. Picking him up, I kiss his soft cheek. "I don't want to be everyone's good time."

Sydney rises, my excitement contagious. "What does that mean?"

"It means I'm done with one-night stands and being alone on holidays. I deserve more. I *want* more in my life." I turn to Sydney. "Despite the rocky road you had to get here, I want what you have—unconditional love, someone to come home to, a family. And for the first time, I'm willing to face uncertainty and the unpleasant for a chance to have something amazing forever."

Sydney places her hands on my elbows, tears welling. "Oh, sweetie. You don't know how many times I've prayed to hear you say that. Not for you to want all those things for yourself because everyone's version of happy and path to get there is different. And you needed to discover yours. But I'm so glad to hear you finally believe that you *deserve* more than what you've allowed for yourself." She touches my arm. "You, my dearest friend, deserve it all."

Emotion lodges in my throat, and I tug her into a hug. "Thank you." William joins in, wrapping his other arm around Sydney's neck, and we relax into the best hug I've ever had. "I have a lot of making up to do first."

"You'll get there," she says, drawing back and collecting William. I miss him already. "They do that," she adds with a smile.

"Who does what?"

"Children. Whether you give birth to them or not, they have a way of filling your heart with a love you can't get anywhere else. It's indescribable, but once you feel it, you'll never be the same."

"I feel it," I agree, threading my fingers through William's thick curls.

"He's quite the charmer…like his dad." Shaking out of her memories, she wraps me in another embrace. "We'll get out of your way so you can finish getting ready."

"Ready? Oh, right. Henry." I'd forgotten about sweet Henry. Walking Sydney and William to the door, I wave goodbye and wonder where to go from here.

―――――

When I slip into Jordan's apartment hours later, I find the group cleaning up.

"Wow," Quinton says, frozen where he stands with his arms full of uneaten snacks and his eyes locked on me. The others follow suit. Guess the back-of-the-closet dress and knee-high black boots were the right choice.

I dial up my best smile. "Looks like poker night was a success."

"Jordan won, as usual," Peter complains and drops his armload into the trash.

"He's had a lot of practice." I shift to find Jordan staring at me, his mouth gaping open. To remind him of the games we used to play, I peel out of my coat slowly and toss it over the back of the couch with a flip of my wrist. This dress hugs my body like it was made for me, and by the way his eyes are taking it in, he agrees.

A heavy silence fills the room until Wes clears his throat. "We were planning to hit the new club down the street. Would you like to join us?"

"You're going?" I ask Jordan, surprised to hear he'd want to go to a crowded dance club with his cast.

"No. Jordan declined," Wes answers for him. "But since you were in the mood for going out, I thought I'd extend the offer."

"Wes," Jordan warns through gritted teeth.

"It's fine, Jordan." I stroll closer until there's only a few feet and palpable tension between me and his friend. "I can take whatever he wants to throw at me. Go ahead, Wes. Say your peace."

I hear feet shuffling behind me, Quinton and Peter getting a better view, no doubt. Jordan's audible breathing nearby has me retreating and leaning casually against the back of the couch. I'm concerned about how this altercation may affect him.

"Choose your words carefully," Jordan warns again.

Wes glares down his nose, his opinion of me deeply rooted already.

"I understand why you hate me," I say to get it over with.

"Oh, yeah? Enlighten me." He crosses his arms, smug danger hardening his features.

"I've hurt a friend of yours, and—"

"You did more than hurt him."

"Don't you think I know that?" I spit back.

"Yeah. That's the problem. You do whatever you want with no regard for him. You won't meet a more loyal, nicer, or caring person—"

"Hey," the other guys chime in, pretending to be offended.

He barrels on as if they said nothing. "He treated you like you hung the fucking moon."

"And I took advantage of that."

"Like a heartless bitch."

"Damn," the chorus in the wings sings softly as Jordan shoots out of his chair with a stifled grimace.

"That's enough," he yells at Wes, his face flushes with fury. I place a hand on his chest to stop his advance and feel his heart throwing itself against my palm.

"I'm not proud of what I've done, you know." Both men relax a bit, and I drop my hand to take Jordan's. We have a lot to work through, but I want him to know I appreciate his jumping to my defense. He didn't have to. His friendship with Wes goes back long before I entered the picture, and it's not like he said anything that isn't true.

"I was a bitch," I agree. "Selfish and cold and rude on a regular basis. I've got issues I'm working on, more now than ever. Hate me all you want. Hell, I hate myself." Straightening and taking a calculated step closer, I point a finger at him. "But that gives you no right to put yourself in the middle of our business and confront me like this. You think you're protecting your friend—"

"Wes," Jordan interrupts. "I think you should leave."

Wes sucks in a deep breath, his nostrils flaring as he stares through me. "Fine. But there's nothing either of you could do to change my opinion. He's too good for someone like you."

"Tell me something I don't know." I hold my ground, attempting to keep those words from affecting me again.

Senior year of high school at my boyfriend's eighteenth birthday party, his mother said that exact phrase to me. It was the first time she told me I wasn't good enough for her son. *Someone like you.* I couldn't care less what she thought of me. Those three little words meant nothing until Tristan agreed with her four months later. He said he loved me countless times. But if he believed, despite his heart, that I wasn't a good person, it must be true. I spiraled after that, doing everything I could to prove them right.

It took finding my college acceptance letter in the trash, tossed there by someone who thought I wasn't worth it, to wake up. After taking a good, hard look at myself, I didn't like what I saw. I could do and be better. My oppressive upbringing didn't have to define me or my future if I didn't let it.

It felt good to set that part of me to flame, allowing a new me to rise from the ashes. But the transformation wasn't without flaws, I've come to realize. Some pieces of that heartbroken girl survived and latched on to the one piece of me I protected the most. All her pain, all her insecurities caused me to do some things that need undoing. Facing the consequences of those actions over the last few days has brought everything full circle.

It's time to start another fire.

Meeting Wes's challenge, I latch my gaze onto his to make my final point. "People can change, and you know nothing about me."

"You've shown me all I need to know."

"Buddy," Quinton calls from the door.

Wes's hands fly up, indicating he's finished with me and strolls toward the door. "I hope you know what you're doing," he says to Jordan.

The door slams behind him, making me jump. I swivel to Jordan, who's lowering to the wheelchair as if every muscle aches. "I'm sorry, Jordan."

"You have nothing to apologize for."

"I shouldn't have encouraged him." I sit on the arm of the couch beside him, suddenly drained.

"You look beautiful."

And there he goes again, destroying all the pressure with his unyielding tenderness. "Thank you."

"How'd it go?" he asks, searching my face.

"Fine. What games did you guys play? Anything new?"

Ignoring my attempt to redirect the conversation, he circles back. "Did you do anything after dinner?"

"Jordan."

"Did you kiss him?"

And with that, all the gooey sweetness crystalizes. I rocket to my feet. "Don't do this."

He rolls after me as I head to the kitchen, the sound of my boots hitting the hardwood floor and echoing through the quiet apartment.

"I need to know."

"You'd already know the answer if you'd get Wes out of your head." I reach into the refrigerator for a bottle of water and hand it to him. Whatever is developing between us doesn't need this. Just like I didn't need to go out with Henry to determine how I feel.

"I want to hear it from you."

To give me time to rally the patience I wasted on Wes, I return to grab another water for me. With more calmness than I feel, the words tumble out. "No. I didn't kiss him."

"Why not?"

"Jesus, Jordan. Do you hear yourself?" Flipping the door closed, I stalk past him to my suitcase in the living room. I need to get out of these clothes. Maybe if I can find some level of comfort, I'll have more energy to prevent another argument.

"I remembered our last break up," he says suddenly.

A weighted silence blankets the room. To keep it from getting to me, I busy myself with the clothes in my suitcase, seeing none of it. I can't think, can't feel. It's another nightmare he had to relive, and I wasn't here to explain myself. Not that I have any good reasons for how I treated him.

"It's why Wes is pissed," he continues.

My hands still. "I'm surprised you're not."

"It wasn't fun, but I'm glad I remember."

Weakened by his gratitude for one of the worst days of my life, I drop to my knees. The unforgiving floor emphasizes the dread seeping into my bones. This is where he tells me it's over. He knows everything now. The good, the bad, and the horrific. I doubt my past transgressions leave any space for building that future I dreamed about.

"That night, you wouldn't tell me what you wanted from me. You just said no to the ring and shut me out." He pushes the wheelchair closer and transfers himself to the couch.

"As I said earlier, I'm not proud of how I handled anything with us back then."

"You also said people change. Do you think you've changed?"

He's gauging me, but I don't dare lift my eyes. We're both vulnerable in this conversation and seeing him like that, knowing I'm the cause yet again, is too much.

"In a lot of ways," I finally say, giving my focus to the hem of my dress to keep tears from forming.

"Tell me." He pats the cushion beside him, but I haven't recovered enough to be that close to him. To smell him and feel the warmth of his body while anger and pain push us apart.

"I will," I lift my gaze to seal the promise and boldly meet his. "But I'd like to change first."

His midnight eyes somehow darken. "Good."

"Good?"

"You wore that for him, and it's getting increasingly harder to see you in it while talking about us."

"Jordan, I didn't—" He looks away, disinterested in a clarification. After all, nothing I say about it will make him feel differently. I grab the first sweatshirt and pants I find and escape to the bathroom.

The edges of this imaginary triangle are slicing through us, inch by inch, the longer he believes I followed through on our plan. After talking with Sydney, it felt wrong to use Henry to placate Jordan's fears, hurting them both. Saying yes may have been Jordan's idea, but he didn't mean it, and his reaction proves it. I thought we could put the whole ordeal behind us. I didn't expect him to demand details, anger fueling his inquisition.

How will he react when I tell him I didn't go?

Frustration, fear, and determination bubbles inside me, competing for control as I take hold of the doorknob. By the time I make the short trek back to the living room, the chaos is poised to erupt. Then, I see him, and everything I need to say dissipates into a cloud of smoke.

"Can I get you anything?" I ask. It's a cowardly move, but the strength I gained from my talk with Sydney earlier and myself in the bathroom has swiveled and holed up somewhere I can't locate in his presence.

"I'm fine."

Resigning, I sit beside him and tuck my legs under me. "Did Wes give you a hard time about me?"

"He did, but I can take it. The hardest part was thinking about you doing what I asked you to do. I regret uttering the words."

I sigh. "Nothing happened between me and Henry. I canceled."

His hand grips the back of his neck as he lets out a long exhale, relief settling on his face.

"I don't want to be with Henry or lead him on."

He places his hand on the cushion between us, palm up, and I slide mine into it. "Then, tell me what you do want, Nora. Why does it feel different between us this time?"

My chest tightens, and I breathe deep to release the knot forming there. "Because I realized something the other day and tonight only solidified it."

"What's that?"

No hiding now. May the truth set us both free. "I don't want to lose you. But I also don't want to hold you back."

"What does that mean?"

I push forward despite the shock altering his expression. "A long time ago, I convinced myself we could never be more than casual. That you'd be happier with someone else. Someone who could give you a horde of beautiful babies and no baggage to trip over. Someone who hadn't stomped on your heart. And that one day you'd find her and never look back."

"I've never given any indication that I wanted anyone but you," he says, his voice rising.

"Not exactly, but you do want the family I can't give you."

"So, you chose to push me away instead of letting me decide? Trusting in us?"

"Yes. At the time." I look down at our hands bound together, surprised he hasn't pulled away. Reveling at my luck and this man with a golden heart, I shake my head.

"And now?" he asks, and I scoot closer.

"If you'll have me with all my issues, I don't want to run anymore."

He pins me with a frown, trying to process what seems like my sudden change of heart. Little does he know that over the last year, I missed him and remained celibate because my body and heart longed for only him.

"Anything else?" he asks flatly, making me wonder if I'm too late. It sends me into a tailspin until a faint grin emerges and alights his eyes.

"Oh, there's plenty more," I tease, letting hope plant a seed.

"Like what?"

"I want lazy weekends in bed, more bucket list adventures, and whatever happened last night on repeat. And I want to remember it this time." I flash him a shy smile. "More than anything, I need to know what you're thinking."

In answer, he hauls me into his lap. I straddle his hips, letting my arms rest on his shoulders while my fingers comb through the hair at the nape of his neck. His eyes drop to my lips, and every cell in my body awakens. I could get used to this view, and everything his hands are saying. But my stubborn brain would like to hear them voiced anyway.

"Does this tell you what I'm thinking?" His powerful fingers squeeze my hips and drag me closer.

"It's been a crazy day. Maybe you should spell it out for me."

His hands trail up my arms and rest gently under my jaw, pulling my lips to his. He takes his time, soft and testing.

"Does this set the stage for a replay of last night?" I whisper against his lips, not letting him get too far away.

"I hope not."

His breath skates over my cheek, and I have to work to deconstruct the walls going up. "What?"

"Nothing happened last night, Nora." His hands relax and drop to my thighs. "Well, we started something incredible, but I stopped it."

"Why?"

"What you just told me...you also mentioned it and more last night."

"You thought it was a drunk confession I didn't mean."

His gaze drops, but I bring it back to me by framing his face with my hands.

"I'm sorry for giving you so many reasons to not trust me. I should have been the one protecting your heart and constantly filling it, not—"

"I've never stopped loving you. I was upset after the breakup, but I'd have found my way back to you eventually. I always do." He leans in for a kiss, but before he can withdraw, I hold him and deepen it. He's less tentative this time, more possessive, hungry.

"Where do we go from here?" I ask, knowing that one taste of him won't be enough and hoping he feels the same.

"Well, we agreed to start over, but I'd rather skip ahead."

"How far ahead?"

"Cool your panties. I'm not proposing again," he confesses with a playful eye roll. "But I learned tonight that I'm not good at sharing you. I won't do it."

"Jordan Jones, are you asking me to be your girlfriend?"

He nods. "In private, public, and every way that matters. No more pretending, Nora. No hiding. I don't need you to marry me, but I do need a real commitment."

My hands slide down his broad shoulders and chest, taking in the feel of him—my sweet, sweet *boyfriend*. "I can handle that."

Bringing me closer, he kisses me until the room spins, and I'm no longer thinking of relationship labels. I no longer care about promises, past mistakes, or future uncertainties. Only him.

Chapter Twenty-Four

Jordan

"We should get ready," Nora says, crawling on top of me, her hands trailing down my torso. The gray light of dawn fills the room, covering her smooth skin in a soft amber glow.

Mirroring her, I slide a finger down the thin space between her breasts. "I'm suddenly in the mood for something else."

"We have plans," she informs me.

"Seems to me like your body is advocating for a change of plans."

"Mmm." She shifts her hips over me, teasing me into wanting more than a beautiful view. "Under normal circumstances, you'd be right, but…"

"We have plans," I repeat as my gaze travels from her face down to her navel, committing the view to memory.

She's tousled and sleepy-eyed from an active night and looking at me with a new affection. One I never thought I'd see.

"You're quite the devoted brother." Moving to her hands and knees, she plants a kiss on my lips for incentive, but it only makes me crave staying put more. I pull her down and roll, pinning her under my arm and good leg.

I cover her squeal with my mouth until her body stops resisting and starts writhing with need.

"We can spare twenty minutes," she concedes.

"Plenty of time for what I want to do to you."

―――

It took three tries, but we eventually made it into the car to start the five-and-a-half-hour trip to New York City. But an hour in, Nora turns off I-95 and heads west.

"What are you doing?" I ask.

"A planned detour." She takes my hand for the first time in our new, actual relationship, and I feel like a teenager again. Back when a touch from a girl felt more like heat from a flame. When simple moments got the heart pumping, not only from the physical connection but from knowing that person chose you. A time when casual gestures meant so much more.

"Detour to where?"

"Cave exploring in a non-dangerous, wheelchair accessible fashion."

I laugh, trying to remember her creative replacement for the activity, but nothing comes to mind. "Tell me."

"Nope. You'll find out soon enough."

Another hour later, we pull into the parking lot at Shenandoah Caverns.

"Clever," I say, and lean over the middle console to offer a kiss. "I love this."

"Good. Let's get you out of here and go exploring."

"Yes. My back is killing me."

"Is that from the car ride or last night?" Her wink reminds me of another night I'll never forget, and it sends a shiver down to my mid-section.

"Definitely the car. You, my darling, made every inch of me feel like a million bucks."

"Damn right." She offers her lips again, and I'm happy to oblige.

After a few minutes of our own gratifying version exploration, we get around to purchasing tickets to enter the caverns.

For the entire tour, Nora stays connected to me—her hand on my shoulder, on the back of my neck, or in mine. It's a new affectionate side I'm loving and praying continues around our friends and family.

"Did you tell Josie when we'd arrive?" Nora asks later as she backs out of the parking space.

"I didn't tell her we were coming at all."

"What?" She slams on the brakes to glare at me.

"I wanted to surprise her and not put any pressure on us."

"You are too smart for your own good." Her smile brightens her face and something inside me.

"Is that a turn on?"

"Oh, yeah."

On the way out of the parking lot, she turns right instead of left to head back toward the highway.

"Are you so turned on that you're on a search for a place to accomplish number six on the list?" I wiggle my brow at her, but she doesn't laugh off the question or change the subject.

Instead, her full pink lips tip up into a grin. "I may know a place we can try."

"Nora Jean Roan Jolene Taylor, you just made my year."

"Don't go getting excited yet. It may not be a perfect spot."

"Every minute I spend with you is perfect." Raising our intertwined hands, I kiss the back of hers. "And ever since writing it down, I've been excited to cross it off with you."

"You remember making the list?"

"I do. And thinking about you."

"Positively?" she asks with a timid smile.

"Positively, sensually, longingly, lovingly."

"Good."

Soon, she turns off the main road, takes another right, and another until we're heading down what looks like an old private driveway. The long, bumpy dirt road is littered with potholes. Weeds and grass, taller than the car, line the sides and brush against the doors.

"I'm starting to worry that you're taking me to a serial killer's house, and I'll have to whip out some of my training to protect us."

"Even in your condition, I have full faith you can take him."

"How sweet."

She lets out a laugh before a deep pothole rocks the car and a dilapidated house with white, wide-plank siding and a crooked porch comes into view.

"Seriously, what is this place?" I ask, taking in the surrounding scene—overgrown shrubbery, boarded windows, peeling paint, a rusted, bent trampoline, and large trees in the front and back yards with fallen branches littering the ground underneath.

When Nora doesn't answer, I glance her way. Her eyes are unfocused and glossy, locked on something in the distance as if reliving memories.

"This is my childhood home. I have many wonderful memories here, but equally as many depressing ones."

"Why did you want to come?"

She shrugs and looks out the driver's side window for a bit before answering. "I don't know. It seemed harmless a few minutes ago—a private way to complete another one of your wishes."

"Does your mom still own this?"

"Yes. It was originally my grandparents'...on my dad's side. He inherited it, and Mom received it in the divorce settlement, mainly because she had custody of me, and it was the only home I knew." She sighs. "Plus, my dad was the one who walked away."

"Do you know where he is now?"

"No. Never heard from him again. Or my first stepfather."

I can't imagine not having my parents on my side growing up. They would have done anything for me and Josie, including working multiple jobs to ensure we never went hungry and had clothes we were proud to wear. When they were around, they made sure we knew how much they loved us. We played games, ate meals together, and made memories I'll always cherish. Nora had only a few wonderful memories from her childhood, all punctuated with abandonment and heartbreak.

"No wonder you hate relationships," I empathize.

"I wish the revolving door of temporary fathers would have made me want the opposite. But ironically, it turned me into what I hate most about my mother."

It takes all of one second to assemble a convincing objection, but she squeezes my hand to stop me from voicing it.

"She can't commit to one guy for very long and when she does, it's never a genuine commitment. She jumps from one bed to the next, chases pleasure, and runs away when maintaining her happiness requires a little effort. The ironic part is she has no clue what makes her happy. She's so terrified of being abandoned that she drives people away before they can do just that. It's maddening."

"Do you believe that happened to us?"

"In a way. For one, the merry-go-round of lovers my mother had messed with my view of relationships. The few good ones she somehow attracted in the beginning treated us both well, and I got attached."

"And you felt abandoned when they left."

She grins in agreement. "When I was young, I didn't understand why. I didn't realize my mother was sabotaging everything until I got older. At some point, she switched to men that were just as crazy and fickle as her." She pauses, and I wait for her to collect her thoughts. "The front door used to be painted a bright yellow. I still can't see that color without thinking about the nightmare this house became."

Air hitches in my lungs. I hadn't thought about the horrific attacks she endured happening here. With her mother's lifestyle, I assumed they'd moved around. An ignorant error. "Nora, we should go. You've been through enough here."

"No. I didn't realize how much I needed to let all this go until I saw it."

"Do you want to go inside? Is it safe?"

"Probably not, especially for you."

"There's no way I'm letting you go in there and through this alone."

At the declaration, tears fill her eyes, poised to spill at any moment, so I continue before she sees how her pain chokes me.

"I will always have your back. When you have mountains to climb, I want to hold your rope. When the weight of the world feels too heavy, I'll carry a load. When you need to cry…"

Her shoulders shutter as tears fall and coat her cheeks.

"Cry in my arms," I finish before a sob burst from her throat.

Throwing open the driver's side door, she jumps out. I watch her jog around the hood and turn toward my side, her hand clasped over her mouth. I swing open my door, and she sits on my lap, her arms locking around my neck with her face buried in my shoulder.

"Let it out, baby. I'm here."

Rocking her trembling body, I run a hand over her hair. As she lets the hurt melt away, I feel it seeping into my bones and becoming mine.

"You're so strong, Nora. However you want to do this, you can let go and find happiness. And I'll be by your side helping you search for it."

She sniffs and sits up, her red, puffy eyes falling to mine. I brush back the hair stuck to her wet cheek and tuck it around her ear.

"I love you," she says softly, and I forget to breathe.

She's never said those words to me, nothing even close, and my own eyes burn from threatening tears. Before I can respond or jumpstart my heart, she presses her lips to mine. Love pours through her body and the fingers framing my face. Whatever I have to do, I'm going to give this woman the world.

"Nora," I manage with a shredded exhale, and gently nudge her shoulders to add some space between us. I need to see her and ensure her confession is as true as it feels.

"I know what you're thinking," she says. "It's not untamed emotion from being here or some other passing sensation making me say it. I've loved you always. I just wouldn't let myself admit it or act on it for fear of losing you. But that's exactly what happened, anyway. I pushed you out the door before you could do it yourself…just like my mother. And I'm sorry."

A lone tear gathers on her lid and spills over. "I pretended not to care, so it would be easier for you to do exactly what I thought I wanted, but it shredded me."

"That's in the past. This is what I want." I wave a finger between us. "Us with no walls or fears or hidden feelings holding us back."

"I know." She combs her fingers through my hair. "It's what I want, too. More than anything."

Drawing her close, I savor this moment, this woman, and our mutual love until she releases me and sits back.

"But to destroy some of those walls for good, I need to face a few things first."

"Need an ax?" I joke to make her smile.

She obliges with a snort. "I might."

"Come on." My palm taps her tight, jean-clad ass to get her moving. "I bet we can find something to help you smash those walls to dust."

"Now, that's an idea I can get behind." She helps me to my feet. When I'm stable, she wraps both arms around my waist, and leans against me, needing the connection. "Afterward, I thought we could check out that tree over there." She points to one in the distance. "It looks mighty sturdy. Maybe you can show me what number six is all about."

"Whatever you want, my love."

"Mmm. I like the sound of that," she says, looking up at me, her eyes soft and admiring.

"What? Giving you whatever—"

"No. I like the way you said *my love*."

"Well, get used to it. I plan on saying it a lot."

Chapter Twenty-Five

Nora

After an impromptu smash session at my childhood home, which was surprisingly therapeutic, Jordan and I crossed number six off his list twice. If I had a bucket list, that little number wouldn't be mid-way down the list. It would be marked at the top in permanent ink.

Holy hell. Jordan Jones could write a book on the activity. Let's just say I'm over the moon grateful he saved crossing this one off for me.

I'm still reeling when we check in at our hotel just outside Manhattan's core and get ready. It took more willpower than I thought I had to not take over Jordan's sponge bath after my shower.

Instead, I opt for the responsible decision since our time is limited and get dressed. When he limps out of the bathroom, I'm standing by the window in his favorite dress. It's too suggestive for an art show—sparkling white with spaghetti straps and a back that dips all the way to my tailbone. One thin strap crosses my back to hold it together. The front falls loosely over my breasts, exposing enough cleavage to make heads turn. But I'm only interested in one man's attention, and he's currently giving me all of his.

He's speechless while his eyes roam over me. As he finds his words, I lift the front slightly, proving the dress is the only fabric on my body.

"In case you get any ideas later," I say, referring to his promise the last time he asked me to wear this dress, and watch his Adam's apple bob with a rigid swallow.

"I have plenty of ideas right now."

He reaches for the towel tied around his waist, and my hands fly up.

"Don't you dare. We have somewhere to be, and we'll never make it in this traffic if we get sidetracked."

"Promise me we'll find somewhere private tonight. I doubt I'll be able to wait until we get back to have you."

"Why do you think I chose this dress?"

"I can't think with you looking like that." His voice is gravely and deep with want. "Tell me."

"I'm wearing it because it's your favorite," I say, inching closer. "And I loved what you did to me the last time I put it on."

A smug smile tugs at his lips. "Ahh. Outside. Behind the bar. I'll never forget it."

"I expect the same treatment tonight...just a little classier, given the circumstances."

"Honey," he begins, leaning on the dresser. "You keep your eyes trained on me like I'm dessert, and you can have whatever you want."

He shifts to his suitcase nearby to collect the items he needs to dress. The muscles in his back bulge and ripple as he moves, making my skin prickle with desire. But it's not only his body that makes me giddy. It's him—his heart, sweet charm, tenderness, and ability to know what I need before I do. He loves me and all my maddening flaws and stubborn scars. With him, I'm a better person and whole for the first time.

"Jordan?"

"Yeah?" he says absently, and I wait for his eyes to find me.

"Just so we're clear...all I want is you."

Saturday night traffic uptown got us to the show forty minutes after opening. We tipped the cab driver double since he delivered us to the Whitney Museum's door instead of a block down the street and didn't complain about the extra time it took to get the wheelchair in and out of the trunk. Jordan claims it's because the driver got a show each time I lifted the chair in my dress.

"Whatever works," I joke, jabbing the elevator's up button more times than necessary.

"I'm having a hard time keeping my eyes off you, too." He reaches for my hand and kisses the top as the elevator door opens.

I follow him inside, and as a few others pile in and gather behind us, I lean down to his ear to whisper, "Ditto. You in this suit makes my knees weak."

His sleek black pants fit over the cast without swallowing the rest of him. The gray blazer over a white button-down shirt accentuates his masculine frame. His dog tags sit proudly over a matching black tie, and his dark blond hair, long enough to curl at the ends now, is combed back off his forehead.

"Good to know. I'll try not to wrinkle it when I f—"

The door opens, and Josie's squeal reverberates off the stone floor and the stark white walls of the long corridor leading to the showroom. She was standing near a sculpture a few steps away, talking to a tall man with salt and pepper hair and rings on multiple fingers when she saw us. After saying something to the gentleman, she takes tiny, hurried steps in our direction, moving as fast as she can in her ankle-length, fitted, black dress and four-inch heels.

"You came." She lunges into Jordan's awaiting arms.

Seeing them together, after all that's happened over the last week and a half, warms my soul. They will always have each other, and even though it's just the two of them, he has family he can count on. There's very little in this world better than that.

"Surprise," Jordan says, retaining her hand as she straightens.

While they catch up, I take a few minutes to appreciate the woman before me. She doesn't look like the carefree, eclectic artist I met in Richmond. She's beyond stunning. Grant has outdone himself, flawlessly styling her from the sparkling diamond clip in her perfect spiral curls to the bright red nail polish on her toes. She's ready for the runway, media interview, or an upscale art exhibit in New York City.

She soon notices my hand on Jordan's shoulder, and the blue eyes that match his trail up my arm and meet my gaze. There's a trace of trepidation in her expression, but for Jordan's sake, she masks it with her usual bubbliness.

"Nice to see you, Nora," she says, stepping around the wheelchair to wrap me in a delicate hug. "You look…"

"Incredible," Jordan finishes for her, bringing a smile to my face.

"That's not quite adequate enough, but since I'm speechless, we'll go with that."

"I was going to say the same about you. That dress is exquisite on you," I gush, while she spins to give us the full view. The back, a web of ribbons matching the pattern on her shoes, is even more intricate and eye-catching than the long strings of diamonds dripping from her ears and neck. "How's the show going?"

She glances between me and Jordan. "It's only been an hour, and I've already sold two pieces."

"And I bet that's only the beginning," Jordan reassures her. "Speaking of selling paintings, you better get back to it. Grant is getting anxious."

She turns to find him waving for her from the end of the corridor.

"He's relentless," she says on a long exhale. "But I love him." Turning back to Jordan, she takes his hand and squeezes it between hers. "I'm so glad you're here."

She scurries off, and Jordan nods his greeting at Grant. "That's her agent." He explains and we watch Grant circle his arm around Josie and drag her toward a group of people examining a framed piece of art, presumably Josie's.

"He looks like a piece of art himself," I say, taking in the bright blue and pink plaid suit, long white scarf, and pink shoes.

"That's Grant for you. Big, bold, and in your face."

"Not a fan?" I ask, using his piercing tone as evidence.

"He's good to Josie."

"But…"

"That's all I care about."

"Got it." As a waiter scurries toward us with a tray of full champagne glasses, I wave him over and take two before he moves on to more important customers. "Come on. Let's go ogle the masterpieces."

The featured artists all have unmistakable talent, but Josie's paintings are the talk of the show. She has a gift of making you feel the emotion she pours into each painting as if you're there in the meadow, on the mountain, at the beach, or on the balcony overlooking the city at dawn with her as she painted it.

There's one piece, a white house in a field of wildflowers, that takes my breath away. I lose myself in it while art enthusiasts disregard and move around me. Although the house is older and in need of repair, it still welcomes you in as if filled with love. The large tree to the left held a swing with two thick ropes tied to a limb. Two black rocking chairs sat on the porch, flanking a lazy dog lounging in the sun near the steps.

"This reminds me of the good times. When Mom and I would bake cookies on Sunday afternoons or play tag with Dad in the field. One fall, I asked for a swing for Christmas, but Dad made and hung one up that same day. It makes me want—" Emotion clogging in my throat blocks the words from escaping. "It's so beautiful."

I stare at it a while longer until someone bumps into my arm. Concentrating on not splashing the bubbly liquid in my glass on the painting and myself, I hold the flute out in front of me until it resettles.

"My sincere apologies, miss," the man says, placing a hand on my elbow.

"It's fine." I flash him a smile and step away to look for Jordan who, I realize, has disappeared.

"There you are," I say after locating him at a table across the room. "What are you up to?"

"Supporting my sister and buying something for the woman I love."

"What?"

"Congratulations, Mr. Jones." A dark-haired woman with thick-rimmed glasses passes him a receipt after stamping it paid.

"What did you do?" I ask.

"Bought the house painting."

His proud grin makes my insides quiver. "You didn't."

"I did. Thank you, slot machines."

Taking his face in my hands, I plant a lingering kiss to his lips. "That's the sweetest thing anyone has ever done for me."

"Where will you hang it?"

"Good question. Maybe you can help me decide when we get home."

His hand slaps to his chest in dramatic excitement. "I'd love to."

"And I'd love to thank you properly."

He lowers his voice, pointing me away from witnesses. "I saw an empty meeting room at the back of the showroom on my way to buy the painting."

"Perfect. I'll race ya."

"You have a little lipstick right there." I wipe the side of his lips with a thumb as we hastily get dressed.

"I'll gladly wear lipstick the rest of the night if it means doing that again."

"We can recreate the moment in my apartment when we get back if you'd like."

"And *my* apartment. And my parents' house after I renovate it."

"Sold." For once, the long-term nature of that promise didn't frighten me. If anything, it gave me an indescribable energy. One I can only interpret to be a rare commodity in my twenty-seven years on this planet—hope.

I help him button his shirt while he tucks in the bottom since my dress took all of three seconds to slip back into place.

He kisses my forehead on the last button and says, "Where's my tie?"

"Good question." I drop to the floor to search for the dark, silky fabric on the dark floor in the near dark room when the door opens.

A museum employee shrieks at the sight of us, shocked and appalled, while I'm grateful she let in some light to help me locate the tie. I snatch it up and jump to my feet.

"Hi," I greet, heat rising up my neck and into my cheeks. "We were looking for…yeah…we're done here." Jordan lowers into the chair, and I roll him out the door and into the showroom.

"That was amazing," he says, waving me down for a kiss. "I love you."

"I love you, too."

He slides the tie into his coat pocket with a smile that could melt my panties…if I were wearing any.

"There you two are," Josie says, bounding up to us as best she can in her restrictive dress. "I've been looking everywhere for—what happened to you?"

"What?" Jordan and I follow her gaze to his shirt. His buttons are one off, making the collar crooked. His hair looks like someone ran their fingers through it—that was definitely me—and a thin layer of sweat shimmers on his upper lip. He looks absolutely adorable and guilty as hell.

Josie turns to me, and I can only grin. "You guys are unbelievable."

"Thanks," Jordan says, making a chuckle spurt out between my pursed lips. "Did you need something?" he asks, slipping the tie around his neck to hide the error we made with his buttons.

"I'm sold out!"

"Josie, that's amazing. I mean, I knew you would, but…" He pushes awkwardly to his feet to give his sister an adequate hug. "I'm so happy for you."

"The white country house was the last one to go and someone paid double for it."

"What?" I jump into the conversation, and Jordan looks over his shoulder with don't-tell-her eyes.

"Yeah. There was a bidding war for it," Josie continues, oblivious to our silent conversation.

"That's crazy."

"I never would have guessed that piece would be so popular. Maybe I should paint more like that."

"You definitely should," I say. "It's magnificent. I knew you were talented, Josie, but your work is truly unlike any I've ever seen."

"Thank you, Nora. That means a lot." She steps around Jordan to give me a hug, then reaches for him. "And thank you both for your support and letting me have this moment. I'm so grateful…and happy. I can't believe I sold out!"

As she returns to her fans, I help Jordan lower back to the chair. "Why didn't you want to tell her?"

"She'll find out soon enough. I want her to enjoy this moment without guilt."

"She's going to be mad at you for spending your money," I say, pushing him toward the bar.

"That's fine. She can be mad at me all she wants later. After seeing that look in your eyes, there was no way I was letting it go to anyone else."

"You're too good, Jordan Jones." I order two glasses of wine and turn to face him. "Speaking of special moments, you were fantastic earlier."

"So fantastic that you're ready to go back to the hotel and do it again?"

"Yes, but there's something I need to do first. Will you be okay here for a few minutes?" I pass him one of the full glasses of wine the bartender set on the counter.

"Sure."

Wrapping my fingers around the stem of the second glass, I march through the expansive room, looking for Josie. I soon find her talking to an animated couple about a commission and wait nearby until she notices me.

"Hi," I say, sounding as insecure as I feel. "Sorry to interrupt, but can we talk?"

"Gosh. I thought you'd never ask." She hooks my arm with hers and leads me into a nearby room, flipping on the lights before closing the door behind us. It's the same room Jordan and I escaped to earlier, making my cheeks flush.

"What happened between you and Jordan?" Her eyes glitter with intrigue, excitement, and a little too much wine.

"What?" With my thoughts focused on the last visit to this room, I'm not sure how to answer.

"This week, he said on the phone that things are better between you."

"Oh. Well, a lot's happened there." Glancing around the small room, I notice for the first time that it's set up for a banquet or dinner—round tables covered with white linens, place settings, and fresh-cut flower centerpieces in expensive crystal vases.

Josie yanks out a chair, and I follow to sit across from her. "He's forgiven me for lying to—"

"I heard that part."

"Oh, right. Well," I try to begin, but her intensity is making the words jumble like a crossword puzzle in my brain. "I'm working through some past issues—and will be for a while—but Jordan has helped so much. He knows everything and has forgiven me."

"That's my brother. You're his weakness."

"And he's mine. I've completely fallen for him, Josie—head over heels and with all my heart. I don't care who knows it. In fact, I want to scream it from the rooftops."

"Wow." She sits back, taking me in. "That's awesome," she says, but I'm not sure she means it. She has residual trepidation. Anyone in her position would, but that's why I wanted to talk to her. Her approval means so much to Jordan, and I'm here to make sure we have it.

"I'm hoping to get your blessing, Josie. You can think about it if you need to. I understand this may come as a shock. You've missed a lot."

"Nora, what are you asking me?" Her eyes are wide as she surveys me.

"I'd like to ask Jordan to marry me."

"You're asking him?" She stands, and I mirror her, keeping a defensive distance as she paces. I'm still unsure how she's feeling about all the changes between us in such a short timeframe.

"He won't ask me. He's a little traumatized, and he's afraid I'll freak out again."

Josie nods, understanding.

"I want to show him how serious I am about us and to set his mind at ease. He's chosen me time and time again, and now it's my turn to choose him." She turns to face me, too stunned to speak. "But I won't ask him until I have your blessing. He'll want to know you're on board, and I need that, too. You mean so much to him. Please, Josie."

I take her hands, but she stares over my shoulder, lost in thought…or in shock. I can't tell which, but I barrel through my speech, hoping she hears me.

"I want him forever, Josie. I love him more than I thought was possible, and however we can make it happen, I want to give him a family. I want our life to be as beautiful and vibrant as the white country house picture you painted. With him, I know it will be full of laughter, passion, and unconditional love. He means the world to me, too, Josie.

And I want to spend the rest of my life showing him and our children just how special he is."

"I think you're pretty special, too," Jordan says from behind me.

I spin around to find him leaning against the doorframe, his eyes glistening with fresh tears. He takes a careful step toward me as Josie leans in to whisper in my ear.

"You have my blessing."

All anxiety dissolves from my body, and I drop to my knees, my face falling into my hands.

"Please don't cover up the beautiful face I love so much."

I lift my gaze. He's standing a few feet away and we're now the only people in the room. Keeping my eyes on his, I shift to one knee and reach for his hand.

"You've shown me what unconditional love is and how it feels to receive it. For the rest of my life, I'd like to return the favor. You have my whole heart, Jordan. All of me is yours forever. Will you give me the honor of being your wife?"

"What do you think?"

"I think I'll be the luckiest girl in the world if you say yes."

Giving me his acceptance, and most importantly, his love, he draws me up and kisses me with a new desire I can feel in every cell of my body.

"Looks like we've crossed another activity off the bucket list," he says softly.

"Make me love you?"

"Yep. Took you long enough," he teases, swallowing my rebuttal with his mouth. "But well worth the wait."

※※※

Leave a Review

If you enjoyed Book 1 of the You & Me Duology, *Make You Love Me*, please consider leaving a review on any or all of these platforms: Amazon, Goodreads, BookBub, Barnes & Noble, social media, and others. Reviews are vital to new authors and help us reach more readers.

I hope you will read Book 2, *How You See Me*.

Thank you!

Alexandra Grace

Printed in Great Britain
by Amazon

41974903R00189